THE DEEP OF THE Sound

AMY LANE

A BLUEWATER BAY STORY

RIPTIDE
PUBLISHING

Riptide Publishing
PO Box 6652
Hillsborough, NJ 08844
www.riptidepublishing.com

The Deep of the Sound

Cover art: L.C. Chase, lcchase.com/design.htm
Editors: Sarah Frantz Lyons, Chris Muldoon, May Peterson
Layout: L.C. Chase, lcchase.com/design.htm

ISBN: 978-1-62649-276-9

First edition
June, 2015

Also available in ebook:
ISBN: 978-1-62649-275-2

THE DEEP OF THE Sound

AMY LANE

A BLUEWATER BAY STORY

RIPTIDE
PUBLISHING

Thank you, Mate, and Mary, and kids.

And especially to my oldest son, Big T, who was diagnosed as Communicatively Handicapped at two years old and has been benefitting from special education programs ever since, even into college.

Thanks, T—You're the best. You work so hard at going to school and having a job and doing all of the grown-up things that people take for granted every day. And every day you tell me about the friends you went to school with. I volunteered when you were young. I know their diagnoses, I know their medications, and now I know what happens to them when they get out of school and the world offers very little safety net to catch them. This is for the parents and the grandparents and the brothers and sister who love their family very much but who just need more help, better help, any help, to keep their family together, to keep their troubled young men and women someplace like home.

TABLE OF CONTENTS

CHAPTER ONE

GOING OUT

"Y" ou going out today, Calladh?" Uncle Nascha sounded surprised. He'd slept in the battered recliner the night before, and the corduroy wrinkles obscured his face so much Cal hadn't seen his eyes were open in the dark of the living room.

Cal had just come in from the boat dock to grab his forgotten lunch, and he didn't state the obvious: he was wearing his hip waders and old slicker, and it was five o'clock on a misty, freezing morning in February. There was nowhere to go *but* out.

"Yeah, Nascha—if I can catch enough freshwater cod, the chef at the Global'll buy 'em from me." Nascha knew this. Cal worked two jobs—one was as a busboy at the Global Restaurant and Casino and the other was his own independent fishing business. Between the two of them, he could just barely afford the payments on Nascha's ramshackle beachfront house and someone to come look after Nascha and Keir.

"Your brother will miss you when you're gone."

Cal closed his eyes. "I know, Nascha. But you need to make him take his pills anyway." Keir didn't listen to Nascha quite like he listened to Cal, but Cal couldn't help that. Cal had set the meds out in the little weekly plastic thing, the white one for day and the black one for night. God, he hoped he'd gotten it right. Adderall, risperidone, Cymbalta—ADHD, Asperger's, anxiety, OCD, possible bipolar—it was a powerful cocktail, and they'd gone through . . . hell, vehicles, teachers, sheriffs, and half the kitchen to get it right. Keir was prone to hitting things with rocks and fire when he was anxious or upset. Nascha used to be able to deal with him, but Nascha had his own drug cocktail now, Exelon ranking high on the list. Nascha didn't always remember that Keir needed his medicine—morning *and* evening cocktails—without Cal or a caregiver around. He also didn't remember to turn off the stove or take the bread out of the toaster or keep Keir inside the house.

Mostly, he didn't remember that Keir was no longer a little boy running down the street screaming in a voice that would shatter glass. Keir was twenty now, with a powerful body and a fondness for all of Cal's fishing knives (which Cal kept locked in the safe out by the boat), and a disturbing habit of tracking the girls in their neighborhood.

"Cherry's rounding the corner, yellow dress, shows her ass when she bends over. Stop yelling, Cherry. Stop yelling, it leads to hitting."

Keir's fixation on girls wasn't limited to the extremely young, but what was Cal supposed to do? He'd told the doctor who dispensed the meds, but *his* only response had been to up Keir's medication.

Cal knew—just *knew*—that his parents would have been able to deal with Keir. His mother and father had been so . . . capable, had such pure hearts and such practical joy in dealing with their fractious, damaged son. But they'd gone for a drive after heavy rains six years ago, and their battered pickup had been washed off the side of a mountain in a mudslide.

Cal's dreams of college, of playing sports, of meeting a boy the way his mother had met his father—all of that had been washed down the mountain too. At barely eighteen, he'd been left in charge of keeping things together, and part of that was making sure Keir had his medication, and Uncle Nascha got his too. And living with that gnawing worry, every day, from dawn until dusk, past dusk, until he was just too tired to see anymore.

"I don't mean go out to work," Nascha said, snapping Cal back to the present through eyes gritty with lack of sleep. "I mean go out tonight. It's Valentine's Day this week, Cal—don't you have a school dance to go to?"

Oh. Okay. So Cal was in high school now. He understood.

"No, Nascha—no dances for Cal. Cal doesn't go to dances, remember?" Cal doesn't go to dances because Cal doesn't really like girls, he thought ironically. Yet one more thing he hadn't been able to talk to his parents about since their car had gone tumbling down into the river.

"If Cal was on the reservation," Nascha said, his voice ironic too as they spoke of Cal in the third person, "Cal could dance with the two-spirit children, and nobody would think less of him."

Yeah, sure, it always *sounded* like Mecca when Nascha talked about the reservation, but Nascha had left when he'd been not much older than Cal. Cal understood that Indian Gaming had improved things somewhat on the reservation—but that didn't mean he was a fan of all the changes it brought about in the *non*reservation parts of the state.

"Maybe I just want to be left the fuck alone," Cal snarled, feeling bad even as he did. Nascha and Keir were his family—his *only* family. He couldn't afford to piss them off, because they were all stuck in this tiny house together, and they were all each other had.

Cal would lie in bed awake sometimes, exhausted and aching because he needed more.

"Maybe you just need to go dance," Nascha said calmly, not taking offense. Just like when Cal had been a fractious kid, losing patience with Keir because he'd been fixating on the same damned cartoon for *weeks*, Nascha had never lost his keel.

Cal loved that about him. It was why, in spite of his increasing anxiety over leaving Nascha alone with Keir, he couldn't bring himself to put Nascha in a home either.

But God, he was exhausted.

"Well, I'll let you know if a dance opens up for me," he muttered, swallowing against the tightness in his throat.

"Calladh!" Nascha spoke sharply, and the long-ingrained habit of responding to his elders with respect crackled through Cal's bones, snapping his spine erect and widening his eyes.

"Yes, Great-Uncle." His hip boots were clean, thank God, so he could walk across the worn brown carpet and into the living room. The old television—36", but pre-flat screen, so it took up about a third of the space in the small room—was set low, but a parade of Viagra commercials and spoiled rich women reflected off Nascha's face, even as he turned his attention to Cal.

"You listen to me. I know sometimes I forget—sometimes your mother is still alive, and your father, bless their hearts. Sometimes you and Keir are boys and your family is staying with me and I am so happy. But when I remember, I see what time has made of you, and you are old before your time."

Oh. *This* was the Uncle Nascha that Cal had loved as a child. The Uncle Nascha who had been young at heart, and kind, and who had offered patience and peanut-butter-and-honey sandwiches and native stories about the gods who fought each other while the people watched, leaving behind mountains in their wake. The Uncle Nascha who would wander away when his parents were having money troubles, and come back in a few days, smelling of cigars and whiskey, with more cash than should be legal in this world.

Cal kneeled in front of his great-uncle's chair. "It's not so bad," he said roughly, thinking that it wasn't anything, any sacrifice at all, as long as Nascha could be like this, be the elder and the confidant and the grown-up all the time.

"You should sell this house, Cal," Nascha said, and his voice warbled, became fractious. "The reservation would pay money for it, set up a casino and a marina—you could make enough money to put me in a home, to take care of your brother. You could go out and live your life."

Cal took a deep breath, and then another, willing his face to stay stoic, willing his eyes not to burn. "But what is my life without my family?" he asked, trying hard to smile.

Nascha sighed. "Is that what I say to you when I can't remember?"

Verbatim. "It's what I know to be true," Cal said, finding his feet again, remembering who really was the grown-up. He bent and kissed his uncle's forehead, hating himself for the brief moment of hope. "Dottie will be here at eight. She'll feed you both. I'll try to get her to remember the medicine."

Dottie was in her sixties—which was good because it made her exempt from Keir's pathological hatred—but she was also apparently from a time when healthy men didn't rely on pills to keep them tethered to the earth. She was good at keeping them fed, at reminding Uncle Nascha he needed to use the john, at getting him out to walk around the neighborhood, and at not taking Keir's shit—but she was just as likely to "forget" the meds and pretend they had no use at all. Those were the days Cal came home to find Keir banging his hand against the wall until it bruised and Nascha in tears because he didn't know who the crazy man in the living room was.

It was really better for all involved if Nascha, when he was bright and alert in the mornings, could remember the medication for both of them.

"Cal!" Nascha called to his retreating back, and Cal couldn't take it anymore.

"*What?*" he demanded, losing control of his voice and his composure. "But make it quick, old man, because my fish today are buying our groceries, and right now there's only about enough spaghetti left for lunch."

Nascha's look of hurt followed Cal out the garage door and into the dory rocking gently on the waters inside.

Some people kept their cars in a garage—but Cal's battered blue Ford F-150 was parked in front of the mossy lawn of the house itself. His parents had been driving the same kind of vehicle when they'd fallen down the mountain, but Cal had long since gotten over his fear. The truck had been cheap, and it ran, and it was one of three reliable things in Cal's life since that rainy April when half the mountain had slid away and carried most of Cal's hopes with it.

The rest of Cal's hopes—and his father's only dream—sat in the little docking bay attached to the house. The covered bay protected much of the twenty-foot dory, and Cal hopped in with the ease of someone who had been steering such a vessel for most of his life.

The back end of the dory was flattened, to make the outboard motor effective and keep it going where Cal pointed it, and Cal handled the craft expertly—and with great wariness. Even in the quiet waters of the sound, the unexpected could turn deadly. Given that Cal's parents had been killed by a simple drive through the San Juans, Cal made that truism his mantra.

He navigated the boat steadily through the mist, grateful for his tightly woven wool sweater. It had been his father's, purchased from one of the reservations in Alaska, and something about the small-gauged knitting of the high-loft wool made the zip-up sweater almost waterproof—and blessedly, blessedly warm.

Cal liked things old school—he wasn't a fan of the casinos or the tourists or the television show, no matter how good those things were for the town. He *really* didn't like all of the strange people mucking about in the pure vistas he'd grown up in. The way he fished reflected that. He didn't have a fish-finder or sonar—just himself, and his nets, and his little boat.

And the fishing territory his father had unerringly staked out, year after year. Just his. Cal knew the landmarks, the distance from his home shore, the line of sight to the Canadian shore, the dimensions of the rugged slopes of Mt. Olympus in the distance—Cal knew the relation of all these things to the waters his father had fished, and he knew that within these boundaries, there would, hopefully, *be* fish.

Cal murmured a prayer to whatever gods his uncle prayed to—Musp the transformer, Bluejay the trickster, and whoever else might be listening—and cast his net. Count, breathe, putter through the black water and mist until the cinch at the top began to close, and stop, allowing the boat to drift while he stood, minding the way the dory would feel like it was tipping over before it recovered.

Then, using a smaller net, he culled the fish, throwing out the salmon because it wasn't their season, and the hake because they were threatened, and hoping for cod or rockfish in the seine net.

His first haul he pulled in a couple of four or five pounders, and these he dumped in the center of the boat, knowing the dory was made to hold nearly a ton, and that odds were good he'd never fill it with that much fish in a day.

Still, he was making a good haul, sorting carefully, his fingers and arms aching with the work. It was good work, a part of him thought. Honest work. Somehow, when he was out on the sound, he never found himself wondering about the scholarships he hadn't taken or the places he'd never seen. Somehow, on the bay, it was enough.

Cast, cull, haul, dump—backbreaking and soothing, his day continued, until he thought he had time for two, maybe three more tries. He was just pulling the net tight, the better to cull the purse seine, when he felt it. A force—a terrific, muscular *pull*, lunging from the side of the boat. The net distorted and the dory leaned dangerously to the port side, and Cal cast about with the culling net, trying to fight off whatever had the seine.

Something huge—gigantic, too big to be in the sound, something that should have been in the open ocean—thrashed underneath his net, knocking it out of his hand. Oh fuck— He floundered, draped half over the side of the dory, trying not to lose a piece of equipment he couldn't afford to replace.

By luck, the culling net had gotten hung up on the purse seine, and he snagged it, pulling the seine close to him and ignoring the perilous tip of the boat. The waters out here were freezing, deep, and unforgiving. If he went so far as to tip over the dory, the odds of getting it upright with him in it before he froze to death were sad and thin.

He fumbled with the net, trying to open the seine to set free whatever leviathan he'd accidentally caught, and found that it had cinched too tight to open, and the weight on the transom was making the bolts creak with the strain.

Holy fucking hell. He had to catch this fucking fish or it would kill him.

He tossed the culling net aside, grasped the seine net in both hands, braced his feet against the side of the dory, and *hauled*.

His back, chest, and shoulder muscles popped with the strain, and still that thing fought, trying desperately to escape, trying desperately to *live*.

Him or me!

Pant by groan, Cal hauled one hand over the other until most of the net was in the boat and the monster's struggles echoed against the outside of the dory, banging a hollow, pounding tattoo across the rolling waters of the sound.

It made a sudden, frenzied resurgence, and Cal screamed, grabbing the fishing gaff, bunching his body to spear this fucker, still it, make it *just fucking stop*!

He wrapped the net around his forearm for stability and leaned over the side of the boat.

Oh holy God. It was huge, ugly, a primal vertebrate, a ridge of bone on either side of its body, and a sharp, prong-like snout—it must have been seven feet long, and oh, *fuck*.

The matte scales were unmistakably green.

Oh no. Not one of those. I can't sell that!

He went to drop the gaff so he could grab the knife and cut the thing free, but it gave a seismic convulsion, dragging him up and almost over the side of the boat. He dangled, watching the fish submerge again, and behind him, he heard a bolt popping as the transom threatened to burst.

It was tearing his fucking boat apart.

Helplessly, he hauled back on the net and hurled the gaff at the thrashing sturgeon, stunning it. The gaff stayed stuck in the creature's skull, and he was reaching into his pocket for his knife, thinking it was best just to cut his net and cut his losses, when the fish gave another titanic heave.

Cal was forced to grab the net with both hands again. The damned thing could still pull him over, even with a gaff in its head.

For a few moments all he heard was his own tortured breathing and the echoes of the giant green sturgeon pounding against the boat. With a groan, deep from his stomach, clenching every formidable muscle in his body, Cal hauled the fish over the side of the boat.

It wasn't dead yet—in fact it threw itself around some more, the rough scales on the top of its body ripping through Cal's waders and through a sizeable bit of flesh on his shin as well.

Cal's scream and kick to the thing's head had less to do with survival and more to do with anger and pain, but it wouldn't have mattered. There was no way—not for one man—to free the fish from the net and keep the boat from capsizing. As it was, Cal finally had a chance to reach for the six-inch serrated fishing knife in his pocket. He unfolded the knife and hurled it with deadly accuracy, splitting the fish between the eyes and cleaving its prehistoric brain in two.

It continued to convulse in weakening cycles, and Cal stood over it, panting, until it finally played itself out.

Oh hell. This thing probably outweighed Cal two-to-one. Who in the fuck was going to eat this giant fucking illegal fish? And more to the point, how was he going to get it from the boat to the back of the truck?

It took an hour to return to shore because the weight was so great the tiny outboard motor groaned and wallowed like a pregnant sow in a mud bath.

He had ice in the back of the truck, which was *great*, because he was going to need to replace his fucking net. The damned fish had torn great gaping holes in it that would let anything *not* the size of a Volkswagen pass right the hell through. He wouldn't have been able to afford to replace the net *and* buy ice again that week, so if he was counting blessings, well, he was still fucked, but at least it wasn't another kick to the nads.

Which were sore, actually, from the herculean effort of hauling that fish over the side of the boat. Jesus, he'd been straining *everything*, hadn't he?

And he needed Keir's help to move the damned fish.

He hated going inside between getting home and hauling the fish to market—usually, he avoided it at all costs. Keir didn't take well to disruptions of his routine, and Cal always seemed to arrive right in the middle of Keir's favorite show, *Avatar*. Cal thought that maybe Nascha had DVRed a bunch of episodes for him and just played them at a certain time because *no* cartoon ran that long. He was grateful, but having Keir's routine locked in that tightly . . .

It meant Cal was going to need to beg, cajole, yell, threaten, and reason with his brother to get those powerful shoulders and thick thighs working in service of the giant fucking fish.

"Cal, you're not supposed to be home right now."

Keir looked up from the television, cupping underneath his chin the giant mixing bowl that they allowed him for cereal.

"I know. I need your help."

"You always come in between one and two. It's only twelve thirty."

Cal took a deep breath and steadied himself on the kitchen counter. It all hurt. All of it—the fucking rip across his shin hurt the worst, but Jesus. "I know, Keir. I'm sorry. I'm sorry I interrupted your show, but I can't manage this fish. Could you please help?"

In his head he remembered his mother explaining how sarcasm didn't work with Keir, and getting frustrated and yelling didn't work either. Keir was a robot boy—you fed in direct instructions, you gave him a specific schedule, and if you fucked with that, you got a confused, angry, muscular fireplug of a man who liked to batter his fists on things.

"I have to watch my show."

"Nascha can DVR the show," Cal snapped, and then took another deep breath. "Please, Nascha, can we tape the show?"

"Yes, Cal— Do you need my help with the fish?"

Dottie was sitting kitty-corner to Nascha on the couch, watching the Cal and Keir show, and when Nascha spoke she shook her head frantically at Cal. But Cal knew—even better than Dottie, probably. The medication Nascha had to take to keep his brain from rotting had the reverse effect on his bones. One slip, and his hip would be shattered, and Cal had heard the doctor when he explained that perfectly healthy people went quickly downhill from there.

"I just need Keir," Cal said, trying not to talk between his teeth. "Keir, could you please put the cereal down, let Nascha tape your show, and join me outside to help me get this fucking fish out of the goddamned boat and into the motherfucking cocksucking pickup."

"You're not supposed to swear, Cal."

"Keir, *please*! We need the money, damn it— We're almost out of cereal!"

Keir actually stood up. "We can't run out of cereal! I eat cereal in the morning and cereal for lunch and then I eat a healthy meal!"

Oh thank God. "Then get your boots on and get your ass out here so I can move this fucking fish!"

"Can I wear my boots with my pajamas?"

Cal stopped and looked at him. He was wearing one of four pairs of flannel pajama bottoms their mother had made him the Christmas before she died. He rarely wore anything else in the house, and Cal got it. Wearing the pajama bottoms meant that his day inside was not over—just interrupted.

"Absolutely. Just . . ." His shin throbbed, and he got a look at the time on the microwave clock. "Please. Just hurry."

At least the fish itself proved a distraction.

"What kind of fish is this?" Keir asked. He had round, brown eyes as opposed to Cal's almond shaped ones, and his hair was straight and black when Cal's was streaked brown and red from the sun and some of their father's blond genetics. But they both had the broad cheekbones and solid jaws of Nascha's people, and the skin that was darker than fair and more fair than rust. Right now, Keir's brown eyes were intent on the flat, tiny eyes of the monster. Cal was pushing it out of the boat and Keir was pulling, and Cal hoped none of the spines on the tail would get him when it slid out—Keir wasn't great with physical pain.

"Green sturgeon," Cal grunted. God, let it come out. Please . . . could he use a winch? Did he have a winch? Could he get the neighbors to help with it? But the neighbors would need to know what Keir had just asked.

"Green sturgeon are protected," Keir recited. "You can catch crabs, cod, rockfish, salmon in season—"

"I *know* what I can catch!" Cal snapped. "But that's not what *wanted* to be caught!"

"But they're not in season. Green sturgeon are protected. You can catch crabs, cod, rockfish, salmon in season, abalone, halibut . . ."

Cal tuned him out, got his legs underneath him, and shoved. The dory tipped just that bit more, and the fish went slithering out onto the waiting dolly, sending Keir on his ass.

Keir hollered because he'd scraped his hand, and thankfully the subject was dropped.

An hour later, after shoving the dolly to the truck and then hauling it up a wooden ramp that Cal had made after Nascha'd sprung his knee, Cal managed to transfer the rest of the catch to the back of the truck as well. He'd bound Keir's hand, and given him stern instructions to comb his straight, black hair out of his face, because he looked feral, like a wild animal, and then Cal took advantage of being home and made sure everybody was medicated before he left.

By the time he got to the Global, it was almost too late to sell the damned fish.

And Smith gave him grief—oh, a fuck-ton of grief.

"What color is this fuckin' fish, asswipe?" Smith demanded, taking off his greasy white cook's hat and running his hand through thin strands of what might have been blond hair.

Cal glowered at him, curling his lip in defiance. "None of your guests are gonna *see* the fuckin' color," he snarled. "Nobody's gonna give a shit. It's not like I set out to kill it, Smith. Wandered into my net waiting to die—"

"Well, wasn't that sweet for *you*, ya fuckin' fairy!"

A delicate crimson veil slid between Cal and the rest of the world. He pinned Smith to the back wall, which was like a sparrow pinning a vulture, given Smith used to wrestle for a living and it had all run to fat.

"You pay me for this fish, you useless piece of puke, or I am taking my business elsewhere for*ever*!"

Smith's fetid breath washed over Cal, and his stomach heaved and turned on nothing, because the fish had destroyed his lunch with all its fighting, and Cal didn't have the pocket money to buy himself so much as a sandwich.

Cal increased the pressure to Smith's windpipe. "What's it gonna be?"

"You know it's probably too tough to do anything but make acres of fuckin' fish salad, don't you?" Smith said in disgust, but he dropped his eyes, and Cal knew he'd won.

"Call it a delicacy. Put it in the smoker. Fucking shave it and use it for toilet paper, but I need the goddamned money!"

Keir was down to his last week's meds, the truck needed a new carburetor, and Cal needed *another goddamned net*!

"You don't expect me to buy the rest of the catch, do you?" Smith asked, whining a little, and Cal knew as a businessman that insisting on that would go too far.

He turned his head and spat. "Naw. I'll take it to the Marriott. It's all rockfish and sole. They always need more."

He hoped.

Yeah, the Marriott on the fringes of town took the rest of his catch, but by the time he got his cash there, he was late for his job back at Global. He still smelled like fish and blood as he hauled ass through the back door of the Restaurant and Casino, running for the men's changing rooms, grateful for the employee shower. He stripped and grabbed a shower sample, lathering up the entire tube in his brown-streaked black hair and under his armpits and creases. The cut across his shin wasn't bleeding anymore and with luck it would draw together soon and heal closed. Or maybe not. It was red and angry and puffy. Oh please God—he didn't want stitches and he didn't give a fuck about another goddamned scar. Just . . . just make it through, he thought somewhat wretchedly. Make it through. If he could make it through, he could get up in the morning, fix the transom, use the money in his pocket to fix the net, to buy the medicine, to pay Dottie, to replace the carburetor, to fix the roof, to buy ice for his next trip out, to . . .

He was holding his face under the spray and trying to order all that shit in his head when he heard George Oswald, supervisor, fuck buddy, semi-scumbag tear-assing through the locker room.

"Cal! Cal—where'd you go, you useless sonuvabitch? You're supposed to be here an hour ago!"

Cal pulled his head from under the spray and shook the water out of his eyes.

"Gimme a sec!" he hollered back. "Had fish rotting in my truck— had to go sell it to Arvin and Smith!"

"I don't give a shit what you had rotting in your truck, McCorkle— you're late for *this* job! Now get your shit together and— Holy fuck, what happened to you?"

Cal had gotten a look at himself when he'd been driving back and forth—he had a bruise on his cheek he couldn't remember getting and his eyes were bloodshot from the strain of hauling the goddamned fish on board. And the cut across his shin was aching like a motherfucker.

"Sturgeon wandered into the net," he snapped. "Outta my way. Gotta go get dress—"

"That's not the only thing that happened, wait—"

"Outta my way, George!" Cal shouldered past him, not wanting his pity. So much easier to deal with his life if he never had to stop fighting, never had to lay down his swords, 'cause when he did that he wanted to put his face between his knees and cry.

"No, man, you can*not* go out there if you're bleeding and looking like death—did you see your arms, Cal?"

Little cuts all over, damned spines on the damned sturgeon. "Don't wanna talk about it," Cal muttered, rifling through his locker for his stuff.

That's when George did a dangerous thing: he put his hand on Cal's shoulder.

"Get your hand off me!"

He didn't like George—didn't hardly like fucking him—but God . . . touch, human touch . . . Cal craved it and hated it at the same time.

He was almost naked, leaning across the bench to the bank of lockers, and instinctively his back arched, his ass thrust out in an invitation he never would have consciously voiced.

George's hand on his shoulder shook, and George ran it down the damp line of his back to the edge of the towel Cal was clutching around his waist.

He snatched his hand back, like he was trying to do the right thing, and Cal glared over his shoulder. "Spare me the gentleman shit," he challenged. "I'm just a piece of ass to you anyway—go ahead and take it! Everyone else's had their bit."

George dragged a deep breath in, exhaling it shakily in Cal's ear. He chewed breath mints between the odd cigarette, so he smelled like a combination of spearmint and tobacco that wasn't bad, really. Suddenly his animal warmth, his muscle and bone humanity, was a comfort Cal craved until his stomach muscles knotted.

Cal didn't like to crave anything.

George smoothed his hand over the towel, and Cal knocked it away.

"You don't get that if you don't work for it," he sneered, and George knew this game. This was the only game they played.

That quick, Cal was thrown face-first into the locker while George fumbled for his belt.

"Not worried about getting caught, Mr. Manager?" Cal taunted. "Gonna take the time to fuck me but not lock the fucking door?"

"It's locked!" George snapped, cracking Cal a good one across the ass. "Now shut up and spread it!"

"Make me, corporate man." Oh yeah—George thought he was better'n everyone else 'cause he went to college, but when all was said and done, he was head of the busboys, just a step higher than Cal who was digging his life out of the mud in the sound.

George shoved two fingers up Cal's ass without lube or courtesy, and Cal saw stars with the pain.

Oh God, the glorious pain.

He rode that pain, rode it as George dropped his trousers and shoved his cock in dry, rode it as George grunted and sweat behind him. His face was mashed into the locker so hard his lip bled a little from a particularly hard thrust, but Cal didn't care.

He was lost in the pain, where bills and duty and family didn't exist, where he was free, like eagles, like crows, flying the red sky of pain above the misty valley of what his life had become.

It was tremendous; he could almost see forever, past the sprung-up town of Bluewater Bay, past the San Juan Islands, to the open waters of the ocean, across the Pacific, to the world.

Almost.

The pain, the roughness, the human contact ended, and Cal was left naked, his cock flopping at half-mast, and George's cum running from the crack of his ass.

George sighed, burying his face in Cal's shoulder.

"Kid," he murmured, his voice almost gentle. "Kid, it didn't have to be like that."

He cupped Cal's scalp then, massaging gently with his fingertips, and Cal leaned his forehead against the metal frame of the locker.

"Sure it did," he muttered back. "It's all I got in me."

George dropped an oddly out of place kiss on Cal's temple, and then zipped up. "You got ten minutes," he said, his voice flat and uninflected. "Then *my* boss'll know we're one down."

Cal nodded, not meeting his eyes. "'Preciate it." He pulled out his clean underwear and his threadbare black slacks and white shirt. Add one more thing to the list, he thought listlessly. One more thing to buy. Clothes for this job he loathed.

No flying for Cal. Just fishing and being a piece of ass for one more lousy fucking day.

CHAPTER TWO

NOT LIKE TV

"Are you going out today, Avery?"

Avery Kennedy rolled over in bed and glared at his phone on the charger. "You're asking me that *now*?" Christ. Six a.m.? Was that even legal?

"We need *milk*, Avery, and *food*—you got a problem going shopping or are you too 'busy' with your 'job'?"

Avery sat up in bed and put on his glasses, the better to squint at Billy Rivera—current boyfriend and giant fucking tool. Yeah, he was still good looking—square jaw, blue eyes, dark-blond hair, square shoulders, swagger—but Avery wasn't nearly as impressed with a good-looking guy in a suit anymore.

"My 'job' is paying for that 'food' you want so badly," Avery said, letting some of his irritation burn through his exhaustion. "And the rent on this shitty apartment—which you are conveniently living in while you go to your 'job' that requires you to buy suits you can't afford and really fucking nice shoes."

Billy jerked, obviously stung. "Look, A—we talked about this. I'm in an internship for the business and I got to look the part—"

"Whatever," Avery grumbled, not wanting to lose sleep over fighting. He took off his glasses and grabbed his phone, making sure it was set for 8 a.m. "You go look the part—I'm going back to sleep so I can wake up and finish the article that's going to buy your groceries."

"You didn't finish last night?" Billy asked idly, going to the closet for one of the really awesome ties Avery had bought from Nordies to celebrate the stupid internship. Oh yeah—they'd been happy at first because sure, it didn't pay as much as getting a job right out of college might, but the possibilities! They'd seemed endless—six months ago they'd seemed endless. Now Avery was wondering when there was an end to the possibilities and a beginning to Billy getting a freaking job.

Which was hilarious, because the more Billy sat and ate lunch (which he bought with Avery's money because his check barely paid for utilities in the little apartment in North Hollywood), the more he complained to his new work friends about Avery getting a freaking job.

"No," Avery mumbled, wondering why Billy was so interested in him all of a sudden. God, where was Billy when *Avery* wanted to talk? Well, usually Avery wanted to talk around one, two in the morning, so that wasn't really fair, but geez, didn't it suck to be woken up and told you weren't good enough. Again. "I was waiting for some data from the company. It'll be here by eight."

"So what was all that typing I heard last night?"

Avery blinked and widened his eyes, playing for time. "You were up? Sorry, babe. Didn't mean to keep you up."

"No—I mean, I was sort of thinking about coming to . . ." Billy raised his eyebrows above his blue eyes and nodded his head in the classic *C'mon baby, gimme sumpn sumpn* gesture, and Avery smiled a little, remembering that Billy's charm and his humor had attracted him in the first place

"Yeah, well—" he yawned "—next time come ask. I was writing some fanfic while I waited for a response. Got a whole story done, was—"

Billy's curled lip radiated disgust. "You mean you're all complaining about being tired and you were just fucking around?"

"I was on the computer getting some crucial data!" God, he was pissed now, and there went any hope of going back to sleep. Urgh, he hated that—fucked his day all up, because first he'd get up and work, then he'd take a nap, *then* when the rest of the world was on the fucking road or in the grocery store or at the post office, *that's* when Avery got to run errands. "I was *working*, and I took a *break* and did something I *enjoyed*. You know, like when you read Buzzfeed at work and send me six thousand stupid links about shit I don't care about?"

Billy's look of hurt was unmistakable. "I thought we were connecting," he said, and Avery sighed and ground his face into the pillow.

"You're right. We were. But you go sit and eat lunch with all your friends and tell jokes, and me and my friends make GIF sets and write stories about Wolf's Landing. It's my chance to play, that's all. I've been working on this piece about fracking for a week—I'm pissed, I'm depressed, and I feel like the world's gone to hell in a fucking handbasket. Let me have my heroes, okay?"

"Yeah, yeah, whatever," Billy muttered in disgust. "Are you going to submit it and get paid today? Because tomorrow's Valentine's Day and I'd really like to go out to dinner—"

"With me this time?" Avery asked suspiciously, because last time it had been to take the boss out to dinner, and there went half a commission in expensive scotch.

"Yeah, with you this time! And with Sandy and Anthony, because I sort of owe them from—"

Avery buried his head in the pillow and growled. "Oh my God. Billy, could you, I don't know, maybe stop spending my money long enough to hear what I was planning to do with it?"

Billy's jaw dropped. "What's it to you, A? Man, the money just appears in the account anyway—why do *you* care how we spend it?"

"Because *I* am saving money for a trip to Washington in March, do you remember that?"

"For what? So you and your friends can all wax your knobs about Wolf Hammer and Greg Sandford or what the fuck ever?"

"*Wolf's Landing* and Gabriel Hanford," he snarled. "And he's played by an out actor, so maybe show a little respect. And you know what? Go to work, impress your friends. But I want to split our accounts again, okay? You are *so* not hearing me when I talk about finances." Oh yeah, Billy thought he was just going to let that "appears in the account" thing slide. Avery busted his *ass* too hard to have his boyfriend spending his money without respect.

"Yeah, fine, you do all that paperwork shit," Billy scoffed. "But when you want sumpn sumpn, you make sure you flash that wallet, big man, because that's the *only* way a guy like you can get some."

With that he threw on his expensive suit coat and slammed the door, leaving Avery wide-awake and fuming.

He knew he wasn't that great a prize to look at—tall, narrow, all angles, elbows, and ears, with a thatch of dark hair he'd rather comb than cut—but Jesus, that didn't mean he had no pride, right?

It took him half an hour in his boxers with his phone and the computer to disentangle his and Billy's finances. It was just a . . . a pulling back, right? A . . . a disentangling, to find something else that worked. They'd done pretty well when they *hadn't* been living out of the same bank account, *right*?

Avery remembered those first couple of months, being so very careful about who had which refrigerator shelf and making sure he treated for movies at least half of the time. Billy *had* pulled his weight then, hadn't he?

They used to use Avery's spending money for shared trips to the movies and weekend getaways to the beach. Nothing too extravagant—Billy had been starting his internship and Avery had been establishing his reliability as a freelancer, but it had been nice. Simple. Avery had liked it that way.

Maybe splitting their finances would get things back to where they'd been at the beginning. Before Billy had decided he was too good to be seen with a guy who looked like a walking haystack and would rather hang with his fanfic forum than people who worried about the shine on their shoes.

He finished the personal stuff and proofed his article, triple-checked his facts and ran it through grammar checker when he was done, just for shits and giggles, and got some preliminary research for the article on women's issues that he had next in the queue. The thing he loved most about freelancing was that he got to make a difference—and he picked and chose the articles that he thought would do that. He'd established a name for himself writing about liberal issues, and a couple of the online 'zines trusted him and asked for him by name. He'd had to work damned hard for that recognition, and damn it if he was going to let Billy or his father or *anyone* tell him he didn't work for his money.

At ten o'clock, he was falling asleep at his computer and still pissed, so he went to the one place he knew would calm him down and cheer him up at once.

To Fandom Landing, the fan archive he frequented, to see how people liked his fic.

He'd been depressed the night before, melancholy, so he'd written something full of longing and choice. Detective Gabriel Hanford had lost his partner, Detective Julia Morris, to a rogue werewolf, and now he was mourning their one sexual encounter and everything it could have been. He'd written a fic-within-a-fic, and the outer story had Carter Samuels—the guy who *played* Gabriel Hanford, in real mourning for Levi Pritchard, who played Max Fuhrman on the show, being comforted by the girl who played Julia. It was a delicate dance between the real and the imagined, the possible and the impossible, the actual actors and the parts they played—made even more delicate by the fact that Carter Samuels and Levi Pritchard were known to be dating.

Avery had been thoroughly ensorcelled by the story, reluctant to leave before he'd wrapped up every end, woven in every spare thread and made it tight and resonant and perfect. *God*, fiction writing was a rush, but not one he wanted to embrace full-time. Writing imaginary scenarios for the show that had captured his attention just *exercised* something important in him, and he read the comments and kudos eagerly.

Perfect, and perfectly haunting.

OMG—you captured the actor from his public appearances so well!

Lord, the sex scenes were so hot—the het and the m/m—how do you do that?

Painful, funny, and very postmodern. Ooh! That last one was from Lone Wolf—he was like *the* fanfic writer of the Wolf Landing fandom! Avery gave himself a moment to preen.

He always read every comment—and because they were his friends and they shared the same obsession, they were almost all positive. He knew that if he veered off his expected path that could change—the internet was a fickle place—but right now? He was going to revel in the glory of having a place that understood him and shared his fascination with one of his few guilty pleasures.

A chat box opened on his fanfic account, and he responded eagerly.

Hey, Gi-Gi—how's the baby?

He liked this woman—they'd chatted a lot, and he estimated her to be in her thirties to his twenty-six, and she had three kids. But she was funny and warm and understanding, and he could deal with stories of dirty diapers and copious gas and vomit because when he was deep into a news story that was breaking his heart, she and her kids and her happy family would remind him why he wanted to change the world for the better.

Hey, Scarecrow! Baby's asleep, Thank God. I had fifteen minutes—I could've take a dump or read your painfully awesome fic, you bastard. Guess what I picked?

Avery laughed and wiggled his shoulders, pleased as a bunny in clover. Billy could have his fucking Nordies ties and leather shoes. Avery had this, and it made him feel good.

Nice choice—you bought your WolfCon ticket yet?

Are you kidding? Mister G bought us two so he can come a day too. Wants to see what the fuss is about.

Aw, man—*that's* the kind of guy Avery wanted. Someone who would share his passions—or at least not think they were stupid.

You've got a good guy.

Yeah, I think so. Speaking of, how's your guy?

We're going back to separate bank accounts. And when he gets home, I'm telling him I'm taking him off the lease, too.

Avery typed that last grimly. It had been a provisional add-on, with the stipulation that Avery had the last say, but they'd wanted Billy to be able to get keys from the super or to use the pool.

Well, now he'd have to ask Avery for permission, and that gave Avery a petty sense of satisfaction, oh yes it did.

Ouch! Why'd you finally go hard-ass on him?

Insulted my fanfic—no one does that to me, bitches!

Damned straight. String him up, cut him off, chop off his—

Not that far. Just maybe don't give him my money.

Good idea. Gotta run—just wanted to tell you your fic was awesomeness. Tonight I'll write you one.

Avery smiled. Gi-Gi wrote the best virgin fictions he'd ever read. Somebody, somewhere, was always losing some kind of cherry, and Avery *loved* that about her.

I can't wait. I'm going to buy my ticket now! Later!

He was still waiting for his credit card to clear when Billy texted him.

You couldn't wait until tonight? I was out at lunch and my card got rejected!

You have your own credit card. Use it.

It's maxed.

The computer pinged at him. Yup—approved by the bank, and yet unapproved by Billy—the transaction had cleared to fund Avery's dream of traveling to Washington to take part of WolfCon.

That's too bad. Go make some more. Mine will just appear in my bank account after my nap, so I'm good to go.

Don't be a smug bastard, Avery. I didn't mean that and you know it.

No. I don't know it. Talk to you when you get home.

Avery stood and stretched—and yawned. Yup. Here it came. Nappy time. Jesus, he couldn't take long—he still had to go get groceries before Billy got home, because they were going to need some protein to supplement this very active fight they were about to have.

Avery thought about Detective Gabriel Hanford, and the noble, no-nonsense way he approached a difficult task, and then laughed at himself. Gabriel Hanford was beautiful, broody, and movie-star perfect, and, for that matter, so was the guy who played him, Carter Samuels. Neither of them probably had problems with a leech-worthy boyfriend or getting taken seriously or being told they'd never be loved again because their abdomens looked more like a xylophone than a six-pack.

Well, Avery didn't need the movie-star perfect, but he wouldn't mind someone who was reaching for a better world or an ultimate truth.

Everybody had their burdens and their strengths, right?

Today, Avery and Billy were going to sort out their burdens, and Avery was going to take a stand for playing to his strengths. Words and Wolf's Landing.

He may have felt trapped in his relationship with Billy for two years, but he was resourceful. He was smart. He'd worked his way through college, and he made a living doing something not everybody could do. Yeah, sure, Billy thought he took trips and got money for sitting around the house wanking, but Avery knew better. Avery's parents thought he was just fiddle-fucking around until he got a job like Billy's, but Avery had no plans to lock himself in a box like that.

He took a deep breath and looked around his little North Hollywood apartment. It wasn't much, but it was all he needed.

Maybe he could live without that much somewhere else.

He'd escaped his parents' colorless house in the San Diego suburbs with his own smarts and a little hard work. His father might think he didn't understand the real world, but Avery got it. The so-called "real world" was a trap, but Avery was a wily creature. If he couldn't make his relationship into something they *both* could live with, Avery was pretty sure he could wiggle his way out of that trap.

CHAPTER THREE

BOTTOM

C al got back from his shift at the Global walking stiffly—and not from being nailed against the lockers by his boss.

His shin pulsed with heat and ague. He'd dumped bacitracin on it before he'd left work, but the skin was swollen and hot to the touch, and the cut—which'd seemed to be healing so well—had actually just scabbed over what was threatening to be a bitch of an infection. Every step brought new sweat popping out on his forehead, and he barely suppressed a whimper as he parked in front of the moss-covered lawn and limped into the house.

Dottie was pacing the kitchen, frizzy dyed hair askew, a worried look on her face, and Nascha was nowhere to be seen.

"He's out in the boat dock," she said fretfully. "You know how he gets when the sun goes down."

"When he doesn't get his meds," Cal supplied darkly, but she was his only hope for a daily caretaker, although the state did supply a nurse a couple of times a week. He didn't want to piss her off. God, sundowning—the curse of the Alzheimer's patient, that terrible disconnect from reality as soon as there was no big glowing landmark in the sky to hang on to when marking time.

"Yeah, well, if he saw more of the world than this crappy house and the mile loop of this back beach road, he'd probably have more to remember!" she snapped back, and Cal took a deep breath, shuddering with pain.

"I'll check on Keir," he muttered.

Keir slept like the dead, most nights, although waking up early had once been a problem. Not anymore, and he was passed out as he should be, on the bottom bunk of what used to be their shared bedroom. Keir's stuffed badger lay clutched in his arms tonight, which told Cal all he wanted about how bad Nascha's night had been. God. Cal would have slept through this too, if he had a choice.

He limped back into the living room and leaned against the wall, fighting a sudden wave of dizziness.

"You okay?" Dottie asked, her irritation gone almost immediately.

"Cut my leg," he muttered. "It's not healing great. Outside? We'll be back."

The kitchen door was slightly ajar, and he could hear Nascha muttering to himself, and the hollow thump of his slippered feet as he paced the dock.

"Well, someone's got to do something. Shouldn't someone do something? The boy is a mess! Football, studying—he can take his damned test next quarter. *Damn it, Owen, get your ass home so you can talk some sense into your kid!*"

"Nascha?" Cal said hesitantly. "Nascha, you wanted to talk to me?"

"Cal?" Nascha swung around, and his thick-wooled, shawl-collared sweater hung crookedly, and the flannel shirt underneath it hung only halfway down. The tails were coming out from the fly of his jeans, and Cal hated that—*hated* it—because Nascha had been the one to teach him to tuck his shirt in when he'd been a kid, and to straighten his collar and make sure his hair was combed.

It was so unfair that basic dignity was deserting Nascha now.

"I'm here, Great-Uncle," Cal said, tears thick in his throat. "What's up?"

"Where's your father? I need to talk to your father. And your mother. That woman in the living room—she didn't know where they were!"

And thank you, Dottie, for leaving him with this tonight. Cal's vision turned gray at the edges, and he fought a groan.

"What did you want them for?" he hedged. God. No. Nascha took it so hard, every time. Cal's mom, Beth, had apparently been the one bright spot in his life. After she'd married Cal's dad and before Keir was born, she'd invited Nascha to live with them, and he'd never looked back. Their deaths had leveled him. Cal was pretty sure that if he hadn't had to help Cal with Keir, he would have curled into a ball and died.

And on nights like this, Cal thought he might have been on to something there.

"Cal, you've got to stop practicing so hard," Nascha begged. He came forward and raised a shaky hand to Cal's face. "Look at you. You're thin and worn, and you're only a kid."

His touch on Cal's face set off a series of fever tremors that almost brought Cal to his knees.

"Well, I'm not feeling great right now," Cal said, his voice cracking.

"You're burning up," Nascha said, snapped into action, perhaps, by Cal's need. "Beth? Owen? Cal, where's your parents? They need to come take care of you."

"They're not here right now," Cal said, trying hard to keep his jaw strong. "Maybe you could help me? I just need to sit down on the couch, Nascha. If you help me there, when you wake up in the morning, it will all be better."

"Where would they go?" Nascha asked unhappily. But he put his shoulder under Cal's arm, and Cal leaned on his frail weight because he had nowhere else to go.

"They went for a drive," Cal said, his throat tight. "You know how they like to do that."

"Yeah, but Cal, they need to be here for you boys. Family—it's all we got!"

"I know, Uncle Nascha."

Slowly, painfully, they made their way into the house. Cal tripped making the slight step from the dock to the front stoop, and Nascha held him for a moment when he howled.

"Are you hurt? That coach of yours, he puts you through your paces—runs you too much. Shin splints, right?"

Cal remembered shin splints. He *yearned* for shin splints. But right now, he was grateful for the old football complaint, because it meant he didn't have to talk about big fish and horrible days.

"Yeah. Yeah. Let me just . . . just sit and stretch," he said, thinking if the pain got any worse he'd throw up.

Nascha's cold hand on his forehead was meant to be tender, but it made all of Cal's skin hurt. He refused to recoil anyway. God, he needed that hand.

They got him inside and sitting down, and Cal shivered for a few minutes while Dottie got him water and some ibuprofen.

"You'll take it easy now, Cal?" Nascha asked, worried. "Because this family needs you."

Cal closed his eyes, and remembered that Nascha meant that even when he thought Owen and Beth McCorkle were still the grown-ups and the breadwinners. It comforted him, even as it broke his heart.

"Yeah," he said, his throat rough. "I'll take tomorrow off, how's that, Nascha?"

He needed to take Keir in for his appointment tomorrow. Sometimes Keir's doctor—who was a good guy, in spite of being overworked and undereducated on Keir's conditions—would take a look at Cal's fishing injuries without a co-pay. Maybe he'd throw Cal a bone and prescribe some antibiotics or something, because Cal's body felt like it was shaking apart, one atom at a time.

"That's wise, Calladh." Nascha nodded sagely. "Your mother will get home and make bread. You need to eat."

Nascha sat at the recliner and tipped his head back, closing his eyes, and Cal relaxed on the couch, his polyester clothes sticking clammily to his skin. He *wanted* to get up and shower and get rid of the restaurant smell, but his body wanted to stay on that couch more. Cal grabbed the afghan his mother had crocheted from the back of the battered couch and wrapped up in it, resting his head on the arm. The television—never off for long—continued to play as Dottie let herself out, and Cal fell into an uneasy, pain-ridden sleep.

He woke up at five in the morning with a crick in his neck and a bloated leg about one bacterium away from amputation.

He made a trip to the bathroom, and then to the kitchen cabinet for more ibuprofen. While he was at it, he woke Nascha up and made him take his medication. The old man was fractious and argumentative. "Why do I need medicine? You couldn't let an old man sleep? Disrespectful little shit—I'll make your father take a paddle to your ass!"

Well, Dad had done that on a very rare occasion, and Cal was none the worse for wear. His father never punished out of meanness, but out of a fear Cal would do things that could get him hurt. The worst time had been when Cal had taken the boat out without permission and without telling anyone where he was going. Cal had worried his parents sick—and that was a lesson he'd learned in his bones. The people you loved deserved respect.

"You make him do that," Cal said, wrestling the pill into Nascha's hand. "You get my dad to paddle my ass, Nascha. But right now you take your fucking pill, okay?"

Nascha slapped his face—not hard or spitefully, but for the obscenity when Cal was supposed to honor his elders. "You watch your manners, boy," Nascha snapped.

"I *will*, damn it, just take your medicine!" Cal yelled back, shoving the cup of water at him.

Nascha tossed the pill in his mouth and dry swallowed, and then threw the water in Cal's face.

Cal screamed.

Oh God, it was *so* fucking cold, and his skin was *so* fucking hot and—

"Cal?" Nascha asked, all concerned. He held his hand to Cal's head. "Cal, are you okay?"

"I'm sick, Nascha," he pleaded. "I'm sick, and you're being awful, and I need to take Keir to the doctor and . . ."

And he lost it, at six in the morning, soaking wet and crumpled in a heap between the couch and the recliner, raging with fever.

Nascha went and got him clean clothes and helped him dress, and then put him back to sleep on the couch, mumbling the whole time about how Cal's parents would make it right.

When Cal woke up again, Keir was awake and ready for his doctor's appointment, and Nascha remembered what year it was.

But Cal wasn't getting any better, and as he swallowed down some more ibuprofen and loaded Keir into the truck, he had the feeling that their precarious little family situation was about to get a lot more unstable.

How was he going to pay the bills if he couldn't work?

CHAPTER FOUR

DOUBT

"Oh yay, the 'rents," Billy muttered, angry as he had been perpetually since Avery had separated their finances.

"My father loves you," Avery said dryly, stepping on the brakes with a frown. God, the stretch of I-5 between LA and San Diego sucked balls. It would be just whizzing along at a decent speed, and suddenly—*bam*. You're going nowhere.

"Wonderful," Billy retorted. "But he's not gay, so where does that leave us?"

Avery sighed. "Look, man. I'm sorry I split our money up without warning you. You're right. It *was* a dick move. But I've got to tell you, you just totally weren't respecting where that money was coming from—and you weren't respecting *me*. I mean, is it so hard now?"

"I have to ask you for a lunch allowance like a little kid!" Billy snarled. "And that would be great if we were roommates—that would at least get me the fuck out of going to see your fucking parents!"

Avery couldn't argue about that. His parents . . . Well, gay might have been a thing in politics, but it was a thing for other people's children. Acknowledging Avery's *own* gayness—hell, his own *anything*—was really a foreign idea for them.

"I'm sorry," he said again, sighing. "I just thought Dad could store some of my stuff. I wanted to thin out the apartment before I went to Washington—"

"Oh, great. So you get to go to Washington and I what? Sit at home and wait to go blow my boss?"

Traffic started moving again, and Avery glanced behind his shoulder, and oh, thank God. He *could* take the next off ramp. Who gave a shit if he was in Anaheim, he needed to get off this fucking road!

He pulled the car onto Valencia and cruised down the main drag until he came to a Denny's by a bus stop. Abruptly, he made a right into the Denny's and looked at Billy, at a loss.

"Billy . . . have you been giving your boss blowjobs?"

That epic fight Avery had been anticipating had never materialized. Billy had come home the night of the big bank job (as Avery now thought of it) and had gone to bed, encased in icy silence. And the two weeks after that had been one long arctic blast of Billy working late and then coming home while Avery was working, and ignoring his existence. This trip to visit the parents had been planned before then, or Avery didn't think Billy would have gotten in the car.

Once upon a time, they had talked, watched television, seen movies, made plans together. Now, they didn't even say good morning.

"What's it to you?" Billy said, but Avery remembered when they'd been boyfriends and not antagonists, and he knew what Billy sounded like when he was hurt.

"I . . . I wasn't trying to break up with you," Avery said. Hurt. There was no other word for it.

"That would have been a helluva lot cleaner," Billy said, still not looking at him.

"Do you . . . do you want to break up?"

"What's sad is that you think we haven't."

Oh. Habit. Avery hadn't seen it, but apparently habit had been what had kept Billy coming home. Habit had gotten him into the car this morning. Oh hell. Avery had been hoping for a reconciliation, and Billy had been relying on a habit.

"I'll. . ." Money. That's what had started this, wasn't it? "I'll pay rent until the lease is up," Avery said softly. "When I go to Washington . . . I'll move up there permanently. That'll give you a chance to find somewhere else to live."

Billy glared at him. "What the fuck ever." But those pretty blue eyes that Avery had once adored—they were spilling over. "What are we doing at Denny's?"

"You . . . you can take the bus home if you want. It'll take a while, but you don't have to go to my parents' house. Not if you don't—"

"Fucking classy." And with that, Billy hopped out of the car and slammed the door. Avery swallowed hard against his own tears and watched him go.

"Now, Avery," Ilene Kennedy said, placatingly, "what's your friend going to do if you don't help him make rent?"

"He's my boyfriend, Mom. Except he's my ex-boyfriend."

"Well, I mean, I know he's a boy, Avery, but didn't you sign a lease?"

Avery blinked at his mother—a short painstakingly thin woman who exercised religiously and clocked every calorie in a diary, but who never looked outside of her diary long enough to see the forest for the calories. Avery thought she *might* have had hair like his—unruly curls—but he'd never seen it *not* slicked back in a ponytail, so he couldn't say for sure.

"Yeah, Mom. I signed a lease. It's up in two months. I'd have to pay the rent anyway, and since I'm moving to Washington, he can just stay there."

Avery had been trying to explain the deal with Billy—which was weirding him out, because it had *just happened.*

"But why do you have to let go of your lease at all?"

"Because I'm moving?" And he'd been saying it a lot since he'd pulled up to his parents' house sans Billy—and it had been making more and more sense the more he'd said it.

"But—"

"Out of the state, Mom. You're not senile—why do you keep forgetting this?"

"Because it's stupid," Avery's father said, walking in from the garage and overhearing. He was wiping grease from his hands as he spoke, and Avery wanted to sneer. His dad worked in a bank, wore a suit, and changed his own oil. Not because he liked to tinker with cars, but because he liked to think he was smarter than the people he'd pay to change his oil for him. He'd actually fried two engines that way, but that was never talked about.

Avery had tried once. In eighth grade—shortly after he'd come out and flush with the victory of getting his junior high a GSA—he'd told his father, "Fred, men who work with their hands are no better or worse educated than you are. They are just talented in different areas." This was an exact quote from one of his teachers.

He'd spent the next two weeks in his room after school, grounded beyond belief. He used the time to write short pieces for left-wing news publications, one of which had been accepted for a fee of $25, and he'd been hell bent on journalism ever since.

"Why?" Avery asked, tired of the argument but unable to stop taking the bait. "The cost of living is cheaper, I like the climate, most of the state is blue, and I don't have any ties here."

"You have *us*," his father said. He'd thrown the rag in the washroom hamper, and Ilene was running in there to make sure that it didn't contaminate everything else in the hamper with grease. Did Avery's father know that one act caused all sorts of havoc in her life? Probably. Did he care? Not particularly.

"That's not incentive to stay," Avery said, meaning it.

"Avery!" his mother complained from the washroom.

"Mom, I'm gay."

"You keep saying that!" she said, laughing. She poked her head out of the washroom, where he heard the sink running. Probably hot water and the special degreaser that he'd seen her use. Spitefully, Avery hoped his dad burned up another engine. God, these people did not bring out the best in him.

"Because it's true. And you keep telling me that all I need is the right girl. I've been *living with a man* for two years."

"But you're leaving him!" his mom said brightly, turning off the spigot and coming back into the kitchen, her duty apparently complete now that the nasty rag was soaking. His father in the meantime was running scalding water over his hands and using dish soap to get the grease out of his fingers. The soap was slopping all over the pristine sink, and Avery's mom was watching in agony as Fred Kennedy wrecked the kitchen she'd just cleaned.

"I'm breaking up with him, Mom. It . . ." Oh Lord. "It actually hurts a lot. And you don't give a shit. So exactly why do I want to stay here?"

"Honey, friends have falling outs—"

"And you're not going anywhere," his father thundered, turning to him, his famous kid-terrifying scowl on his face. Avery was pretty sure his father wore that scowl when he destroyed working-men's dreams.

"I am," Avery said, nodding. "I have the hotel reservations, the route, and the money in the bank. All I need to do is drive up there and find an apartment with wi-fi. I can do that even if I pay Billy's last two month's rent."

"Why the hell would you do that?" his father asked. "Ilene, you're driving me bug-shit. Get away from me with that towel."

Avery's mother retreated in wounded, antsy silence, and Avery thought that maybe he should stop for some Advil on the way home. He felt a massive headache coming on, and he had to go home and tell the whole world he was moving. Oh geez—his editors, his landlord, *Gi-Gi*!

His head gave a violent throb. He was going to have to tell his best friend why he was moving, and admit to her that he'd been part of the doucheyness that had become his and Billy's relationship.

How embarrassing.

"Because we're breaking up, and I'm trying not to be a dick about it," Avery said patiently. Jesus!

"No, not that—that's your personal business, I don't want to hear about it." Of course Fred didn't want to hear about it. He didn't even acknowledge it was true. "Why would you want to move?"

"Because (a) I don't want to be near Billy anymore, and (b) I don't want to be near you," Avery snapped. Both things were the truth, but he felt sort of bad about saying them.

"Don't be a smartass, Avery. Do you really think you'll get past the California border by yourself? God, you're fucking incompetent. Have you *seen* that thing you drive?"

"I drive it, Dad. I see it all the time. And you're forgetting that I go out of state periodically—"

"I don't mean flying across country!" God, the way Fred said it, he made it sound like Avery was getting on the kiddie carousel. "I mean *driving*. You can't get your head out of your computer long enough to take a fucking leak!"

"That only happened once," Avery said, crossing his eyes. He'd been in the seventh grade, and damn his mother for telling Fred anyway. God—like he'd been the only kid to play video games to the extremes. "And you know what? I've done a whole lot of growing up since I was twelve—it's what happens in *fifteen years*." Oh God. What was it about his parents that made him feel like a little kid—and not in the wide-eyed, *Yes, there's still a Santa* way, either. "Seriously, Dad. I'm a grown-up. I've paid rent, put myself through school, had a couple of relationships—"

"But no one you can bring home," his father growled.

And even though Avery knew better, he was *still* surprised into saying it. "I brought Billy over once a month for two years!"

"That's not what I'm talking about!" his dad retorted. "And you know it!"

"No, no I don't," Avery said, trying not to cry out of sheer frustration. "We paid bills together, we slept in the same bed and we had penetrative coitus—"

"Don't you talk that way around your mother!" Fred Kennedy thundered.

Ilene put her hands over her ears, distressed. "Avery! That's not polite!"

"Neither is ignoring who I am!" Avery turned to her, thinking that before he fled the state, he might be able to get this across. "I'm a grown-up, mom. I've taken care of myself since my third year of college. I pay bills, I hold down jobs—I'm even sort of good in my field. And I've had two relationships that meant a lot to me, that you and dad keep pretending you don't understand."

"That's because—"

"And now I'm leaving. I'm moving away because you two don't know who I am, and my boyfriend"—*ex*-boyfriend—"is apparently blowing his boss." Billy had gotten home at two in the morning every night since the "disentanglement." How could Avery not have known?

God.

He tried to bring himself back to that moment when he thought Billy had been a good guy and their relationship could work. But spending time with his parents just reinforced that he'd apparently been living with a guy just like his dad.

And he was in no way, shape, or form his mom who would put up with that crap.

"Avery Sanders Ken—"

"Dad, Mom, I'm leaving in two weeks. I'm going to ship my books here until I find a place—you don't have to do much with them—just keep them dry, and I'll pay for the postage, okay?"

"You're asking us to—"

"To please let me use your garage for a couple of boxes. Are you going to charge me rent, because if you are, I can always rent a storage space—"

"You can use the garage," his mom said, smiling hesitantly like that was going to make all the rest of it go away. "Will your friend want to leave his things too?"

"No, because we just broke up," Avery said, scrubbing at his face with both hands.

"No, because he's not going to make it past Crescent City," Fred said in disgust, throwing a grease-covered dishtowel into the sink.

"Okay," Ilene said brightly, scurrying past Avery's father's wide-shouldered body to grab the towel. "We'll just count on that, then. Can you stay for dinner, Avery?"

"No," Avery said. "I've got a headache."

He got home, partially hammered on Motrin and a giant triple cheeseburger from In-N-Out, and let himself into the apartment.

Billy wasn't there, but then, Avery imagined, he probably hadn't had to catch a bus from Anaheim to North Hollywood, either. Not if he'd been blowing his boss for the last two weeks. Feeling sad and lost and thoroughly beaten, he drifted to his computer and tried to wrap his head around what he'd just decided to do.

Gi-Gi was online. Oh, thank God. Gi-Gi was online.

Heya, Avery. How goes things?

How goes things?

Avery poured his heart out on her, from the short, painful resolution with Billy to the frustration-fest of his parents. He finished feeling silly and guilty and all sorts of dumb for sucking up her time with his personal problems.

So, you're moving to Washington in two weeks?

He laughed to himself. *Yeah. Why the hell not?*

That's awesome! We live north of Portland—we can come visit. You and me, we can see each other more than just at the convention! Won't that be awesome?

Oh my God.

YES! He found himself laughing semihysterically in his empty, bitter apartment. *Gi-Gi, that's the best news I've had all day.*

And it was the news that would get him out of California and up past Seattle. It was the news that would let him start his life all over again.

Out there, in the great wide beyond, Avery had people who would understand him. He would have friends.

CHAPTER FIVE

TIME OUT

"Yes, Cal, I took my medicine," Nascha said mildly. "Did you take *yours*?"

Cal squinted at Great-Uncle Nascha through his fever, and tried not to snarl. Oh, the fucking irony of being home and being too goddamned sick to take care of Keir and Nascha while he was there.

"I think so," he admitted, pulling in a painful breath. "What time is it?"

"Noon. Did you take your morning antibiotics?"

"Yeah," Cal muttered, remembering because they'd sat so badly in his stomach. "I took my antibiotics." They didn't have any milk in the house, or any cereal or, well, *anything* for that matter, because Cal hadn't been able to fish *or* bus tables for the last two weeks.

Goddamned motherfucking, cum-sucking, bitch-smacking, cock-biting, spit-roast-me-on-a-skillet, God-are-you-*trying*-to-kill-me, piece-of-shit, illegal green fish.

"What about your pain meds?"

By the time Cal had gotten to see Keir's doctor, the infection on his shin had been dire. Not just red-fleshed, *Ouch, maybe I should wash that?* sort of infected, but *Holy Jesus God is your skin turning green?* kind of infected. Fever, shakes, body aches, and vomiting—for days.

Keir's doctor had diagnosed him and written his prescription without a co-pay or a visit fee. The bad news was, he'd had just enough money for Keir's antipsychotics and his own antibiotics, but not enough for the full prescription of painkillers. He'd compromised with the doc by buying half the Vicodin, and then doling them out for those times when a handful of over-the-counter ibuprofen wasn't going to cut it.

"No," Cal said shortly. "Sorry, Nascha. Don't have enough to just down them like candy."

Nascha grunted, and Keir, who had been flipping through the cable channels on the television suddenly stopped.

"Noon? Doesn't that mean it's lunchtime? Nascha, I need lunch. Is there any cereal?"

"I don't remember," Nascha said vaguely, and that was enough to propel Keir up off Nascha's chair so he could start rooting through the cupboards. As soon as he was there, Nasha took his place on the corduroy recliner and looked at Cal seriously. "We're completely out of food," he said quietly. "There's a package of ramen in there, and he's going to make it and eat it, and we're done."

Cal closed his eyes. "Nascha . . ." Oh God. "Here—hand me the phone. I'll try to pick up a shift at the Global."

Nascha grunted. "If I had five dollars . . . I swear, Cal, I could turn it to five hundred. I've been taking my meds since you got hurt—I could make it happen."

Cal grunted. He knew it. Nascha *could* make it happen. He'd done it when Cal's parents were alive. But now . . . "What about when the sun goes down," he asked, wishing he could sound gentle. "You can't see the sky in the Global, Nascha."

Nascha let out a growl. "God," he said, with feeling. "I haven't sundowned in weeks, Cal—"

"Yeah, but you'd be in a strange place, and I couldn't be there for you," Cal said, voice fraught. God, that last time had sucked. Cal didn't want to think of himself, weeping on the floor, sick and helpless, and Nascha, confused and hurt and pissed off. In six years that hadn't been easy in the least, that moment ranked at the bottom.

No. Just *no* on the whole *Nascha can make their rent with his gambling cash* idea. It wasn't happening—not now.

"I'll go in to work," Cal said, holding out his hand for the phone. "I'll take a Vicodin and go. It'll be great. I can get groceries on the way home."

If he went to the 7-Eleven, he could get groceries on credit. Of course, if he went to the 7-Eleven, they'd charge him twice what the groceries cost at the supermarket. Okay—he'd go to the supermarket, because thanks to the tourists—and the damned TV people—the supermarket stayed open until twelve now, right? Cal felt a little guilty about taking advantage of that. Until he'd been forced to watch *Wolf's Landing* while he'd been laid up here, he'd sort of hated all those people.

Well, you had to let go of petty grievances against the world in times of need, and he figured this moment right here qualified as a time of need.

Nascha must have seen the resolve in his eyes, because he handed the phone over without protest. In the background, Keir made a delighted noise and started to fill a pot with water, so he could eat the last of their food.

Cal knew the number at the Global by heart, and he had Kendra at the front desk route him to George.

"I thought you were sick?" George said suspiciously, and Cal let out a short bark of laughter.

"I feel like crap," he said, hating that he had to admit that. "I need the shift, George. My little brother is eating the last food in the house."

How was that for honest?

George grunted. "I could bring you some—"

Oh no. "I'd rather go catch fish," Cal muttered, the threat to hang up implicit in his voice.

"No!" George snapped. "Jesus, I'm sorry my help is that repugnant to you!"

It wasn't the help—it was the selling his ass to get it. "I'm not for sale," Cal said stiffly.

On the other end of the phone, George blew out a sharp, painful breath. "I didn't mean to imply—"

"Can I have the shift or not?" Cal asked shortly. He wanted to add, *And sex is out of the question*, but Nascha was listening.

In fact, Nascha was looking at him oddly, like he was getting a feeling from the conversation alone.

"Yeah. Here. We've got a four-hour shift today—heavy work, but heavy tips, and you can go home and sleep. Do you want me to start putting you on the schedule again, too?"

"Maybe the day after tomorrow," Cal conceded. God, the big bills were piling up—the mortgage, the ice bill for the fish, power and heat. The least Cal could do was get everybody food and maybe pay up the heat and power. The cable wouldn't shut off for another two months, but they needed to pay that too. The *least* he could do to take care of his family, right?

"We'll see how you look when your shift is over," George conceded. "I'll see you at four?"

Four. That meant Cal had three hours to sleep, a half an hour to shower and get ready, and then he could make it to work. "Yeah," he said, thinking only of that three hours of sleep. "Four is fine."

George hung up, and Cal gave the phone to Nascha, who hung it up on the wall and then came back to sit. Keir was still in the kitchen, watching the pot boil—they had a few more minutes.

"You know that young man?"

Cal grunted. "We don't like each other. He's my boss."

Nascha grimaced and shook his head. "That sounded personal."

Oh God. No. On top of everything else, let's not make Cal tell his uncle about the fuck buddy he didn't even like. "It shouldn't be," he murmured, barely awake anyway. "Nascha, could you put my clothes in the wash and wake me at three? I'll take a pain med then, and my antibiotics too."

Nascha wiped Cal's sweaty hair from his forehead. "I wish you didn't have to go," he said softly.

"Yeah, well, me too." Cal was comforted in spite of himself.

He woke up feeling marginally better—and then took his pain med and felt *much* better.

And then went into work and felt way the fuck worse.

He managed to keep his ass moving, which was good, because every time he slowed down he saw spots in front of his eyes. By the time the four hours—and the dinner rush—were over, he was queasy, still feverish, and his leg felt like it was going to fall off.

George came into the locker room as he was counting the forty dollars the servers had left in his apron, holding a small bottle and a no-bullshit look.

"These are from Kendra. She didn't take all of them when she sprained her ankle. They're standard-issue Vicodin, so you can take them when your prescription runs out."

Cal took the bottle numbly and shook out a tab to dry swallow. "Thanks," he said, too drained to keep up any hostility.

"You're welcome."

"I can't put out for you right now."

George jerked back like Cal had slapped him. "That was a shitty thing to say!"

Cal sucked in a breath. "God. Yes." He closed his eyes. "You're right. I'm sorry. Thank you. I'll go now."

"Jesus, Cal—you won't let me help you even a little?"

"No," Cal said, eyes closed. "They're mine."

George let out a sigh. "I can't let you work the day after tomorrow. But I'll have you on the schedule, same shift, the day after that."

"Thanks, George," Cal said—the second time in five minutes. "I'm sorry."

"Sorry for what?" George asked.

"For being a douche bag. For saying shitty things. For not being who you wanted."

George grunted. "Well, I'm obviously not who *you* want. I guess we're even."

He left, and Cal spent another five minutes letting the painkiller take effect, and thinking about what George had said. They weren't even, not really. George had all the power—he was Cal's boss. Which was why Cal was so shitty to him. But that wasn't George's fault, really.

God.

Cal was really not a nice person when he wasn't with Nascha and Keir. When had *that* happened?

He shifted off the locker room bench and groaned.

Well, he wasn't going to fix it tonight, that was for damned sure.

Nascha was waiting for him when he got home. Dottie was there too, and she only took half her usual fee of $20, which meant Cal could have bought gas along with the milk, bread, ramen, peanut butter, and jelly he'd brought home. Bananas too, because who couldn't use a good banana once in a while?

Well, apparently Cal, because the only banana he'd been getting was George's, and that hadn't made him feel good at all.

Dottie put away the groceries while Nascha applied a hot mustard poultice to Cal's leg. The searing heat made him muffle a scream in his fist, and hope Keir hadn't heard it.

On his shin, he felt something burst, the infection breaking the half-healed wound of the skin, and the pus began to run. He started to cry, the relief and the pain mixed together were so terribly acute, and Nascha handed him a paper towel so he could clean off his face.

"Oh fuck," he sobbed, exhausted and sweating through his clothes. "God, Nascha. That hurt like fucking hell."

"Take off your clothes," Nascha murmured. "We've got clean sheets on the couch. Lay down here and sleep, and I can put cloths on your head."

Cal nodded, helpless. George didn't get to take care of him. George wasn't family.

But Nascha was, and right now, Nascha had forgotten more about how to be family than Cal had ever known.

CHAPTER SIX

Vision Quest

The car that Avery's father despised so much was an eight-year-old Honda hybrid—it was fuel efficient and handled like a dream. Alas, it was not roomy. Two weeks after Billy *hadn't* made it to Mom and Dad's for dinner, Avery pulled out of his apartment parking lot with all his earthly possessions. He'd left the furniture in the apartment, because it had been cheap and secondhand anyway, and he'd left Billy in the doorway, after trying to shake hands.

"I paid up the rent," Avery said for the umpteenth time.

"I don't give a fuck," Billy told him rudely. "Why don't you just go already."

"You know, you had something to do with this too!" Avery burst out, finally unwilling to bear the brunt of the entire breakup.

Billy shook his head. "Why didn't you just kick me out, Avery? You split up our finances, why didn't you have the balls to just kick me out?"

Avery sighed. "Because I thought if we went back to the beginning, we might remember why it was good."

Billy sighed. "Don't get eaten by a fucking bear," he muttered.

And that was the closest Avery would get to "good-bye."

He made it to Sacramento that first day before he absolutely had to stop. He checked into a cheap motel with a pool and excavated the overnight case he'd put on the front passenger seat. After a quick swim and some time spent surfing aimlessly through his laptop, he got a call from Billy.

"You coming back yet?"

Avery frowned, wondering what it was about him that said "stupid" and "irresolute." "You done blowing your boss?" he asked, wondering if he'd get a straight answer this time.

"He's got a giant dick and a giant bank account, Avery. And you cut me off!"

Avery was going to apologize one more time, but he couldn't. "I'm sorry we both got like this," he said finally. "I want to be a better person than this guy. I hope you can too."

"Fuck you!"

The end-call beep pretty much killed any productivity buzz Avery had going, and he stopped surfing the internet and pulled up his bank account. Looking at the reassuring (if not robust) numbers, he tried very hard to take stock of his life.

Oh holy hell.

What had he done?

Not with Billy—he'd pretty much ended that himself.

But what? He suddenly decided to move to the Pacific Northwest because he happened to be going there anyway?

What the hell had he been thinking?

He sat at his computer desk in the hotel and tried not to hyperventilate, comforting himself with facts.

He had enough in the bank account to cover the convention, and *probably* enough to cover the deposit on an apartment and some basic furniture while he got his feet under him. And he had two weeks reserved in the hotel in Bluewater Bay to do that. Yeah, four days were going to be the convention, but hopefully while he was there he'd be able to get some advice from locals about where to eat cheap, where to buy groceries, and where he could find an affordable, nonsleazy apartment with wi-fi. Of course, he was spending a few days traveling to get up there, too—there were no guarantees he wouldn't find a place on the California coast, or Portland before he cleared Seattle. The Pacific Northwest was his oyster, right?

As long as he had a computer hookup, he had a job. In fact, the convention actually *was* a job—he had a line on an article about fandoms that he was *dying* to write. All he needed was to hang out in his hotel room the day after the con and he'd have that done.

Some of his panic receded, and he looked around his little single-bed hotel room long enough to relax.

He could do this. Yeah, it was true—nobody in his *old* life thought he was capable of getting himself from point A to point B. But he'd proved them wrong a thousand times already—they'd just never seen him in the first place.

Avery could see himself. He was not going to be stuck, small and anonymous, in a place he didn't love with people who didn't even know him—and he was getting the hell out of Dodge to prove it. Hell—*getting*? He'd *gotten* the hell out of Dodge. All he had to do was get past Seattle and into Bluewater Bay, and he would have proved to all of them that he was far more capable than anybody thought he was.

His father had thundered at him that he didn't have the guts to make it past Portland—he could *at least* prove him wrong about that, right?

He almost didn't make it to Portland.

He fell into the classic trap: he took the scenic route to Crescent City because he wanted to see the ocean, and he stopped there for an early dinner. He had slightly less than half a tank when he got back into the car. High on the sweet ocean breezes—and the fact that he hadn't *killed* himself maneuvering the twisty coastal roads in the afternoon drizzle—he decided to refill in Medford. And if not, there had to be a stop along the way, right?

Wrong.

Oh God.

Longest three hours of his life.

The road wasn't bad, actually, but as the sun went down, leaving him in the great shadow of the redwood forest, Avery made a terrible realization.

He couldn't see any lights.

He couldn't *see* any *lights*.

Oh as God was his witness, mile after mile crawled by, and he couldn't *see any lights*.

His gas tank pinged about twenty miles from Medford, and he passed his umpteenth closed gas station with something like despair. Where were the *fucking lights*?

His car rolled to a stop in front of the next gas station and died. And the place wasn't just closed—there were weeds growing around the old-fashioned, nonelectronic pumps and everything. When his car died, Avery was left alone in the quiet dark. He'd never slept out of doors before in his life.

He pulled a blanket from the pile in the back and huddled under it, peering into the thick trees that ringed the station. He'd seen them as the sun went down, great towering redwoods, and he'd already passed up the opportunity to drive *through* the trunk of one. Right now, looking up into the night sky through his windshield, they were terrifying, giant guardians, looming blackly between him and the only light on earth.

In the few spaces between the treetops, the stars glittered, copious and myriad, and he stared at them, willing the moon to drift into their sphere and give some light to his surroundings. He turned off his headlights so his battery didn't die and thought dolefully of pulling his iPod off the charger so he could at least listen to some music with his earbuds.

But what if someone walked up to the car and he didn't hear them?

The thought of someone walking up to the car and knocking on the window was terrifying—even if they had friendly intentions. He *needed* to hear what was coming.

He pulled some of his softer luggage down so he could lean against it, and tried to make himself comfortable. He'd sit and wait, right? Someone would come down the road with a gas can. *Some* psycho, *you mean!* The locals had to carry gas cans, right? Why wouldn't you carry a gas can if there weren't any gas stations for seventy miles? *Maybe the locals are cannibals, and they all hang out waiting for prey.* He couldn't have been the first tourist stuck between Crescent City and Medford, right? *The others were never heard from again.*

Maybe he should call somebody, let them know where he was? *Your parents will laugh at you. Your ex-boyfriend probably* hopes *something bad happens to you. Your editor will want you to call the police and get a story. And the whole discussion is moot because there's no signal anyway.*

"So there!" he said out loud, and the sound of his voice startled him so bad he almost wet himself.

Five minutes later, he'd turned the headlights back on so he could make sure there were no snakes, bears, coyotes, or ghosts in the place he chose to urinate. When he was done with that (and of making free use of the Purell tucked into the side of his door), he turned off the lights and cuddled resolutely under the blanket.

It was time to give himself a pep talk.

He had mace. He had water. He even had healthy granola bars and bags of sunflower seeds. If someone saw him and stopped, he had two options.

Option A: This person was a serial killer who would skin him and eat him and wear his messy brown hair as a hat.

If Option A showed up, Avery had mace and sharp elbows. It wasn't much, but it's what he had, and scaring himself stupid wasn't going to make that any better.

Option B was a nice person who wanted to help him.

But after his boyfriend had turned out to be a douche bag and his dad had turned out to be mostly right about him not being capable of getting past Portland, he was sort of more leaning toward serial killer.

He fell asleep eventually, his tired eyes not able to take peering into the darkness anymore. *It's quiet. I can hear the wind in the tops of the trees and that's about it. Wow. Even my thoughts echo.*

It was his last thought before he fell asleep.

The next day he was *literally* rescued by a cowboy with a gas can. The guy had a Stetson and a giant gleaming black truck, and three extra cans strapped in the back with bungi cords. He said very little, accepted Avery's thanks in taciturn silence, and pushed aside Avery's attempts to pay him.

"You're not local," he said, spitting casually through a missing tooth on the side.

"No, I'm sort of traveling up the coast to—"

"Always fill up in Crescent City or Medford," the cowboy muttered. "Every gas station between them has closed up shop. You got a chance to refuel, you take it. You get a chance to eat, you take it. This ain't the fuckin' city."

"Yessir, thankyousi—"

Avery's obeisance in the direction of the Stetson-wearing forest god was cut short by the sound of a truck door slamming. After another stop behind a tree (and a hope he'd have a chance to contemplate the other God in a *real* bathroom sometime soon), Avery was on his way again.

Medford to Portland wasn't a bad trip really, if a guy could ignore the "Jesus Saves" billboards back to back with the advertisements for "XXX Porn!" (There seemed to be a chain—at least all the signs were similar in yellow and black. Avery was reasonably sure there'd be no rainbows in those porn stores but he was not once tempted to test this theory out.)

He did, however, find the cultural center in Portland and venture in for a visit. He wanted some books on legends and the Native tribes in the area. As he'd driven in, he'd been taken by the great volcanoes in the distance—Mount Rainier, Mount Hood—and he wanted to learn more. They enchanted him, all of that power, the snow in late March, the broadness of their bases and their hubris in reaching for the sky.

Avery couldn't wait to read him some of *that*.

He checked into a hotel in Portland, thinking he'd follow random flannel-wearing cowboy's advice and enjoy the downtime while he could. Avery found himself the tallest building in Portland and the best restaurant, according to the locals. He was going to eat himself some *steak*.

His cellphone buzzed just as he got back to the hotel room with a doggy bag.

"Hello, Avery Kennedy, this is Stagecoach Bank—you have an account with us?"

"Yes . . ."

"We seem to have some odd charges on your card. Were you at the Cultural Center in Portland today, address . . ." The young woman on the other end of the line rattled off pretty much everything he'd done in the past twelve hours, and Avery was *very* glad he hadn't gone to the porn store, just to "see" about the right kind of porn.

"Yes, yes," he cut the girl off. "All those charges are mine. I'm on vacation—"

"Okay then, sir, we'll just freeze your credit card to make sure there's no other theft involved!" Her chipper voice was reciting words by rote, and Avery panicked.

"No! Wait! Don't— I'm on vaca—"

The dial tone seemed to mock him, and he sank dazedly onto the bed. Oh hell. Motherfucking hell. How much cash did he have? He'd been paying for everything with his bank card, but he'd taken out a good $300 and added the odd twenty to the total at gas stations. With a firm swallow, he dialed the number on the back of his bank card and tried to maybe undo the damage.

"No," he said patiently for the third time. "All of those charges were normal. I left town two days ago from LA, drove to Sacramento, then through Redding, then I took the back way to the ocean, through Crescent City, to Medford, and now I'm here."

There was a frustrated sigh on the phone. "Well, sir, you've just paid your hotel charge for the night, and you seem to have your hotel paid up in Washington, so you're doing okay. Is there any chance we can send you your new card at your home address—"

"I'm in the process of moving!" he muttered in frustration, ripping a hand through his curly hair. "I was going to find a place while I was up in Washington!"

"Oh. Okay, sir, so what I can do is this . . ."

Avery listened in disbelief as he was given the post office address closest to the hotel and told that his card would be sent there, and that he'd better not lose his birth certificate or his driver's license or then he'd *really* be in trouble.

Oh God. "I'm going to be without resources for a *week*?" he asked, a little panicked. He reminded himself again of the money in his pocket, of the fact that he had a roof over his head, and of the fact that he had a place to go and someone to see. It wasn't that bad, it wasn't that bad, it wasn't that bad . . .

"Yes, sir. We'll send the card via registered mail, and you will get a call from this number when it arrives. We're so sorry about the mix-up, sir. Do you have anyone you can call to help you out?"

Avery tried not to moan, and threw himself backwards on the hotel bed. "You mean like the ex-boyfriend who's been blowing his boss or the parents who were sure I was too dumb to drive across country? No. No I don't have anyone I can call!"

"Oh. Uhm, we're sorry, sir. Uhm, let us know if there's anything we can do to make his situation better."

"Reinstate my card?"

"Except that."

"Augh!"

"Good-bye, sir. Have a nice day!"

And with that, Avery was stuck in the hotel, wondering if the gods weren't telling him something really dire.

He crossed his arms and pouted. Well, fuck them if they were! He'd survived a night in the woods, no tent, no running water. He'd just tucked in and survived. Yeah, he didn't want to make a *habit* of living in his car, but he thought he could deal. He *had* money. He just needed to exist without it until he found another branch of his bank.

He could do that. He could live lean. Hell, didn't need much beside his computer most days anyway, right? And cheap food. God, you could get two cheeseburgers for three dollars at McDonalds—look! For Avery, that was two meals alone!

Or a stop at the grocery store, and some peanut butter and jelly, right?

Avery gulped some air, and stared at the really nice artwork on the wall.

This was a *really* nice hotel room. He was treating himself—he'd gotten a room with a view and the good soap and the big television.

He'd better take advantage of this good hotel room.

And he'd better put his leftovers in the minifridge, because that there was breakfast.

Two days later, he was driving on 101 through Olympic National Park, thinking that Bluewater Bay was only another hour away. The road wound surprisingly, around mountains and small lakes, and although the terrain was beautiful—green, full of life and water—he couldn't enjoy it.

His car was making a knocking noise. It sounded like the washer in his apartment, which had been falling apart just like his relationship and had tried to do a *Saturday Night Fever* outside his washroom during the spin cycle.

Which was funny in a home appliance when you just *forgot* to call the repairman, but not so funny in a vehicle when you had no money with which to get the damned thing fixed.

The day after Portland, Avery had stayed in the hotel until checkout time, then driven until it was dark. He'd pulled into one of the smaller towns with a "No Services" sign, and found a deserted parking lot behind a gas station and parked there. After eating a self-righteously lean meal of peanut butter and jelly with a small carton of milk, he'd slept in his car, waking early enough to pee in the bushes behind the station, and leaving before anybody else was stirring.

The next night, he'd used his cell phone to find a YMCA, so he'd at least had a swim in the public pool to stay clean, and a sleep on a paper-lined cot. He was sort of proud that he'd spent very little besides gas money, but oi! Gas money was going to kill him!

If his car didn't die on him first.

Knock . . . clonk . . . BAM!

Oh. Oh fuck.

Rattling and coughing, the usually reliable Honda sputtered to a stop on the road shoulder, leaving Avery to lean his head against the steering wheel in exasperation.

Oh. Well, damn. He sat up and adjusted his bladder. Well, good news was? He had to pee.

He relieved himself on the side of the road, used the Purell again, before making himself a sandwich. He sat on the hood of the car, cross-legged, munching on peanut butter and jelly and staring south at the mountain range thinking, *Dear God, how do we even exist next to something that big?*

He'd apparently bought some perspective with the wheat bread and discount peanut butter. Somebody probably not a serial killer would be along eventually. He could wait.

He was two peanut-butter sandwiches in, contemplating the Hoh Glacier and wondering what species were specific to Olympic National Park, when it started to rain.

CHAPTER SEVEN

STRANDED

The doctor cut another incision in Cal's shin to let even more pus out, and the cut hurt like a motherfucker. Cal was still rationing his Vicodin—he had half a bottle in the glove compartment, and he was thinking if he could make it through the next few hours, the pain would fade, just like it had when Nascha had applied his poultice. In fact, overall, he felt about a hundred percent better than he had two weeks before, when he'd first gone back to the Global. Which was good. Not using the painkillers was good too. If it was a choice between stopping his brother's antipsychotics or his grandfather's meds to prohibit Alzheimer's, Cal was going to suck it up, take the Advil, and retain his ability to drive the damned truck.

In this case, he had to drive the damned truck from the ferry in Seattle, because that's how they got to and from Keir's doctor, the one who was nice enough to see Cal free of charge, and the same one who had just given him shit about trimming Keir's fingernails.

"The doctor said I needed to use the square trimmer," Keir said from the passenger seat. "And that if we weren't careful I'd get an infection."

"Yeah, Keir. Infections blow."

"He said your infection almost went septic. I looked that up, Cal. You almost got your leg cut off. That would have been messy."

"Yeah, Keir. I know. It was bad enough being off the leg." Or, off the leg instead of *fishing*. God, every shift at the Global had completely destroyed him. He hadn't been able to fish; he'd been too busy recovering.

"You *lied* to him!" Keir accused, and Cal scowled.

"Yeah, I lied."

"You said you'd stay off it!"

"Yeah, I did."

Keir's straight black hair was bowl-cut around his broad and earnest face. Awake, he looked like a colossal manchild, since he stood at 5'8" and had wide, sturdy shoulders and solid, no-bullshit arms. But anyone who had needed to fight Keir and pin him to the ground was no longer fooled by his innocent face, or the sincerity of his intentions. If Keir sincerely wanted to do something, it took a powerful body and a will of iron to stop him.

Or Cal's bitterroot refusal to give up.

Given all of Keir's *myriad* problems, it didn't put Cal in a better frame of mind when his little brother nagged him about *his* health.

"You need to stay off of it," Keir said insistently.

"And you need to eat and take your meds," Cal responded smartly. "Now tell me about the wildlife in the park."

"There's black bears, Olympic marmots, black-tailed deer, cougars, mountain goats . . ."

Cal let Keir's recitation wash over him. Keir loved natural science and history—Cal always thought it was fortunate that he'd been born in this part of the country, with miles and miles of national park land as his backyard. If Keir could just live in a cabin, deep in the recesses of the park, with no people anywhere—and no girls in particular—Cal was pretty sure he could be happy.

The rain that had been threatening since they'd pulled out of Seattle began to piss down, and Cal sighed. He never forgot that his parents had died in a mudslide—even though his parents had been driving around mountain roads and spectacular bridges when the slide hit, for Cal it was always the rain that was frightening.

This part of Washington got one hundred fifty inches of rain a year.

Cal reminded himself that they were nowhere near the mountain where his parents died, and as he squinted through the spring deluge, he gritted his teeth against the irrational frustration—and the fear he refused to give in to.

"There's a car," Keir said. "Cal, there's a car. The hazard lights are on. You need to stop."

"Oh hell."

"You need to stop, Cal. You need to—"

"I know, I know, I know."

Nobody was on 101 this late afternoon. If this person needed help, Cal had sort of a moral obligation. Bluewater Bay was forty miles away—if cell service was out, and it often was, this person was stranded but for the kindness of strangers.

Cal left the truck running as he grabbed his slicker from the back and threw it on. And even though it had only happened once, when Keir was six years old, he continued with the regular litany of warnings.

"You can't touch the steering wheel."

"I won't touch the steering wheel."

"You can't touch the brake pedal."

"I won't touch the brake pedal."

"You can't touch the gas pedal."

"I won't touch the gas pedal."

"You can't get out of the car."

"I won't get out of the car."

Cal paused, standing on the tarmac, leaning into the cab. "You absolutely cannot try to drive unless there is a serial killer in there and you see me beheaded."

Keir nodded. "I understand, Cal. Once I drove the truck into the house and took the support off the garage. It's where I got my scar."

He rubbed his forehead, and Cal nodded. Everything with Keir was absolutely literal, including the need to state the memory that had become family legend. Cal's father had shouted, "Keir, damn it, get in here!" from the garage, and six-year-old Keir had gotten behind the wheel and tried to drive the car into the house.

"Right, and we're not doing that again."

"No."

Cal nodded and slammed the door, trotting around the truck to the little white Honda. He knocked on the steamed window, and backed away, giving whoever was inside some room.

The door swung open and a scarecrow got out.

He stood taller than Cal by at least two inches, with a riot of curly dark hair quickly plastering to his narrow face. He squinted at Cal through thick-framed glasses, which were held up by ears that stuck out a little. His plain blue hooded sweatshirt was growing quickly sodden in the rain, and he took off his glasses and grimaced at Cal in apology.

"My car just died. No cell service. I've got no idea how to fix it."

Cal nodded. "Hybrid?"

"Yeah."

"We've got a couple of garages in Bluewater that can fix that. I'm headed into town. You got a place to stay there?"

He saw an ironic twist to the young man's mouth. "I actually do, but I don't have any cash for a week. I've got no idea how I'm going to pay for a tow."

Cal grunted, thinking. "Yeah, well, I'll get you to town, you can tell Clarke where it is. The tow will be between you two, but right now, I can get you out of the fucking rain."

He was surprised at the strength of the young man's smile. "That's *amazing*!" he said, nodding his head like Cal had just affirmed something important about the world. "Thank you! Thank you so much! Here—can I get some clothes?"

"Nothing too big—it's three of us in the cab."

"Oh. Uhm, hang on a minute."

Cal watched the young man think fast, then reach into the car and rummage. He came out with a backpack, the kind with the softened pocket that held a laptop. It was bulging out the front—probably with clothes and toiletries—and he killed the hazard lights and slammed the door.

He smiled hopefully at Cal. "Hey—I'm Avery. Avery Kennedy." He stuck out a long, bony, pale hand. "Thanks so much for the lift into town."

Cal took that white hand in his own, not needing to look to see the contrast of his Native American brown skin. "Cal McCorkle. You got all your shit?"

Avery nodded, not seeming to be put off at all.

The truck steamed up the minute they got in, and Cal had to let the engine idle a minute so the defog would compensate for the extra body. Next to him, Keir and Avery were staring at each other.

"I'm Avery." The cab was pretty crowded, so Avery's attempt to stick out his hand to shake was ridiculous, really.

"I'm Keir. I'm Cal's brother. What happened to your car?"

Cal darted a glance at Avery, to see if he'd be alienated by the abrupt speech pattern. Odd or truncated speech patterns often defined the severe Asperger's part of Keir's diagnosis, and introducing Keir to new people was always a challenge.

Avery blinked at him through his steamed glasses and shrugged. "It broke down. You and your brother were nice enough to give me a ride."

Cal put the truck in gear, and risked a sideways look at Avery. He was peering at Keir speculatively but not unkindly.

"My brother isn't nice. He yells a lot. It's why he likes to be alone."

Cal swallowed. Wow. If you wanted to know what Keir thought of you, apparently just sit next to him and look at him funny.

Avery made an understanding sound. "Well, sometimes what people do for us is more important than what they say."

"What does that mean?"

"Well, like my ex-boyfriend. He liked to tell me I was really smart. But then he'd make fun of me to all his friends about how I hunched over my computer all day and didn't know how to do real work. So he said really nice things to me, but he made fun of me behind my back. It made it feel like basically none of the nice things he said meant anything."

Avery sounded bitter, like the wound was fresh, and Cal grunted. Wow, could he have found anything more helpless in the rain?

"My brother earns money for the house. He pays for food and medicine. He works two jobs."

"Keir, maybe not tell all my business?" Cal said gruffly.

Avery ignored Cal and responded to Keir. "Well then, he must be a good guy. Even if he yells."

There was a moment of silence, for which Cal could only be grateful. God, Keir could talk a subject to death.

"He is a good guy. He lets me watch *Avatar*. Do you like *Avatar*?"

"*The Last Airbender* or *The Legend of Korra*?" Avery asked, and if Cal hadn't had a death grip on the wheel, he might have wrecked the truck. "Because I like them both, but I get really frustrated with Korra's character."

"*The Last Airbender* is my favorite, but I like that *Korra* has moved into the steampunk world. What's your favorite episode?"

Avery responded easily, because apparently he really *was* as much of a nerd as he looked, and Cal fought the temptation to weep tears of gratitude. Keir's focus was so very narrow. Natural history, that damned show, and Cal. Cal hated talking about his own life, could only quiz him so much on natural history, and only knew the very basics about the show. God, finally, someone who spoke Keir.

For a good half an hour, Cal got to listen to them talk about everything from voice actors to animation houses to world building, and for that half an hour, Cal was both stunned and happy.

His brother was really freakin' smart. He analyzed this show with all the passion and intelligence of a literature major analyzing the works of Milton or Shakespeare. Cal remembered his old AP classes—Keir talked about dialog, conflict, theme—and Cal wanted to cry. All of those beautiful tools in his brain, all of that *incredibly specialized function.*

But hearing another adult responding, understanding everything Keir was saying—that was a beautiful thing. Cal had seen the California license plates, and for a moment he was tempted to break into this freaking perfect storm of conversation, this gift of heaven for his brother, and demand to know if the A+ in geek was a California thing or an Avery Kennedy thing.

About five miles before town, Keir's ability to interact with Avery completely dried up. Fortunately, Cal had managed to institute one habit—and one habit only—into Keir since their parents had died, and that was the ability to warn someone before he decided to tune the hell out.

"I'm sorry," Keir said in the middle of Avery's sentence. "I can't talk anymore. I'm going to listen to music."

And with that he popped the earbuds of Cal's ancient iPod into his ears and hit play. For a moment the sound of the wipers and whir of the concrete in the descending darkness were the only sounds in the truck.

"What does he listen to?" Avery asked.

Cal kept his attention on the road. "Cello music. You know, the cellos doing the rock covers. No words, but lots of bouncy chords."

"My favorite writing music," Avery said, his voice dry.

"You're good with him," Cal felt compelled to say. God, he'd just spent a half an hour listening to this stranger talking to his little brother like a human being who mattered. *Cal* sure as shit couldn't do it. If he had any money—or any *time*—he'd be tempted to fix Avery's car for free.

"Yeah, well, one of my first articles was on Asperger's kids. I went to a CH class—you know, Communicatively Handicapped—to ask the teacher some questions. I ended up volunteering once a week for a year and a half." Even across the cab, Cal could hear Avery's happy noise. "I had to get fingerprinted and everything, but it was totally worth it. Nobody talks geek like an Aspy kid. I fit right in."

Cal grunted, feeling like a dirtbag. "I didn't know a fuckin' thing about Aspy's or OCD or bipolar or ADHD until my folks died. Suddenly I'm up to my eyeballs in bills and acronyms and Keir. I suck at dealing with him."

"I doubt it!"

The light was almost completely gone, and the headlights battered feebly at the rain. For a moment, Cal wanted to look at his temporary passenger and *see* what his face did when he talked. That "I doubt it!" sounded so fucking sincere. Jesus, it had been a long time since anyone had seen the best in Cal.

"Yeah? What makes you say that?"

"'Cause he worships you. You're on his list of five."

"You know about his list?"

"No—I mean yes, most people with really severe Aspy's have a sort of list of things that they really obsess over, whether they write it down or not. The categories get broader as they get older, which is how most of the time they function fairly well. But still—it's all in the category, you know? A certain kind of book, a certain type of show, a certain branch of science—just, you know. Not so much single-minded, but minds like a really deep, strong canal. Everything else they want to think about gets swept away."

Cal nodded. Next to him, Keir was sitting, eyes closed, dark hair falling across his forehead, swept away in cello music.

"I've never heard the term CH before," he said, not wanting to talk about Keir anymore. Avery was nice and all, but he was a stranger.

There was no reason to bring up Keir's violence, his obsession with girls, or the meds. Cal wasn't going to talk about his bone-deep terror that his brother was going to hurt someone and then the institution wouldn't be an option, it would be a necessity, and it wouldn't be the nice place, even if Cal could afford it. That was the stuff that kept Cal up at night when his body screamed for sleep. That stuff was private.

"Yeah, well, not every kid has a definable diagnosis, you know? Or even several specific diagnoses, like Keir. Sometimes, all the stuff sort of train-wrecks together, but what it really comes down to is the person has trouble communicating. No give and take. So they can be really smart, but getting what's in their heads to the rest of the world isn't going to happen. So, like, there was a girl there with a seizure disorder, and the seizures kept her from acquiring language. There was a boy there who had no actual diagnosis, but he had some physical weaknesses, fine motor problems, some gross motor problems, some difficulties enunciating—they just sort of put the blanket term over him, right? Communication Handicap. It works—'cause not being able to talk with someone, not being able to hear what they're saying—"

"Sounds like the bane of fucking human existence," Cal said, with feeling.

Avery made a hurt sound, and Cal wished again that he could actually see the guy's face.

"Yeah, well, sometimes communication is overrated," Avery muttered, his voice soft and bitter.

"Yeah, I know how that goes." Cal wanted his boat so damned bad. Since his father had died, he'd gone out damned near every day in the dory. Having to sit and . . . *veg* with his family the last few weeks had really left a scar on his psyche. He'd been an island of incommunication in the middle of Nascha and Keir every day, and he'd hated it. For some reason it kept that fight with the prehistoric fish fresh in his mind. Cal didn't *ever* want to be that helpless again.

"I imagine you do," Avery said, irony dripping from his voice, but before Cal could ask him what the hell he meant by that, the ungrateful bastard, they were there.

Since the advent of the damned television show, Cal had felt like the town had been divided into parts. There was the part with the big hotel overlooking the sound, with the attached casino. Down the road were the old 1920s touristy stores that looked old town and historic because they were, and for some reason managed to charge really outrageous prices for shit because of it. Then there was the actual rundown part of town that existed in the tiny streets *behind* those historic, marketable kitschy streets.

Clarke's Auto Repair and Fortune Telling Service was one of *those* businesses. Avery was squinting through the rain, his attention stolen by the hotel in the distance with the attached glitzy casino that called so irresistibly to Nascha.

"That's the hotel for the convention, right?" he said reverently.

Cal didn't need to see where Avery was looking. "Yeah. I work there. Gonna be busy." Fucking convention was putting off the time he could take his boat out into the water. But it could help him not lose Nascha's house, if he could work his ass off enough for the tips.

"Yeah, well, that's the only place I've got to stay for the next two weeks. Think I can walk there from here?"

Oh hell. "No," Cal told him, thinking that he owed this guy some sort of Samaritan debt for making his little brother happy. "You get out. Do what you have to with Clarke. I'll drop Keir off and change. Pick you up here in an hour. Deal?"

"You don't have to do that," Avery said softly, but it was for form, and they both knew it. He was out of options.

"Nope," Cal agreed. "Don't have to. But I will." He swung the truck through the main street with all the tourist attractions, and took a left at the one intersection in town. Clarke's Auto Repair and Fortune Telling Service sat one block back from the main stuff, and it wasn't as flashy as that place with all the race car drivers, but Rob Clarke had kept Cal's pickup from falling apart for the past six years.

"Here," he said, grateful that Clarke still had his lights on. "Back in an hour. Don't let him talk you into paying him up front. Tell him I said you could work it off. He owes me."

Well, more like Clarke owed Cal's *father*, since Dad had worked there to supplement his fishing income much like Cal worked at the Global. But occasionally Cal would come and help Clarke when he got busy, just to keep the connection with someone else who knew and remembered his parents. He got free maintenance on the truck, and Clarke didn't have to fork over the money for the help. Since he used his extra money to pay for his wife's business permit for fortune telling—which Cal did *not* understand—Clarke was his extra-special buddy in all things mechanical.

Cal stopped the truck in front of the little blue and white station, between the pumps and the minimart/office that Clarke kept trying to make money out of. Cal kept telling him he needed to buy more than three kinds of candy bars and two kinds of soda, but Clarke insisted that the whole world either drank Coca-Cola or Diet Coke, and there wasn't much more he needed to sell beyond that and coffee. If the guy couldn't fix any motor that ran, he'd be *so* out of business by now.

"See that guy in there, fiftyish, bald, big gray and black beard?" Cal said, looking through the truck window to the well-lit office.

"Yeah, I see him."

Cal listened for reluctance or some sort of judgment on the scary guy in the shop, and was relieved he didn't hear any. "Good. Tell him you left your car out on 101 about fifty miles southeast, and he'll tell you when he can tow it, and how much it'll cost. You tell him when you can pay him, and tell him I vouched for you. Don't pay him up front. Like I said, he don't make none of the locals do it."

"Okay," Avery said. "Thanks, uhm, you know. Thanks aga—"

"You talked to my brother," Cal snapped, cutting him off. "You got no idea. Get out. I'll be back in an hour."

Avery hopped out of the truck and strode into the shop, his backpack clenched tightly in his long bony hand. Cal realized that he still hadn't gotten a good look at the guy, unblurred by rain or dark or Avery's big steamed up glasses. He wanted to. Suddenly those ears that had seemed so wide seemed a lot more symmetrical, just from hearing his voice for the last hour.

He pulled away from the garage, and Keir popped awake like a jack-in-the-box. He yanked out his earbuds, glanced around him, and said, "What did you do with Avery?"

"I let him off at the garage."

"That was stupid. I want to talk to him. You couldn't even tell me?"

Cal fought the temptation to glare at him. Just because he knew the small roads with the little houses on the backstreets didn't mean anyone was safe, even for a minute, when driving in the rain.

"You were listening to music, Keir. That's usually the 'don't talk to you' time."

"Will we see him again?"

"I will—I'm giving him a ride to the hotel."

"But I want to see him!" Keir's voice rose to a querulous pitch, and Cal instinctively checked his watch. Fuck. Fuck fuck fuck.

Making sure he wasn't blocking the driveway of the house he pulled in front of, he skewed the pickup to a slippery halt and gathered the little white bag of prescription meds he kept in the side of the door. He was late. They'd been just pushing the schedule by hoping to get home before having Keir med up, but after stopping for Avery, and then going out of their way to drop him off, Keir was half an hour late for his meds, and if Keir couldn't hold it together, Cal was fucked.

"Here," he muttered, pulling the remains of the giant soda he'd given Keir on their way out of Seattle from the cupholder. "Start drinking."

Keir liked soda, so that was easy, but Cal's hands shook as he dumped the medication in his hand. Part of that was that he hadn't eaten, but part of it was the knowledge of what Keir could do if he didn't get that mix of antipsychotics and stimulants into his body. One thing—one small thing—and Keir would focus and obsess and, possibly, need to fix the object of his obsession. Cal had once caught an elbow in the throat trying to keep Keir from destroying Cal's fishing net because he'd seen one hole, and he knew that the net couldn't function with one hole, so it needed to be thrown away.

They'd spent the day together, and Avery had been right—Keir liked spending time with Cal. He would *not* be happy Cal was going to his job that night, and God help them both if Dottie hadn't medicated Nascha too.

"Here," Cal said gruffly. "Swallow."

"Swallowing," Keir said dutifully, gurgling. "You almost forgot, Cal."

"You can remember too, you know," Cal retorted. "You're smart."

Keir looked at him slyly. "But you have to talk to me when you're giving me my meds," he said, and Cal felt a double slug to the gut.

"Yeah, well, I'm not good at talking to anybody."

"Nascha says it's 'cause you have no practice."

"Nascha's a smart old guy when he remembers what day it is."

"What day *is* it, Cal?"

"Wednesday."

"Because we had our doctor's appointments."

"Yep. Show me your mouth." Keir was not above pretending to swallow and spitting out his meds, just to see if he was crazier today than he was yesterday. (Those had been his exact words when Cal found out. It had taken a week to get him back on schedule, and twice that long to get him to stop saying "crazy.")

Keir opened his mouth and moved his tongue around, knowing the drill. When he was done, he looked at Cal levelly.

"I took my meds. Where's Avery?"

"Avery is going to the hotel, where he can get some sleep and try to figure out his life. We are not in Avery's life. Period."

If Avery had still been jammed into the cab of the truck with them, Keir wouldn't have had the room for the cock-back, and the swing wouldn't have had quite so much power.

He had to drive fast in the rain to get Avery by the promised hour. As he turned up to Clarke's garage, he saw that the lights had been turned off, and Avery was leaning patiently against the store under the eaves, munching on what looked like a peanut butter sandwich. Apparently Clarke had left on time for once, which was nice of him, because hey! That left the out-of-town guy alone in the dark.

The relief on Avery's face was blatant, even through the glare of the headlights in the rain. He looked up, tied the neck of what appeared to be a loaf of bread, shouldered his backpack, and smiled gamely at Cal as the truck powered to a halt. As he trotted around the front, Cal got his first good gander at a narrow little face and pitcher ears that could actually be called charming, and as Avery swung into the cab, a grin split his face that even deepened the impression.

Cal's rescue puppy with the evil ex-boyfriend was actually sort of adorable, in an innocent, geeky, lost-kitten sort of way.

"I'd almost given up hope; I thought you'd forgotten— Oh holy God what in the hell happened to your face?"

That quick, the throbbing in his eye returned with a vengeance. Well, if the pain meds for his healing infected cut hadn't knocked that shit off, nothing would.

"I told Keir he wouldn't be seeing you again. He was . . . unhappy."

Cal had needed to drag him into the house by the hair. Keir had Velcro restraints by his bed, because Jesus, Nascha and Cal had to sleep sometimes, even when Keir was pissed off, right? Keir was currently restrained in bed, while Nascha fed him and read a serialized novel version of *Avatar* that Cal had pretty much stolen from the public library.

"That's rough," Avery said, his voice deepening with sympathy. He threw the last crust of bread in his mouth, and Cal's stomach gurgled. And, among other things, he'd been running so late he'd left without eating.

Avery glanced at him, a small smile on his face. "I, uhm, have two more sandwiches in here." He shook the bag. "You, uhm, want one?"

Cal's stomach gurgled again. Oh Jesus. This was embarrassing. *Stranger*. He started to shake his head no, because he *could* get food at the restaurant, but Avery stopped him.

"I mean, you gave me a ride into town, set me up at a garage—you know. Rescued me. Let a guy pay you back."

Okay. Paying back. Cal could do that. It wasn't charity. The first sandwich was gone so quickly he didn't notice Avery was shoving the second one in his hand until he felt the brush of his fingers. He froze for a moment and risked a look at his passenger.

Avery was smiling at him guilelessly, grooves cutting into cheeks that Cal found reasonably attractive.

"Thanks," Cal mumbled through a hurried mouthful. "It would have been a long time before I got my break."

"So, you work at the hotel?"

"Bus tables and bar back at the restaurant."

"Don't wait tables?" Avery asked, his interest friendly and nothing else.

"Gotta talk to people," Cal told him frankly. "I really fucking hate people."

Avery laughed softly. "I never would have guessed. So, what else do you do?"

"Fish," Cal said, because he was proud of this. "Fish the sound in my father's dory." Without meaning to, he found himself adding, "Got my leg sliced open a month back, fucking green sturgeon. Got infected. But I got the okay to go back tomorrow."

Oh God yes. Back out in the sound, where there were no bills, no great-uncle with Alzheimer's, no kid brother with a snaky mess of problems Cal had no idea how to handle. The calm waters of the sound, the majestic rise of the islands around him, and his own sweating back. Peace.

"You alone?" Avery asked.

Cal grunted. "For hours," he said, longing in his voice.

"Sounds . . . lonely," Avery said thoughtfully. "But interesting. I'd like to go out and do that though." His voice grew dreamy. "I know you don't get it, 'cause you probably grew up here, but I grew up in a concrete desert, you know? Not really poor, but lots of apartments and small houses, lined up and down hills, tiny lawns, tiny rooms. This place . . . man, I know it started raining, but I could have just sat there in my car, looking at that fucking mountain for hours."

"Don't think it's uncivilized?" Cal asked, because he'd heard some of the tourists talking. Words like "unspoiled" and "untamed" were usually followed by, "Yes, but you have to drive three miles to get coffee." Considering that the Stomping Grounds was better than anything that could be found in the hotel Starbucks, Cal thought people might just like to complain.

But not this guy.

This guy had just finished a peanut butter sandwich and was talking about what a rush it was to get stranded in his car.

"Civilized is my boyfriend in a suit, blowing his boss for kicks," Avery said glumly. "I've had plenty of civilized, you know?" He shook himself and then looked at Cal covertly, like maybe Cal had forgotten he'd talked about his boyfriend before, and was now all stunned about the gay.

As. If.

"Lots of gay guys here this weekend," Cal told him. "Like that actor—what's his name?" Cal really *had* caught a lot of *Wolf's Landing* when he'd been laid up, and even though he wasn't excited about the tourists, or even the hotel and the casino, which helped him make a living, he *was* pretty impressed with how respectfully his town seemed to be treated. The town had been making a big deal about the shooting crew not leaving a mess when they did location shoots, and how the cast and crew had been making a point of using local businesses. Cal's pathological hatred of new people to talk to did not keep him from appreciating that the town he'd grown up in was getting a lot of good out of this show, and it didn't hurt that the show was entertaining as well.

"Carter Samuels," Avery said, sounding excited. "You mean the guy from *Wolf's Landing*, right?"

"Yeah, him. Should be lots of gay fans. Maybe you'll catch yourself a new one."

Avery shook his head and gazed out the window where the big lightless gap between the town and the hotel was filling the darkness with an ocean of tall grass. "Naw. I'm not here to find a boyfriend. I'm here to declare my independence."

"From what? Your ex-boyfriend?" Cal's skepticism must have shown—and why not? He'd been plenty independent, and as far as he could see, all independence got you was enough antisocial attitude to make you hate your *own* company.

"From . . . from everything I grew up with," Avery said, gesturing broadly now that Keir wasn't there in the truck to cramp him. "From the concrete cultural desert of LA, from my boyfriend who thought the only good work came from wearing a suit, and from my shitty apartment which had the only view of the sky you could get in LA, but it wasn't enough."

Cal had to smile at the same time he was almost queasy with envy. "You left all that to come somewhere new?"

Avery's enthusiasm crashed to the floorboards. "Yup. And in four days I pretty much proved to my whole family and my ex-loser that I was too helpless to be on my own. So, you know, not as awesome as I just made it sound."

"Whattya mean, 'helpless'? 'Cause your car died?"

"And my credit card got canceled because . . . I don't know. It was fucking *weird*. I mean, I travel about once a month, but this time, the bank decided that apparently I'd spent my *entire life* in the LA basin, because my bank card *leaves* the LA basin, buys a couple of books on Native American legends, and I get the phone call that says, 'Sorry, Avery, but since you've been such a completely boring human being from high school until now, we're going to have to assume someone stole your fucking bank card and you are no longer a person. And good luck eating. Hope you get to Bluewater Bay, 'cause that's where we're sending your bank card! Have a nice trip!'"

Cal laughed—he had to, because Avery was gesticulating wildly for one thing, but also because it was just dumb, stupid luck. He could relate to dumb, stupid luck.

"So, a month ago," he said, out of nowhere, "I was out fishing. Go every day. Have a place I sell the fish, then I go to my night job, right? I don't poach, don't fish out of season, I'm doing it right, yanno?"

"Yeah, Inno." Avery was looking at him avidly, like he'd never in his life heard anything this interesting, and Cal kept his eyes on the road and his flush to himself and plowed on.

"So, suddenly, my boat starts to tip, and there's this ginormous fuckin' fish in it, and I . . . I mean, I wanna cut it free, but if I let go of the net, it's gonna capsize me, and I'm way too fuckin' far out to swim to shore. So I reach for my knife and it threatens to pull me over—this thing, it's like, when we weighed it, it was like four hundred pounds, right?"

"Holy fuckin' wow!"

Cal hadn't told this story to *anyone*—not a soul in his life knew how that fish got on his boat, mostly because he was pretty sure no one would believe him. But Avery—Avery *liked* stories. He'd said something about being a writer, and Cal suddenly felt good about talking. It was like he'd found the one guy in a million who might hear this story and believe it.

"Yeah—I still can't believe I landed that monster by myself, but the thing was, I wasn't trying to land it. It just . . . I mean, I hauled it in the boat using the side as leverage, right? I had to— We were going over, and every time it went in the water, it was that close to just busting my transom and fucking ripping my boat apart. I tried to kill it or stun it or whatever, but my gaff got stuck in its skull and . . . nada. Didn't notice I'd even touched him. So I get this fucker in my boat and . . . it hits me. There's no way I can get it *out* of my boat. And to make matters worse, it was a fucking illegal fish. If it hadn't been trying to kill me, I would have fucking let it go. It was endangered. So I've got this . . . prehistoric buffalo in the bottom of my fucking boat, and it slices me across the leg. And I don't give a shit because I have to kill it—'cause I'm not getting it off the boat again, right?"

"Yeah," Avery said, sounding like Keir did when he watched his damned cartoon.

"Anyway, so I get the stupid fish to the hotel—I have no idea how they served it, by then I just needed someone to buy it and not ask questions—and go to my job and I'm thinking, 'God, I almost got screwed by this giant fucking fish, but I survived!'"

"Hooray?" Avery asked, and he must have had practice with stories because it helped Cal tell the rest.

"No, not hooray. Hooray, my fucking leg got infected, and I was off it for a month. And I get to go back on the water tomorrow. But the thing is . . ." He was surprised to find he was smiling. "I have that story."

Wow. That felt pretty fucking profound considering he'd been cursing the goddamned fish since February.

"And now so do I," Avery said with a chuckle. "Nicely said. And I gotta tell you, you are *not* killing my enthusiasm about getting on a boat and going fishing."

"It's not all big green sturgeon," Cal warned. "And you don't sit there with a rod and reel, either. It's a net, and it's hard, and the boat's really small."

"Would you take me?" Avery asked, and just when Cal was going to say, "Yeah, why not," Avery's enthusiasm dimmed.

"But it would have to be next week. Not this weekend. I'm, uhm . . . I mean, I signed up to go to the convention, and I sort of paid for all of it."

"So you did all this for a week?" Cal asked, absurdly disappointed.

"No, actually. I, uhm . . . Well, I decided my breakup would be best accomplished if one of us moved out, so I booked the hotel for an extra week so I could find a place to live."

Cal's heart gave a little thump, which was stupid, because, hey, skinny writing ex-desert dweller—how much fun was he going to find *Cal's* life?

"So," Cal said, thinking that even with the new TV people, Bluewater Bay was still a small town. He should probably let Avery know it would be okay to ignore him. "I guess I'll be seeing you around."

He was pulling into the employee's entrance at the hotel now, and not only was *he* late for work, he'd spoken more in the past ten minutes than he had in the past ten months. He was ready to let this stranger disappear into the hotel and maybe forget Cal had ever given him a ride in his truck.

"I'd like that," Avery said brightly. "And seriously—let me know if Keir ever needs company. I'd be happy to do that. He's great."

Like an iron vice, Cal's real life clamped down. "Yeah. Well. He's not easy." He winked his swollen eye.

Avery nodded his head. "Yeah, well, I had to learn the three-point restraint for a reason. But still, let me know, okay?"

Cal nodded, with no intention of trying to contact one Avery Kennedy ever at all. He was almost embarrassed to talk to him now.

"Your entrance is around the side in the front."

"Thanks!" Avery said, seemingly oblivious to all the reasons he was never going to see Cal again. With a little hop and a wave, he was striding (he had *long* skinny legs) around the side of the employee's entrance toward the front, where the guests came in. No matter how out on his luck he was now, it was best if Cal remembered he was a guest. Guests didn't stay at this hotel or come to the conventions if all they had to do with their lives was hang out on fishing boats or babysit Cal's terrifying family.

CHAPTER EIGHT

OLD FRIENDS YOU NEVER MET

A very had managed to grab two changes of clothes, an extra pair of underwear, the last of his food, his laptop, and his charger while Cal was standing behind him, tapping his foot in the rain. Everything else he owned on the planet was in the car he'd left on the side of 101.

Given that, he was feeling surprisingly chipper as he checked into the hotel, a thing he had to credit to the amazing story his knight in a rusted pickup truck had just dumped in his lap.

It was better than fan fiction, better than the best article, it was *what writers dreamt about*, not even to write but to hear. Avery had just met a real-life Hemingway hero in the flesh, and damn, who could be upset about that?

Well, Avery could be upset about *something*, but he couldn't be upset about *that*.

"I did already pay for my room, right?" Avery asked, trying really hard not to let his voice rise.

"Yes, sir, but you need a credit card on file with us in case there are any room incidentals incurred."

The young woman—blonde, pretty, slender as a willow—replied to all of his queries professionally and courteously. He sort of wanted to scream in her face because professionally and courteously just wasn't fucking doing it for him.

"Okay—I *have* money in the bank, right?" he said, a little desperately. "But the bank—through no fault of my own—canceled my bank card. I don't have any credit cards because I'm trying not to get swallowed by debt, and I just left my home to find a home up here. The *one thing* I had going for me was that I had prepaid my room for two weeks. Are you telling me I don't have that now?"

Ooh—there was that crack in professional and courteous. "We, uhm . . ." The girl looked around, and Avery looked around too. The appointments were nice—the check-in desk was faux black marble, and the carpeting and accessories on the walls were a pretty shade of antique gold. A little baroque, maybe, but it also spoke to a warm, clean room with maybe some pampering for Avery who was starting to remember that a good story didn't give you a place to sleep at night. "Okay. You're reserved for two weeks—maybe we could take the last three days of your reservation and apply it to your incidental fee? If you don't use that money, it will show up in your account—"

"Which I can't access!" Avery remindered her sourly.

"No, but that's not my fault," she snapped, and then looked around, probably to make sure nobody caught her standing up for herself. "Look—I'm supposed to not check you in at *all*, but the bank did the same thing when we were taking my son to Disneyland. If my husband hadn't had *his* bank card, it would have been a really crappy trip. So if your card arrives in the next week, go ahead and give it to us, and we'll reinstate your next three days, but for now? You got a week and a half, okay?"

Avery nodded. "Yeah. I got it." He took a deep breath and remembered the four years he'd spent working as a barista to help make it through college. He was going to try very hard not to be this woman's worst customer. "Thank you. That really *is* nice of you. I just . . ." He shook his head, not wanting to talk about the car and the money and the fact that his life had apparently fallen to shit the minute he left LA. "That's awesome," he finished. "I can check in now? 'Cause I'm telling you, I don't smell so great." Wet dog, with a side of BO and a soupçon of stinky feet. No wonder Cal couldn't wait to kick him out of the truck. He stopped for a minute. "And hey—you wouldn't know where the post office is, would you? Because the bank was supposed to call me sometime in the next three days to tell me my card's arrived."

The girl looked at him blankly. "Why didn't you just ask them to send it to the hotel?"

Avery stared back, feeling stupid. "I . . . uh . . . you know, I didn't ask." He felt a bubble of hysteria rising in his throat. Resourceful, apparently he was not.

She frowned. "Well, way to make things hard on yourself." She typed on her keypad, and then grabbed a stack of post-its and started scribbling. "Here. This is the post office number and their hours. They're located on Main Street, with that address—that way, you can check with them, how's that?"

The exasperation that had been building in Avery's chest and behind his eyes melted, and he found himself giving her the same smile he'd given Cal when the sturdy truck had rolled up out of nowhere.

"You know? When I started this trip I was terrified of all the people and absolutely sure the technology would help me survive, but you know what?"

She looked up from her screen and smiled slightly. "What?"

"My technology is trying to kill me, but the *people* are seriously rocking my world. Thank you so much. I'll take that room key and that shower now."

The woman—Kendra by her name tag—looked around again. "Here," she murmured, pushing something into his hand. "It's a room service voucher—it'll get you dinner twice, as long as you tip."

Avery grinned at her. "If I wasn't gay and you weren't married, I would *so* have your babies," he said baldly.

Her burst of laughter was totally worth it.

An hour later, he'd showered, changed, and rinsed out his dirty clothes in the bathtub. That last part felt a little low-rent for such a swank place, but then, so would going downstairs in moldy socks and the baseball jersey that had seen two days' wear and the epic soda spill of the Oregon/Washington border.

When he was done, he looked at the clock, pulled out his laptop and his cell phone, and tried to figure out his life. He was doing okay for money—he had $200 left in cash, which, while it would not pay to get his car towed or to lengthen his stay, it would definitely spring for food as long as he was conservative. Now, as for carfare to the bank so he could withdraw enough to survive . . .

Damn. He should have asked Kendra about shuttles into town. They *had* to have something, right? He knew there were a couple of big tour buses coming up from the airport in Seattle for the convention, so in order to get from the hotel/casino to the little tourist trap, folks would need *something*, right? What was it, nine o'clock?

Figuring Kendra would still be on duty, he slid on his dry jeans and still-wet sneakers and went walking to the elevator to ask her. When he came out of the elevator, he glanced right toward the restaurant instead of left toward the concierge desk, and pretty much stopped in his tracks.

There he was. The restaurant looked out over the sound, which meant the bus stands were close to the entryway on the inside of the hotel. Leaning against one of the bus stands with his arms loaded with full dish tubs was Avery's fisherman in the rusty truck, getting his ass grabbed by a guy wearing a hotel uniform. Cal sneered at the guy, and the guy leaned in and whispered in his ear. Cal shook him off without friendship, and turned around to take his laden tubs probably to the back, limping slightly.

On his way, he glanced up and saw Avery's stunned regard.

A terrible thing happened then.

His lips parted, a sort of mesmerizing brown-pink color in his dusky face, and his dark-brown eyes grew wide and round. He looked away, and Avery didn't need super good superhero vision to see that he was blushing.

Someone must have called Cal's name, because he jerked suddenly and went trotting to the other side of the restaurant, and Avery felt lead in the pit of his stomach.

He was upset because he was inconvenienced for a couple of days. Cal's whole *life* depended on working this job in the restaurant, on getting his ass groped by the guy he apparently didn't like very much, and on fishing.

He must hate us. The thought came out of nowhere, but Avery was sure it was true.

He had to force himself to go talk to Kendra, but he was rewarded with a shuttle schedule and a travel tip that he *must visit* the Stomping Grounds, on account of them having excellent coffee and maybe being able to let Avery work for extra cash if the bank card didn't arrive in time. Avery smiled a little.

"Yeah—I haven't done the barista thing in a while. That's actually a pretty good tip."

Kendra grinned and gave a mini-bow. "My pleasure. Now are there any *other* questions, my liege?"

Avery's head tried to jerk around so he could peer through the hotel lobby to the restaurant overlooking the bay. "Yeah, uhm—the dinner rush has cleared out. Would anyone mind if I just sat and had a cup of coffee?"

She shrugged and waved her hand. "It's Washington. We gave *birth* to Starbucks. Not taking the time to sit down for coffee is the sign of an alien outsider who cannot be trusted. Knock yourself out."

Ah, good, Avery had made a friend.

The restaurant was . . . Well, he supposed most hotel restaurants were like this. Nice but not too nice, bland furnishings, very comfortable, meant to be sat in for a while and lingered over. Excellent. Avery had enough money for a cup of coffee, and since the place really had cleared out, he got to drink it looking over the still waters of Puget Sound.

A full moon had risen, and he caught the fractal reflection in the tiny waves, under the breaking cloud cover.

In the distance he could see two smaller islands breasting the water and rising in abrupt mounds. There was something sinuous and surprising about those islands, about the thought that there were myriad islands, with houses and ferry docks on each. What would that be like, to live out there, to be a human turtle, with your home as your shell?

He was so captivated by the scenery he didn't even regret not bringing his laptop to work. His brain was doing enough busywork as it was, deluging him with words and comparisons, possible questions, angles for his article, angles for future articles, description for his fan fiction—any place, any event, any circumstance was a seed in a dry garden, waiting for the rain of his imagination to make it grow.

A reflection flickered in the window, so he was not startled when Cal slid across from him, a plate of pie in each hand.

But he was surprised.

"Thought you'd be happy to see the last of me," he said, but he was smiling openly when he said it. "And Jesus, thank you. I was *dying* for something this bad for me. The ice cream makes it perfect."

He saw a brief flicker of teeth in Cal's undeniably attractive, clay-tinted face. God, this guy had the Native American thing going in a big way—cheekbones, square jaw, even white teeth and almond-shaped obsidian eyes. Avery had never been particularly into one kind of guy—hell, with his looks, he knew he was lucky when someone noticed him at all—but when Cal smiled and regarded him from that inscrutable face, Avery couldn't help hope he would maybe *develop* a type.

"You're welcome. They were going to throw it away."

"Well, that would be a shame," Avery said sincerely, taking an exquisite bite of apples, fat, cream, and sugar. He swallowed and then grinned at him. "You on break or done for the night?"

Cal's weary smile told him all he needed to know. "Break. I go back and help wash dishes at the end of the night. More clock time."

"Damn, you work hard!" Avery took another bite and shook his head. "You should meet my ex-boyfriend. He thought blowing his boss on his lunch hour counted as overtime."

Cal cringed and shoved away his plate, and Avery wondered how stupid he could get.

"Forget that," he said hurriedly, reaching across the table and putting the plate back in Cal's hands. "I didn't mean to be crass. I'm sorry. I'm bitter—it's unattractive, I know it."

Cal regarded him distrustfully, but Avery felt a chamber of his heart crush quietly into powder and let the other three labor on without it. That grope he'd seen, the manager with his hand on Cal's ass—that apparently meant exactly what it looked like.

"I . . . Yanno, people get fuck buddies," Cal muttered over his pie, and Avery's heart thought about rebuilding itself a little.

"Yeah. Absolutely." Avery had never had a fuck buddy.

Cal raised an eyebrow. "Right." It was like he *knew* Avery had been living boyfriend to boyfriend since he'd lost his V-card in college. No casual hookups for Avery, no one-night stands, just a sort of sad attempt to live just like his parents, no matter how unhappy they seemed to be.

Avery changed the subject. "This is really beautiful." He gestured to the silver-dark out the wraparound windows. "Do you ever get bored with it? Living on the water? Being able to see this every day?"

Apparently he chose a good topic. Cal's jaw lost its tightness, and he stared out the window dreamily. "Naw. I mean, I'd like to go other places someday. I was picking out colleges when my folks, uhm . . . died, but even then, I always wanted to come back here."

"What's it like?" Avery asked, partly because he wanted to see Cal talk again about something that made him happy, and partly because he *always* wanted to know the answer. "Going out on a fishing boat in the morning? I mean, cold? It's gotta be cold. Foggy? Is it—"

"You ever been in a plane?"

Avery looked at him in surprise. "Yeah—couple of times. Not all my research is on the net. Chicago is my favorite."

Cal nodded, like he'd expected that. "I got to go on a trip to Washington DC when I was in high school. And I was looking forward to that plane ride so much, you know? But we got inside, and it was a little box, and looking outside was boring, like a television show with no plot. Once we left Washington airspace, I didn't care what was under me. See, I thought flying was going to be *flying*. Like the birds. You see the birds fly, and you just *know* they're having fun. The wind feels good in their feathers. They can smell water and woods." He took a bite of pie, chewed thoughtfully. Took another one and chewed some more.

Avery waited, because he'd been interviewing people since he was in eighth grade, when he'd asked the conservative superintendent of their school district why *couldn't* the junior high have a GSA? The man had scrambled for an answer, and Avery had let him. In the end, he'd simply granted the junior high the rights they'd had coming, just because Avery hadn't stepped in and tried to answer his own question.

Cal finished his second bite and looked out the window again. "Used to be, before the big fish, that's what fishing was like. Like flying on the water."

Ah. That was where a good question would come in. "What's it like now?" Avery asked softly.

Cal sighed. "Like that," he said, gesturing with his chin toward the window. "Big and dark. You don't know what's out there anymore. I thought I did, and I caught a monster. What if there are more monsters in the sound?"

Avery tried to wrap his mind around his schedule the next day. God, registration opened at nine, panels started at ten, lunch was served at one, prepaid with the ticket. But to go out on the sound . . .

"Do you want me to come with you?" he asked, before he could back out. "I mean, for real? Tomorrow, not just next week. I'd like to see it too, in the morning."

Cal tilted his head. "Fishing's hard work," he said dismissively, and Avery wanted to curse his spaghetti limbs and complete lack of muscle tone.

"I'd stay out of the way— You know what? Never mind. I mean, why would you want to—"

"Your thing—your TV show thing—starts tomorrow, doesn't it?"

Avery nodded, feeling stupid. "Yeah."

"I figured—it's why everybody's been driving in tonight. Probably could have left you there on 101. Someone would have come along after me."

He didn't sound sorry, though. Avery smiled, making it as winsome as possible. "Aren't you glad it was you though?"

A corner of Cal's mouth pulled up in derision, but his eyebrows rose like he really *was* glad. "Almost. Have your convention—do your . . . whatever. Your fan thing. Maybe meet Carter Samuels and get laid."

"As if," Avery muttered, rolling his eyes. "He's dating Levi Pritchard. But afterward—it ends Sunday morning—"

"I'll take you Monday," Call said, nodding. "Pick you up early, bring you hip waders and a slicker. You write articles. Maybe you can put it in an article or something."

Avery smiled at him. "Thank you—wait. Do you have a phone?"

Cal shook his head. "No good out on the water. Can't afford one on land."

Avery stared at him. "That's . . . *terrifying,*" he said, his brain completely tweaked by the idea that . . . OMG. *No cellphone?*

Cal was unimpressed. "Here. Give me your phone."

Avery slid his unimpressive Windows phone over, turned on, password typed in already.

Cal punched some numbers and hit Save, then slid the phone back. "That's my home phone. Call me Sunday night if I don't see you earlier."

With that Cal took their two empty plates and stood up. "I'll have Alicia come by with more coffee. You're welcome to stay as long as you want, but service dries up in fifteen minutes."

Avery nodded. "Maybe tomorrow I'll bring my laptop."

Cal shrugged. "Tomorrow there'll be lots more people. See you tomorrow, Rescue Puppy."

He left, and Avery drank one last cup of coffee, laughing to himself. Rescue Puppy. Well, maybe. But Cal seemed to be taking care of him just fine. Avery made his way back to his room then, because as tempting as it would have been to sit and watch Cal work and wonder if his black khakis could get threadbare enough for Avery to see his ass, the fact was, it had been a full couple of days.

Avery slid into bed that night absolutely positive that coffee, pie, and clean sheets were the blessings of every god in the book.

The next morning Avery gave his ID to the lady sitting at the registration table and looked around a little guiltily. When he'd first signed up for the convention, he'd had delusions of dressing up in character because hey, if anyone could lose himself in a well-made world, it was him. But after that surprising breakup, well, he'd had enough on his plate getting ready to move. That didn't mean he didn't appreciate the assortment of werewolves, elves, vampires, wendigo, and alternate shape-shifters that populated the checkout line. He'd have to be content with wearing one of his five Wolf's Landing T-shirts and admiring other people's ingenuity for this round.

"Avery Kennedy?" the woman asked, searching her list. She was dressed in the characteristic blue trench coat, black turtleneck, and jeans of the female lead on the show, and she had her dark hair pulled back into the same sort of ponytail. Her features—broad cheeks and a clearly Latino complexion—were nothing like the lead actress's crystalline bone structure and pale Irish skin, but Avery appreciated the hell out of the effort. It didn't matter if you *looked* like the actor— did you *feel* like the character? *That* was the question, and this woman even had the hair-flip out of the eyes.

"The name on the tag is 'Scarecrow,'" Avery told her self-consciously.

The woman's face brightened. "Oh! Okay! I'm looking in the wrong place." She riffled through a long box for a second and came out with an ID card with a cartoon shot of a wolf leaning against a tree and drinking a martini. "Here, Scarecrow—you get a lanyard, and a swag bag and *oh my God*!" She stopped suddenly while handing Avery the swag bag, and Avery startled, looking around him to see if something was wrong.

"*Scarecrow? Avery?*" The woman stood up (well, not very far, she was maybe 5'2") and gestured to herself. "It's *me*, Gi-Gi!"

Avery couldn't stop the grin that split his face. "*Gi-Gi? Oh my God*!" He took a step around to the end of the table and tried not to jump up and down like a little girl. "Wow! You said you were volunteering at reg, and I completely forgot! Lookit you, all dressed up like Julia! You said your husband was going to dress up like—"

A squat, balding man who had been standing behind Gi-Gi and blending into the background looked up at Avery and grinned, pointing to *his* trench coat, matching black turtleneck, and plastic martini glass peeking out of the pocket.

"Mr. Gi-Gi!" Avery crowed, delighted. Gi-Gi rushed him and he got the most amazing hug—it was like the hug a mom or a sister would give him, but he was an only child and his mom wasn't a hugger.

Gi-Gi was, and the weight of two years of late-night conversations gave his arms strength as he bent down and returned her hug with interest.

"Oh my God! Honey! I'm *so glad* to finally meet you!"

"Mr. G!" Gi-Gi cried to her husband, "Take over for me, okay?"

And just like that, he sat down and took over her job, while Gi-Gi guided Avery away from the line and to a quiet place by the stairwell where they could talk.

Avery couldn't stop looking at her, because he'd spent the last two years thinking she was six kinds of wonderful. She'd been there for every fight with Billy, for every victory celebration when he finished an article, and for every piece of fan fiction he'd written.

He'd complain about Billy and his mother would say, "Well, Avery, this is why men are made to date women!" and Gi-Gi would write, *Avery, if the guy's a pig in a restaurant, you have the right to be embarrassed.*

He'd talk about work, and his father would say, "Nobody can make a living writing. When are you going to get a real job?" and Gi-Gi would type, *I read your article this morning. Man, you are gonna change the fucking world.*

He'd write fan fiction, and his boyfriend would say, "Jesus, Avery, if writing is your profession, could you maybe stop writing the stupid stuff and stick with the stuff that's going to make you money?" and Gi-Gi would IM, *People don't understand that sometimes our fantasy lives are what get us through our real lives. The kids had me in absolute tears getting them out the door this morning, but I'm telling you, that piece of fiction you just wrote me, that was worth getting up for.*

When Avery went to Chicago to do a piece on urban upkeep, he'd bought two books' worth of postcards and sent them to Gi-Gi's kids so they could see where their mom's friend Avery went on his trip. He knew their names, he knew their birthdates, and he and Gi-Gi had IMed about *Wolf's Landing* at three in the morning when Gi-Gi had been in labor and her husband had been asleep, saving his strength. Neither of them posted their pictures online—both of them kept most of their social media restricted to the fan fiction archive—but damn.

Avery felt like he was meeting his very best friend for the first time in his life.

Considering the way Gi-Gi was misting up, she obviously felt the same way.

"Oh my God, Avery! Lookit you! You're *adorable*!"

Avery couldn't stop the aw-shucks blush that washed his face, and his cheeks were scrunched so high, they interfered with his vision.

"You look amazing!" he said, completely sincere. The rest of the world might not see an angel in this chunky little housewife, but that's because the rest of the world was *blind*. She had a smile that stretched her cheeks and a warmth that just emanated from her body. She hadn't stopped clutching both his hands in hers. "Man, I had no idea you'd be right there. Were you here last night? If I'd known you were here last night, I would have looked you up!"

"Oh!" she waved her hand. "Forget about it. We got in at like ass-crack-o'clock—there were a bunch of tour buses that were late to greet the ferry passengers and we were exhausted, which was sort of good because otherwise I woulda been too keyed up to sleep. So lookit you! You know, you told me you were leaving and just sort of dropped off the map. I was worried, but Mister said you were probably just living the high life on the way up—so what. Tell me. How was your trip?"

Avery pulled one hand away to scrub at his eyes.

"Gi, you would not fuckin' *believe* the bullshit I had to deal with to get here."

And like *that* he had a buddy, someone he could complain to about the fucking bank card and the fucking car and running out of gas before Medford and living on peanut butter and jelly and not knowing how he was going to get his car out of hock from the taciturn, irritable man that Cal had left him with. And God. *Someone* to tell about the gruff man who'd picked him up in the rain, called him Rescue Puppy, and had almost been killed by a giant fucking prehistoric fish.

"And he's good-looking?"

"Yeah, Gi—he's totally out of my league, that's not the—"

"That's *totally* the point. Is he available? I mean, is he *interested*, if you know what I mean?"

Avery remembered the manager's hand on his ass, and the way Cal had said, "People get to have fuck buddies."

"Yeah, I think he might be available—which would be a fucking miracle to have, you know, gay guy rescuing gay guy in the rain, but it's still not the point."

"What's the point?" Gi asked, looking at him with wide, interested, melty chocolate eyes.

Avery adored her so hard right then, he completely forgot. "The point," he said, feeling a little misty himself, "is that I just got to tell my best friend about my stupid adventure. *Jesus*, it was rough, keeping all that to myself."

They both went in for the hug at the same time.

"I am *so* glad to meet you!"

They both said *that* at the same time too.

They probably could have talked for another hour—hell, another *ten* hours—but Gi had to go finish her stint at the registration table, and Avery had committed to a couple of panels for his article.

"How about we meet at the restaurant at two," Gi-Gi said as Avery left her with her beleaguered husband who was staring at a woman dressed as a were-wendigo with a slightly shell-shocked look on his face.

Avery hesitated, and she hurriedly inserted, "*Our* treat. We can take lunch tomorrow and go see what's up with your car, and maybe visit the bank for a cash withdrawal, okay?"

Oh Lordie, how Avery was glad to have a friend here.

"You're a lifesaver, Gi. Thanks, sweetheart. My treat as soon as I get cash. I swear, I didn't even think about going to the bank itself."

Gi-Gi waved her hand—she did that a lot. It was like her body was a little short-ish, so her gestures were a little grand-ish. He loved that about her too.

"Oh, hon—no. Let us treat. Mister is gonna go gamble tonight, so you and me, we're on for long meaningful talks, right?"

Avery nodded. "And plot mapping and—"

"I got the tablet—we could go back and watch episodes twenty-six, twenty-seven, and twenty-eight, all in a row, if you want?"

Avery couldn't help it. An ecstatic shudder rocked his body, and he gave her a shiny-eyed smile. "It's like *you* are the sunshine I always needed in my life but never knew."

She gave him a smug smile. "I like that in a man. Now go work. Lunch at two—see ya!"

By the time two o'clock rolled around, Avery was suffering from serious sensory overstimulation. He'd never realized how working from his kitchen every day had left him open and sensitive to noises, crowds—hell, even fluorescent lighting. That said, he'd enjoyed the panels immensely. Having a press pass helped him get into the celebrity panel, and watching Carter Samuels and Levi Pritchard laugh and flirt with each other, and generally clown around with Marianna Talbot who played Julia Morris with the crowd was enough to make him forget his own troubles for a while.

Carter and Levi's chemistry together was just as impressive in person as it was on film—which was a good thing, since they'd just gotten very publicly engaged. Seeing Carter's blond boyishness and Levi's dark, broody thing going on up close, Avery couldn't believe they'd ever planned to hide it. Plenty of people were asking about how hard it was to play will they/won't they between Carter's character Gabriel, and Gabriel's partner Julia, while Carter and Levi were definitely will they! All three stars were candid about that, and Marianna played it classy by confessing that she'd been kind of disappointed she didn't get any romantic scenes either on or off page—after all, she got to play opposite two handsome leading men. Who *didn't* have their fantasies?

But those weren't the only questions, either, and Avery listened with interest. Did the additions to the writing staff make the scripts more exciting? Did Marianna ever feel overshadowed by her two costars, or did she have other projects out there to showcase her formidable talent?

Even Avery got a chance to ask a question. As interested as he was in Carter and Levi's sex life, he contented himself with asking if the stars enjoyed living in the Pacific Northwest or if they missed Hollywood or New York or some of the bigger places where TV shows were usually shot. That's when Carter Samuels surprised him with some candor.

"Honestly, I love it here. I mean, I never thought I would. When I first showed up here to shoot, I thought I'd go crazy with nothing to do—but it turns out there's stuff here I love to do, I just never knew it." There was a chuckle from the crowd, and he flattered them with a smile. "The people here, the scenery—it's a good place."

"Absolutely," Levi interjected. "Grounds you when you need it. One of the problems you have in Hollywood is that nobody knows your real name. Here, you can walk on the set and *be* someone else, but when you walk outside, you're in this sort of real place. It's hard to get a big head or forget who you are here. That's a good thing for an actor, you know?"

There was more laughter, and the panel continued, but Avery took a good look at Pritchard's face while he was speaking. He seemed . . . content. He was not the boyish action star who had fled Hollywood, licking his wounds in his twenties. He had some years, some perspective, and Bluewater Bay had helped him find it.

For Avery, who was hoping to find a home here too, their happiness was a place to find inspiration.

So that was a bright moment, and so was the panel on the use of CGI in the show, and the other panel on makeup. But by the time two o'clock rolled around, Avery was exhausted and *so* ready to brave the restaurant for the late afternoon lull.

Gi-Gi was waiting there, and so was Mr. G, and as Avery slid into the booth, the waitress arrived with two baskets of chips and queso.

"I am such a freeloader," Avery breathed before shoving the first handful of chips in his mouth. He'd discovered that the hotel was about two miles from any sort of convenience store, and the one inside was as expensive as the coffee shop. His breakfast had been a triple shot latte, extra cream.

Gi-Gi and her husband laughed, and then Avery and Gi-Gi got down to the serious business of being best friends for life.

Sometime after their food arrived, Mr. G (whose real name was, go figure, Gregg) bent and kissed his wife's cheek, and then disappeared, probably to the hotel casino. Gi-Gi waved at him distractedly, and she and Avery continued talking about . . .

Everything.

From her kids to his love life to a giant coauthored fanfic that they would write if they only had the time.

And finally, to the series of disasters that left him stranded at the convention of his dreams with nowhere to go afterwards.

Sort of.

It was weird, how resourceful Avery felt now.

"So," Gi-Gi said with some concern, "Avery, what are you going to do now? I mean, besides clear up the bullshit with the bank."

Avery shrugged. "God, I still feel stupid about forgetting I could get cash without my card."

Gi-Gi laughed. "Yeah, well, you're young. As far as you're concerned, you stick the plastic in the place and the money pops out. Natural mistake to make. But I mean . . . you know. Making a living."

"Lots of things," he said frankly. "They've got a coffee shop in town—I can go earn tips there if I need to, and maybe find an apartment or a house or a roommate. I mean, I make a pretty good living freelancing, but it's not all I can do. This bank thing is temporary. What matters is I find a place to live and find a way to get around. I've got clothes and stuff in my car, and when I get *it* out of hock, I'm pretty much set. I mean . . ." He peered out at the water through the same window he'd been looking through the night before. The view didn't get worse in the daytime. "Look at where I am," he said simply, smiling and shrugging. "I'm here, and I can earn a living, and how bad could that possibly be?"

Gi-Gi cocked her head. "I thought you'd be more upset," she said bluntly. "For months, all I get is 'Billy did this!' and 'What if Billy's cheating on me' and—"

"He was," Avery said, feeling surprisingly calm. "I told you that. He totally confessed before we broke up and I left him at the bus stop."

"Well, that was fucking sweet of him."

Avery grinned at her, all teeth. "Yeah. It actually was. Let me leave him in Anaheim with no guilt whatsoever." He sobered and sighed. "Which was also sort of a dick move."

She patted his hand. "Your heart was in the right place—I mean, you know. Saving him from seeing your parents—that was actually pretty considerate."

He beamed, relieved because she understood that part. He wasn't *trying* to be a dick or a moron—it was like the thing with the plastic card. He just hadn't thought that move through. "Thanks, Gi," he said softly.

"Has he tried to contact you?"

Avery held up his phone. "Once. As I was pulling out of Redding he called and told me he'd give me one last chance." God, he'd almost forgotten that. Running out of gas after Crescent City had completely overshadowed it.

Gi-Gi made a moue of distaste. "Again, what a fuckin sweetheart. He's a doll. He should apply for sainthood."

"St. Big Dick of Assimus?" Avery said, tongue firmly in his cheek. "Don't we all know that guy?"

Gi-Gi rolled her eyes and shook her head, and Avery drained his umpteenth glass of water. He was going to have to pee soon, and as he glanced around to find the bathroom, he got a glimpse of the employee's hallway.

A guy who looked a lot like Cal was hauling ass that way, being pursued hotly by the manager Avery had seen groping that selfsame. Their raised voices could be heard from Avery's table, but not their exact words.

Avery frowned and then looked at Gi-Gi.

"I kind of got to pee, hon. I'll be back in ten, okay?"

She nodded. "My turn when you get back."

He trotted off, grateful that the restrooms were to the right of the employee's hallway.

He *really* wanted to hear what Cal and his fuck buddy were saying to each other. Instead of taking a right into the bathroom, he took a left toward the changing rooms, stopping just outside the door and leaning against the side.

"You're late, McCorkle, and you look like you've been in another fight."

"Yeah, well, the first one was my brother and the second was a big fucking tree limb in the net."

To his credit, the manager made a pained noise. "Cal . . . damn it—you're going to get *hurt* if you keep going out there!"

"Like a month off my feet wasn't hurt?" There were noises then, like Cal was getting undressed and thumping around a locker room.

"You spent a month off the *water*, Cal. You were back here as soon as you could walk."

"You're not my mother, George," he snapped. "I'm gonna shower, do you mind?"

George's voice dropped, became intimate. "Do you, you know, want me here when you get out?"

The sigh Cal let out wasn't promising. "No. Man, I think that thing we were doing, you know, before I got hurt . . ."

And surprisingly enough, sleazy manager sounded sad. "Yeah. Yeah, I hear you. Just . . . you know. You ever want to make it . . . a thing. A real thing. A dating-and-shit thing—I'd do that, Cal."

And Cal's next words were so characteristic of the man who'd called him Rescue Puppy that Avery actually felt sorry for the guy he was dumping.

"That's . . . Really? Well, fuck. Sorry. I mean, I thought we were just—"

"Yeah," George said bitterly. "We were just using each other. Carry on, oh mighty fishing god. You're on in five."

Avery hightailed it for his own bathroom, did his business, and was on the way out, drying his hands, when he bumped into Cal.

Who looked genuinely surprised to see him.

"Jesus, do you trip little old ladies in grocery stores?" Cal snapped.

Avery backed up, sheepish. "No— I didn't mean to get in your way. Just, you know, lunch with a friend—"

"I thought you didn't know anybody here?" Cal asked suspiciously, and Avery had to smile.

"Well, I only knew her online before, but she dragged her husband along—they're great people, do you want to meet her?"

Cal stared at him, blinked, and then stared at him again. "You just had lunch with someone you met *online*? And you *trusted her*?"

Avery smiled sunnily. "Yup. And I'm talking to a guy I let give me a ride to town even though I'd never met him *at all* before that. And I *trusted* him. Isn't that a kick in the balls? Do you want to meet her? C'mon—follow me, you can meet her!"

Cal grunted. "Avery . . . man, I appreciate that I'm the only person you know in this town, but—"

Avery turned to him, and felt his expression sober. "Yes, but I *want* to know you," he said. A smile pulled at his mouth. "And I feel like Gi-Gi wants to meet you."

Cal scrubbed at his face, and his shoulders slumped, like he had no will to fight. "I'll be out in a minute. I gotta get my tub and pretend to be working."

Avery was going to turn the wattage up on his smile, but something in that defeated set to Cal's shoulders stopped him. "You uh—I mean, how's Keir?"

Cal shrugged. "Got his meds today. So did Uncle Nascha. Win." But his voice didn't sound like it was a win. His voice sounded like he couldn't win.

"What about fishing? It was your first day back, right?"

Cal held up his arms, which had deep scratches, some of which looked as though they'd barely stopped oozing. There was a gouge under his chin and across his cheek, to add to the brutality of the shiner.

"Tree limb," he said, sounding still puzzled. "I . . . The water is my place. I *thought* the water was my place."

Avery's stomach took a thump and a dive. "You . . . Maybe you need to find a place with people too, you think?" God. He didn't know this guy. It was great to play at *let's make friends*, but Cal's life— Avery had a feeling Cal's life was just so much more intense than that.

The bleak expression on Cal's face only confirmed that idea. "I've got people. I've got Uncle Nascha with Alzheimer's, and I've got Keir. My entire world is those two people. Can't say I don't got people."

Avery's heart joined his stomach on the roller-coaster ride. "Well, you know. I'm in town now. You got me."

Cal's derision didn't quite reach his eyes. "Okay, Rescue Puppy. I'll feed you until you run away on me, how's that?"

He turned away, probably to go clock in so he didn't get fired, and Avery watched him go.

Yeah. Too late. Don't know how easy it's going to be to run away.

Thinking carefully, Avery walked back to where Gi-Gi sat, texting on her phone. It was probably her parents who were watching her kids, and the fact that she'd be worried about her kids made his heart get warm all over again. He'd texted his mother the night before from the hotel, and he hadn't gotten a response yet.

He needed Gi-Gi in his life. If nothing else, his entire trip up had taught him that while there might be some awful, evil souls out there in the world, there were also some really frickin' decent people.

Cal needed to do what he had, and rediscover people.

CHAPTER NINE

THE TREE LIMB
FOR THE FOREST

When he was fishing, Cal's day started at 4 a.m., and the day he met Avery and his friend in the restaurant at the Global was no exception.

The sky was black, and the air was just cold and damp enough to make his chest hurt, but oh! He was going out on the water. And yes, he'd been honest with Avery the night before when he'd said all he saw was black water and shadows instead of blue skies and freedom—but even black water and shadows held a certain depth in which to hide.

But Nascha had been getting wilier this past month since Cal had been laid up with his infection. Cal had been able to impose the medication regimen on both of them, Keir and Nascha, since he'd been home more often, and Nascha had used his clarity to do what the old man did best: meddle in Cal's life.

It had started innocently enough—Nascha would bring Cal orange juice or milk, bring him the remote, tell him where the good shows were. But Cal would wake up from a sudden nap, because Nascha had doubled his Ibuprofen dose, and he'd find that Nascha had called in to the Global and postponed his shift, or, even worse, called in sick. He'd only done it a few times, but it was enough to make Cal leery of taking food or drink from the old man, much less letting him control the television.

One of the reasons Cal had stayed away from the water until the doctor had given the okay (when it was not in his nature to do *anything* on the authority of a doctor, administrator, or even policeman) was that Nascha had spent a week sabotaging his alarm clock. Cal would wake up, heart pounding, and see that it was full light outside, which was hard to do in Washington in the winter.

He'd tried sleeping with the clock under his pillow, but Nascha must have had an alarm clock of his own.

"Ridiculous" was the word that came to mind.

It was *ridiculous* that after a month on the right medicine, suddenly Nascha would be taking the same route Cal's mother had used when he'd been taking too many classes and practicing too many hours on the field.

But Cal finally had his doctor's clearance, and the night before he'd gotten a promise from Nascha (and the old man didn't take those lightly) that he'd let Cal go out and try to earn a living so they didn't lose Nascha's house.

Cal didn't count on Nascha being awake when he ventured into the living room while wearing his long johns, socks, and flannels. He was ready to go out and put his hip waders on before he got in the dory—but he wasn't ready to confront Great-Uncle Nascha.

"Nascha?" he asked uncertainly, peering into the living room from the tiny kitchen. "Why're you up again?"

Before Cal had gotten hurt, Nascha had started falling asleep in the living room and waking up there as well. Since Cal had gotten laid up, he'd begun to go back to his own bed again. Said something about how they *all* needed to remember what was night and what was day. If Cal didn't know better, he'd say Nascha was giving him a subtle reminder about who was the elder and who was the younger in their household.

But Cal *did* know better, and Nascha's advice as well as his ability to care for his beloved grandnephews hadn't been that on point for years.

"I'm up to talk to you, Calladh," Nascha said. He was sitting in his customary corduroy recliner in front of the television, and Cal grabbed an apple and a bagel from the counter and wandered into the living room, gnawing on the apple first.

The living room looked the same as it had for the past six years. There were no tchotchkes or pictures on the mantel or on the walls because Keir got destructive in a temper, and it was wearying to try to restrain him from breaking something he'd broken the day before. The plain tan carpet had worn spaces, and in particular the path between kitchen and the recliner was bare to the warp and weft of it.

"What's up?" he asked, feeling happy for the first time in a month. The water. For a month, he'd been trapped in his own home, on constant vigilance with Nascha and Keir. He was horrible at it, growly, irritable, and helpless. God, at least on the water, he was *doing something.* He was catching fish—how primal could you get? Catching fish, providing for his family. *He was useful.*

He was not useful with his leg up on the couch, watching hours of television that he had no idea existed.

Hell, until his leg had gotten infected, he hadn't seen a single episode of that damned show. Fact was, he sort of liked it. The show, that is. Being helpless ate his stomach like battery acid, but watching the show was like watching some sort of alternate reality. *If* there were werewolves . . . *If* handsome men like Gabriel Hanford really populated Bluewater Bay . . . *If* the good guy could make hard choices but win in the end . . .

Then Cal might be able to find a way out of the family finger trap in which the two people he most loved were effectively strangling all of his hopes and dreams.

So he got it. He got why someone like Avery—someone who had a good life, and this sort of boundless enthusiasm—might come to a place like Bluewater Bay to find out more about a show that celebrated the place.

But that didn't mean he was going to spend more time watching it.

"You are going out too soon," Nascha said, and Cal smiled through his mouthful of apple.

"Naw," he said when he'd swallowed. "I always go fishing at four, Nascha. I know I took a month off—"

"I'm talking about your fear. The water doesn't treat fear with compassion, Calladh. That's what people are for."

Cal swallowed hard, even though he didn't have any apple in his mouth.

"Nobody's got compassion for a late bill, Nascha. I need to go—"

"Yes. You need to go. You need to leave Keir and me, and fly."

Oh no. Not this discussion again. Cal sighed and squatted in front of Nascha's recliner, hating this and loving this at the same time. When Nascha's medication was working, when his mind was sharp, he was . . . *wonderful*. God, Nascha had always given the best advice. He'd always, always, held the roadmap to Calladh McCorkle's heart.

Why aren't you going to the dance, Calladh? There are lots of pretty girls there.

Uhm, you know . . . girls, whatever—

Don't bullshit an old man, Cal. Your brother will never marry. Be honest. Will you?

Probably not, Uncle Nascha. Not, uhm, unless the world changes.

The world *had* changed since that conversation—but so had Uncle Nascha, and the passage of marriage equality was the last thing on his mind. In fact, anything that happened in the recent past was pretty far from Nascha's mind.

Unless he'd had a straight month of medication, and someone in the house to keep him rooted in the present, and someone to talk to who didn't obsess over the same damned television show he'd obsessed over eight years ago.

Apparently Nascha needed Cal to be there in the present, and Cal needed to be gone to keep him there in the house.

"I love you and Keir," Cal said, the words coming easily, as they should. Here with Nascha, he couldn't lie, and he didn't need to front. He could be open and honest with that one truth. But only that one.

"But you don't love being trapped here," Nascha said bluntly. "You don't like not being able to date, not being able to leave the house, and not getting enough sleep because you are working too hard."

"Well, what am I going to do without you? Work too hard to make sure you two are in a nice place, and be alone?"

Nascha scowled. "You wouldn't be alone if you talked to other people! Keir hasn't shut up about the boy you picked up on the 101— Wouldn't you like to be able to sit down with him and have dinner?"

Cal smiled faintly. "I sat down with him and had pie, Nascha. He's a journalist, and he's sweet as a puppy—"

"Perfect. Maybe you can take him to dinner, and discover real sweetness afterward, yes?"

Cal made a child's sound in his throat—a whine, but deeper. "And who will be watching you and Keir? Who will be making sure you eat? Who will be paying for your medicine while Cal gets all the sweetness—"

Nascha was maybe the one person who could smooth Cal's coarse dark hair back from his brow, and Cal fought the urge to rest his head on his uncle's lap. He also fought the urge to scream and stomp away.

He settled for closing his eyes for a breathless, warm moment, and he let Nascha's words rock over him like waves.

"Sell this house, Cal. The tribe wants the lands here to build a marina and a casino for tourists. Dottie will sell if you sell, and Keir and I—we can have the good places, a place where Keir can wander in woods, and I can smile at the pretty orderlies, the girls *and* the boys. And you can go to school, and only fish because you love it and—"

Cal stood up abruptly, angry for having heard so much.

"And live with the idea that I *left* you?" he snapped. "That you and Keir loved me and I *left* you, because I couldn't cut it, couldn't provide for my family, couldn't—"

"How much love is going to be left!" Nascha struggled to his feet, another thing that had apparently gotten easier for him over the past month. "How much love will you have for us when we kill all the promise in your life?"

Cal thought about Avery and how badly he'd wanted to sit with him the night before. He could have bought him dinner, and confessed to his new television addiction and talked to him about being a high school football hero, and keeping up with the edicts of Fish & Game and how he'd once wanted to be one of the trainers, like they had in the animal shows, had wanted to feed the injured birds by hand and see them fly again.

Such a simple thing—to sit down with the boy who peered through his thick glasses and grinned at you like he knew the sun would rise behind you, and he'd study your face in shadow or in light. And it was a thing he couldn't do—because the sacrifice he'd have to make for that simple date was . . .

"You're thinking, aren't you?" Nascha said soberly. "You will fight it, Calladh. You will fight and you will rage. You always have." He smiled faintly and balanced himself on the back of the recliner. "You were six years old when we told you that you'd have a little brother. You *hated* the idea. For months, you broke toys and had tantrums and screamed at your mother. You stomped out of the house one day, your school pack on your back. You were running away from home, where there wouldn't be a baby to take away the love you were surrounded with. We let you go, because that's what you do with children—especially children like you, with such an independent heart. And then—I don't know what happened." He sighed and lowered himself back down into the recliner, apparently tired from standing. "You came home in the afternoon, full from the lunch you'd packed, and dirty from playing in the pond, and happy."

Cal reached for the memory. "Puppies!" he said, thinking about it. "Remember that family that lived out by the pond? The Hernandezes? Three boys—Mark, Luke, and Paul, and they had puppies. And they invited me to play with the puppies, and they were . . . you know . . . puppies! And just having brothers there made the puppies better." *Oh, damn you, Nascha.* Cal was smiling in spite of himself. In spite of the black eye from the fight about bringing Avery home, in spite of how badly he'd wanted to sit and talk to Avery himself—Cal was smiling. "I wanted a brother because he could help me play with . . ."

They'd had a dog, about the time Keir had started to get angry. Keir had kicked it in the stomach, and they'd needed to put it down. Cal had cried for days, and Keir, unable to cry with him, had simply sat in a corner, staring, glassy-eyed, repeating Outlaw's name.

Nascha closed his eyes. "Cal. Cal. You have got to get away from us, or pretty soon, memories like that one will be the only ones you have."

Cal didn't even have words. "I need to go," he said gruffly. He bent down and kissed Nascha's weathered cheek, feeling his uncle's coarse, straight, gray hair under his hands. How soon would his hair turn that color? Would he know love by then? Would he know a family that didn't hurt? Or would he still be out in the water, casting his purse seine, trying in vain to sort the good from the bad?

"I took my medicine today," Nascha said, his voice firm. "And Keir will take his too. And tomorrow you and I will have this conversation again."

Cal turned away before he could say, *That's what you think!* and made for the water.

But Nascha had been right about the water having no compassion. He'd been fishing for a couple of hours when the tree limb had gotten tangled in his net. He hadn't seen it until he bent over the dory to try to sort the fish, pull out the salmon and the sturgeon, which were still on the watch list, and pull in only the rockfish, flounder, and sole, which were legal if not plentiful. He heard the bump first, the scrape against the hull of the boat, and then the first branch had broken the water as he'd hauled on the net. The branch ripped a stripe down his neck and his jaw, and by the time he'd untangled his net from around the half-submerged nightmare, he had a number of deep gouges down his shoulders and arms. He'd given up then, so he'd have time to doctor his hurts before he took the fish to the hotel kitchen to sell, but his time in the bathroom with the peroxide and a washcloth hadn't been a lot of fun either.

"You need to wash it," Keir said about a million times. "You don't want an infection."

"I know, Keir, I'm washing—ouch!—it!" God, the one across his throat hurt. It was such a personal place. Mother Nature hadn't exactly kicked him in the nads—no. She'd tried to slit his throat.

"But you need to get out everything—the grit, the grime, the bacteria—"

"I'm using peroxide, Keir. And antibiotic ointment and everything."

"Good, because you don't want an infection."

Sigh. "No. I don't want an infection."

"Because infections can kill you."

"Because infections can kill me."

"Like the girls—they're an infection. They're going to hurt me."

What infection is killing you, *Keir? Why do you keep obsessing about the girls in our neighborhood?*

"The girls don't want to hurt you, Keir. Not these girls. Some other girls might have, but they're all gone." He'd said it before, but Keir never seemed to register.

The sound of Keir's fist going through the first layer of laminate on the cheap bathroom door startled Cal so much he ripped open the scratch he was cleaning. For a moment he stared dumbly at the blood dripping from his collarbone down his chest before he registered Keir's howl of pain. Feeling sluggish and completely incapable of managing his own life, he opened the bathroom door and brought Keir in, sat him down on the toilet, and spent the remainder of his spare time picking splinters of wood out of his hand.

Keir sobbed quietly while he worked.

"Why?" Cal asked for maybe the hundredth time. "Why do the girls—"

"I don't know," Keir moaned softly, rocking against the back of the toilet. "I don't know. I don't know, I don't know . . ."

One of Cal's best weapons in his arsenal was a sedative. They didn't like giving it to Keir in the day because when they did that they had to give it to him at night as well, to keep him quiet and let him sleep until the next morning. Feeling weak and overwhelmed, Cal gave Keir his first capsule and sat him in front of the television. He would stare blankly at the screen for the rest of the day. God, his brother deserved better—his brother deserved sunshine and flowers, and long rambling walks where he could hold his arms open and let the wind bear him up.

He wasn't going to get that. Eight years ago, when Keir had first started to act out, Cal, his father, and Nascha had gone around to every neighbor for a mile around, knocked on their door, and given them a picture of Keir.

"This is my brother. He's got problems, but there are no good places to put him. If your kids see him without an adult nearby, tell them to run for the house, and call us. If we have anything to do about it, he will *never* be without supervision."

And barring the few times Nascha had fallen asleep, before Cal had started asking Dottie to come over to watch him, Keir had never gotten out without supervision.

But Cal was starting to wake up in a cold sweat, dreaming of the police knocking at his door. Dreaming of living with his brother hurting someone, or dreaming of seeing him locked in a criminal facility, or one of the really shitty places that used straitjackets all the time and stank of pee. Unless he sedated Keir and dealt with *that* guilt, he lived that other nightmare every night.

He'd sleep tonight—but there was a price.

As Cal was changing his shirt—yet again—Dottie let herself in. In her sixties, with brightly dyed ginger hair, Dottie was the epitome of the good old broad. Cal imagined that after her gig at the McCorkle house of horrors was over, she sat back in her recliner at home, poured herself a highball, lit herself a cig, and watched something with pretty young men doing the thing while her man of the week went down on her like a Saint Bernard going for peanut butter. Not that the last part of the image didn't make him want to hurl a little, but Dottie was just that no-bullshit. She'd had a good time in her life, would continue to have a good time in her life, and wanted the people around her to have good times in *their* lives. Of course the caveat was still that she thought antipsychotics were for wusses.

He worked around Dottie's limitations and knew that if he kept his end, she'd keep up hers, and she wouldn't charge him extra if George kept him after hours.

Not that George ever really did that, because what George wanted didn't last more than a minute or two.

And that thought sent a surge of frustration and self-loathing under his skin.

"You going to be late tonight?" Dottie asked, taking stock of the counter, the dishes (which had been done), and Keir's zombie stare at the television.

"No," Cal said, looking at Nascha's disapproving glare as well. "I'll— Everybody's happy when I'm here more." Oh God. He was going to have to suck this up. "I'll try to make it earlier at night, since I've got a good haul to sell."

Nascha nodded his head, like Cal was making a giant concession to his demand of . . .

Of what?

Cal so didn't want to think about a life without Nascha and Keir.

"Well, Keir will like that. What'd he do to his hands?"

Cal sighed. "Slammed them through the bathroom door. Watch out when you walk by it. It might snag your shirt or your arm. I'll fix it tonight."

He'd need sandpaper, wood fill, a small patch, wood glue . . . He used the list to loop through his mind instead of his emotions.

It was easier that way.

By the time he'd finished selling his fish to Smith and was heading to the employee room to change, his brain had jumped the chain of the comfortable loop. He'd made money on the fish—that wasn't a problem—but three people, including Smith, had asked him if he'd been in an auto accident and had sounded concerned enough to shake his faith in the indifference of man.

He hadn't thought he'd be missed when he'd been taken out with the infection. Not only were they worried—apparently people were worried that it would happen again.

And God, that included George.

"Cal—what in the hell?"

"I don't want to talk about it!" Cal muttered, stalking past him.

He didn't want to see George's bland, open face. But it had been nearly two weeks since Cal had stumbled back to the Global to work when he was sick and he hadn't been with George that whole time. Maybe he should get the courage to at least look the guy in the eyes.

"You're late, McCorkle, and you look like you've been in another fight."

There was something in George's eyes, something proprietary and soft, and Cal knew, without a doubt, that he really was being an asshole.

The conversation with George was short and to the point, and the look on his face as Cal well and truly broke off a relationship that had never been sort of slugged Cal in the gut a little.

Enough so that when Avery came bounding out of nowhere, skinny face alight, hazel eyes burning beneath the thick glasses, Cal didn't have any fight in him. Yeah, sure, he'd meet the internet friend (and who let Avery out of the house—seriously, just *meeting* somebody at a convention in a strange town?) when he got a break.

Because when he'd slipped the chain of his own thoughts, somehow that weight he'd been bearing up for the last six years slid off his back. Sometimes married people who had affairs said they just "forgot" they were married. Well Cal, for a minute, "forgot" that he was married to his present.

He clocked in and grabbed his tub, then met Avery out by the bus stand.

"I gotta run around and clean up," he reassured his rescue puppy. "But I'll swing by in ten minutes, okay?"

"Okay," Avery said, still smiling. He had a wide, mobile mouth, and teeth that had been straightened with braces. Cal kept wondering who was it who gave this kid braces and let him buy a hybrid car and then sent him traveling through the Pacific Northwest all by his lonesome. "Just not too long—she's going to try to catch a panel this afternoon."

Disappointment crept into Cal's belly like a roly-poly bug. "So you both need to—"

"No!" Avery said, grimacing like he just fed his friend to the wolves. "No. I was going to hang out here. I need to call your friend at the garage, and call the post office and the bank. I might even go up to my room and bring down my laptop and try to put my notes in order."

And he'd do all that so he'd have a chance to talk to Cal? Yeah, Cal was pretty sure that was the deal. The open-faced, shiny-eyed disappointment on George's face wasn't going to leave Cal alone. People *looked* at him with affection. He hadn't counted on that, not with George. But with Avery, who didn't have any power over Cal, and who wasn't wielding said power like a mace to get Cal to bend over for him, Cal felt like he had to be much more careful.

For all his bounce and open-faced friendliness, Avery probably had a heart that could crumble.

Cal did his job conscientiously, not wanting to take advantage of George's sufferance anymore since they weren't going to be fucking in the locker room, and when he'd finished his opening duties, he managed to swing around to Avery's table.

The woman he was sitting with, wearing her dark hair in a low ponytail and dressed in a trench coat and FBI clothes, looked comfortable, normal, and no-nonsense. For a moment, Cal forgot that he'd been imagining a serial killer getting ready to take advantage of his rescue puppy.

"Cal, this is Gi-Gi. Gi-Gi, Cal!"

Avery looked from one of them to the other, and Cal had the urge to tuck his shirt in under his waistband. Gi-Gi eyed him coolly and he was suddenly reminded of the scratches on his face and neck.

"Hi, Cal," she said, smiling a rather fierce smile with a gap between her teeth. "Lovely to meet you. So you're Avery's knight in shining armor?"

Cal darted an uncomfortable glance at Avery, who grinned back. "I just gave him a ride to town, ma'am," he muttered. "I was on my way anyway."

"Yeah, yeah, that's what he says. Says you might take him out on your fishing boat—"

"It's a dory," Cal burst in, feeling the need to qualify that he wasn't in a fully powered, great big boat with a mast, etc. "I go out every morning."

"Hmm." Gi-Gi took a sip of coffee and eyed him over the cup. "Sounds dangerous." She paused. "*Looks* dangerous."

Cal shifted uncomfortably. "Uhm, tree branch. You know . . . they don't happen a lot."

"But they'll get ya," Gi-Gi said, uncompromising.

Avery was the one who snorted disbelief. "Everything's dangerous, Gi. I drove up here on a route that was supposed to be perfectly safe, but I'm telling you—if people weren't nice most of the time, I'd be dead."

Gi-Gi shook her head. "You are not inspiring me with confidence, Avery. I mean, I know you were trying to make a stand for independence and all, but I'm telling you—you should have at least filed a flight plan."

Avery shrugged. "Yeah, well, nobody expected me to get past Crescent City anyway." His mouth twisted. "Besides—you're the only person on the planet who'd miss me right now."

Cal felt a sudden pang. "Are you kidding?" he asked, remembering when he'd had a sense of humor. "You're the only person on the planet who thinks I'm a knight in shining armor. If it wasn't for you, I might have killed my little brother just on general principle."

That geeky grin from behind those thick glasses—God. Cal's hands started to sweat, and he was sure his face flushed.

"He adores you," Avery said loyally. "I'm sure you're great with him."

Cal shrugged and gestured to his still-swollen eye. "I think he would beg to differ. He, uhm . . . I mean, if you go fishing with me, you should . . . I mean, you could visit if you wanted."

He remembered dating. Once upon a time, during his senior year in high school, he'd been out on a few dates. He'd ask about a movie or a meal, and they'd usually end up kissing and groping in the front of his dad's truck for an hour, and then the date would be over. He'd given his first blowjob in that truck, and lost his virginity when one of his dates had parents who were out of town for a weekend.

He didn't seem to remember it being this *hard*.

"I'd love to see your brother again," Avery said, and for a moment Cal's cold sweat broke, and then it got suddenly worse, because, hey, *Keir and Nascha*, fuck his life. But Avery was smiling and nodding, and Cal didn't think he could disappoint him for the world.

"Yeah, we'll set that up before you leave today," Cal said. He smiled at them both again, conscious of the late-afternoon crowd beginning to thicken. "I'll be back," he said. He held up his bus tub and gave a game smile. "Got some work to do!"

He turned around and started clearing tables, running back and forth from the kitchen to the dining room. Work. Easy, brainless, muscle-exerting work. Try to anticipate the servers, make sure coffee was filled, don't slop too much food on your apron when you're unloading the dish tubs. God—sometimes even the Global was a blessing.

He was so intent on busting his hump that he almost ran Avery's friend over when he rounded the corner from the kitchen.

"Oh God—"

"Oh no—I'm sorry!"

"Oh hell!" Cal stopped a skid across the tiled section of the hallway and threw himself against a wall so he wouldn't plow over the sturdy little woman. "God. La—" he wanted to impress this person "—deeeee," he finished, keeping his voice from growling. "Sorry. I'm sorry."

"No, no!" She smiled apologetically. "I'm the one who was lurking, waiting for you to come out. I should have known—you've been running your ass off, I needed to stay out of your way."

"Yeah, uhm . . ." He paused, confused. "Why *are* you here?"

She regarded at him from under lowered black brows. "My friend, Avery—"

"Who you just met—"

"No—we've been talking online for over two years, Mr. Smarty Pants. He's a friend—my late-night buddy, my writing friend. If I start getting too cranked up or bitchy, my mister tells me to go talk to Avery, 'cause he makes me laugh."

Cal could imagine that. Avery as a late-night confidant, someone to chat with when the rest of the house was asleep.

"Yeah?"

"So the last two years, I been listening to him bitch about his boyfriend. He didn't think he was bitching—he was embarrassed, 'cause the guy was sort of a douche bag. Mean to people, catty, and Avery—he's, like, not a looker. He thinks Billy's as good as he gets. And Billy? I may be a little bit biased, but Billy was happy with Avery as long as Avery kept out of sight, paid the bills, and gave him head."

Cal recoiled. Oh. Oh, poor Avery. "Ouch."

"Yeah. So his ex-boyfriend was a good looker, but he was a douche bag."

A douche bag. Behind Gi-Gi, George walked, darting a hurt glance at Cal before looking resolutely ahead.

A douche bag, just like Cal.

"Oh," he said, feeling like crap.

"So, we know you're a looker. How you doing on the douche bag thing?"

Cal's stomach knotted. "I, uhm, I'm sort of too busy for a relationship." It felt like he was wearing Avery's glasses backwards, and Avery was getting farther and farther away. "I just wanted a friend, really. Avery's good with my brother." Cal's voice sank wistfully. "And, you know. He's . . . he's really good to talk to."

Surprisingly she reached up to his whole 5'9" height and patted his cheek. "You sound so sad!" she said. "You can't sound that sad if he's just a friend, can you?"

At that moment, George rounded the corner and looked at him meaningfully, which meant that the failed fuck-buddy thing *was* off the table and Cal's job was the whole meal.

"I, uhm, I gotta go," he said. He'd picked a guy up in the rain. That's all. He looked at George and nodded. "It was real good meeting you."

"Well, I'll probably see you again. Avery's moving here, and we don't live too far away. Now that I've got my buddy just a quick flight away, I'm not gonna go so long without a visit."

"Good," Cal said, surprising himself. "He needs someone to look out for him, you know?"

She nodded, that gap in her teeth flashing again. "I do. Maybe you could be up for the job."

She walked away before he could tell her that he did a shitty job taking care of people, period—witness Nascha trying to get rid of him—but why would he want to spill that to a stranger anyway?

"Who was that?" George asked, and Cal was going to just blow him off.

But he couldn't. Was he a man or a douche bag?

"That kid on table fifteen—I gave him a ride into town the other day. He's sort of new to around here, wanted to introduce me to his friend."

George grunted. "You know, you could have given Sasquatch a ride home for all I know about you."

"George?" His voice quavered and he hated that.

"What?" Oh God. All that Cal *hadn't* been for George, and he was concerned.

"Look—I meant what I said, about us not doing the thing anymore. But . . . you kept trying to be decent to me. It's not your fault I didn't take you up on it, okay? Just . . . I'm sorry I'm a douche bag."

George's soft gasp sort of ripped at his stomach a little, and he let George stop him with a hand on his arm.

"You . . . just . . . I wanted to be there for you." George looked away. "But I'm, you know, your boss. It probably wasn't awesome for me to be banging you in the locker room either."

Awesome? No. "I . . ." He expelled a heavy breath. "I needed . . . need . . ." God. He couldn't even put a name to it.

"You think I don't know that?" George asked bitterly. "It's a small town, Cal. I know why you were using me. I don't even blame you for it. Just . . ."

They both stood in the hallway for a moment, looking at each other. Cal realized how much George's face *didn't* fascinate him, and never had. It wasn't because he wasn't handsome, or because he wore his shirt buttoned down the front and all the way up to the collar, or because his blond hair was thinning on top.

"It was never gonna be us," Cal said, and he felt bad for saying it, because it was a shitty thing to do to someone, but there must have been something in his voice, something kind.

"No," George said with a quirk of the lips. "But I'll tell you what. I'll put you on the schedule for a half an hour later every day, you can stop being late, I can stop yelling at you for it, and we won't have a reason to go at it in the locker room."

For a moment, Cal wanted to scream about money, but then it wasn't really fair. He wasn't earning that money if he was always late, was he?

"That's a deal. I appreciate it."

He extended his hand and shook George's slightly clammy one. It occurred to him that poor George must not have been enjoying this conversation any more than he was.

"I gotta go," he said abruptly, pivoting on his heel.

"Cal?"

Cal turned for a moment and saw all that he could have been to this very decent, very average man quirking on George's full mouth. "Yeah?"

"You're not a douche bag. Don't . . . just don't go off thinking you're the bad guy, okay?"

Cal couldn't help it. He smiled.

By the end of the evening, Cal was learning to disdain the word "convention" entirely. *Christ*, it was busy. He thought the damned television show kept him hopping during most of the rest of the year, but apparently they were full up at the Global, and the Marriott down the street was getting their overflow.

Avery had given up his table when the dinner rush hit, but he'd waved to Cal and pointed at his phone, indicating he'd be back when things got sane again.

Cal had waved back, pretty sure that wouldn't happen because who did that? Money or not, who did that?

He certainly wasn't expecting Avery to return, around eleven thirty, half an hour before close.

He'd changed and had apparently charged his laptop because he sat down and started typing, not even waiting for the waitress to come ask him what he wanted.

Cal was pretty sure he'd take anything free, so when George told him he was off, he grabbed two more pieces of pie and a carafe of coffee. He still had some time before Dottie expected him, and damn it, what was one more half hour?

CHAPTER TEN

BOTH HANDS
AND A TIN CUP

B less Gi-Gi, bless her children, her children's children, and all the increase of her house.

Her husband had actually hit a $200 jackpot in the casino, and because he was apparently Gi-Gi's awesome mate, he got the hotel to comp him a rental car.

After the restaurant began to fill up and Avery was forced to stop staring helplessly at Cal's ass as he tried valiantly to run it off, he *thought* he was going to his room to work. Instead, Gi-Gi and Mr. G ditched out on stuff they'd originally planned to do and took Avery the two miles to town.

In the light, the town held a certain Pacific Northwestern charm. The sidewalks of main streets were hewn logs, and most of the store facades boasted log cabin exteriors as well. Yeah, sure, he had to *bypass* the fun stuff, while Mr. G steered them to Clarke's Auto Repair, but it was at least pleasant to look at.

Clarke had taken a look at his car and had a quote for him. It was something Avery could afford—but it would take a chunk out of what he'd been hoping to use to find a place. The good news was, it would probably take a week to fix, so he had some breathing room before he had to come up with some way to pay.

And for the moment, Avery could get the rest of his clothes out of the back and bring them to the hotel, along with some of his reference books so he could write the article, as well as his blankets, DVDs and other things. He had to admit, having his stuff around him in the hotel room comforted him on some basic level. Hotels weren't quite as much fun when you didn't have a home to return to when you were done.

Mr. G also stopped at a little grocery store on the way back. Avery was able to buy enough groceries to last him, so he didn't have to buy food at the hotel restaurant, which would break him in short order, which was real helpful after the Gs (whose real names were, apparently, Gina and Gregg Gillespie, God *bless* them both!) both left to change for a romantic dinner at an intimate little steakhouse down the road. Oh wow—the possibilities! Food, some quiet time to work, and then, if he'd been really ambitious, he would have headed down for the convention and the costume contest ball. He hadn't actually bought a ticket for the event, but he understood a lot of the action was filtering into the indoor pool, and if he'd cared to put his scrawny pale body into a pair of swim trunks, he might have had a hookup—at least for the con.

But as tempting as anonymous sex might have been (and it wasn't), the fact was, getting a chance to talk to Cal, no matter how much of a long shot, was worth giving it up.

Cal had broken up with his fuck buddy that afternoon. Wasn't *that* interesting?

And the guy hadn't seemed to be that pissed off.

Avery had watched them both as he'd sat through the afternoon lull and outlined his article. No lingering looks, no scowls—just two guys who were used to working together. If Avery hadn't talked to Cal the night before, he would never have guessed about the fuck buddy thing.

But Cal had blushed while standing in front of Avery's table, oh yes he had.

Interesting.

Very interesting. There was just no other word for it.

So when Cal came sauntering up to his table with a plate of pie in each hand and his apron stuffed in his back pocket, Avery gave his most blinding smile. He was well aware it wasn't movie-star quality—all it really did was deepen the grooves in his cheeks until they sort of pointed to his pitcher ears—but he hoped the sincerity shined through.

Cal let a small smile slip, and his eyes slid sideways as he set the pie down, like someone might have caught him looking happy.

"So, uhm . . . pie. And free coffee?"

Avery nodded. "Yeah."

Cal set everything down before sitting across from Avery and pouring.

"You know," Avery said, savoring the chocolate cream and lard-laden crust, "I totally appreciate the sugar, but you don't have to feed me pie just to sit and talk."

Cal's red-toned skin grew even darker at the cheekbones. "I was trying to be . . . nice," he finished with dignity.

Avery sent another of his best smiles out into the void. "Well, you are. Thank you. You've been very kind."

Cal scratched fiercely at the back of his neck, until his blunt-cut hair stood out in spikes from behind his head. "Uhm, what are you working on?"

Smooth. But Avery left the abrupt change of subject alone.

"Well, before I came out here, I found an online 'zine that wanted an article on fan fiction and conventions. I got their permission, so when the con's done, I'm putting it together and hopefully I'll get a little commission with which to start my new life here in the great Pacific Northwest, and some expense money to boot."

Cal dumped some sugar and cream in his coffee—it was like he was making his own food group. "Why here?" he asked.

"Don't you like it here?"

"I like it fine, smartass. *You*. Why here?"

Avery thought about it for a moment. He usually wasn't the one getting interviewed. "Because . . . it's beautiful. And because, to date, nobody's given a shit about the gay thing. And because it's not North Hollywood, and nobody's going to give me shit about my crappy car and the fact that sometimes, if I'm driving somewhere to interview someone, I leave my clothes in it for weeks." Avery waited to see if Cal would crack a smile, but he didn't. Oh hell. His mouth was running now, so he may actually have to go with the truth. "And hopefully the world will forgive me a little for not looking like a movie star." He wrinkled his nose. "Although given how many TV stars are floating around the hotel just like—" he flailed his hands "—like *lint*, I'd have to say maybe I picked the wrong place."

Now Cal smiled. "You picked the right place," he said mildly. "Nobody's going to kick you out of Washington for wearing glasses."

Avery rolled his eyes—which was really a stupid thing to do, because he was fully aware he looked sort of like a bug from behind the thick lenses. "I hate sticking stuff in my eyes," he said apologetically. "And they're getting weak from being behind the computer so much, so I have to wear bifocals."

Cal scowled. "Doesn't anybody make you take breaks?" he snapped. "Jesus—who's watching out for you!"

"I can watch out for myself," Avery defended, hurt. "God, you sound like my parents. *And* my ex-boyfriend. 'You'll never make it in the real world, Avery!'" he mimicked. "'You can't do it alone! You need a real job!'" Avery pushed his glasses up the bridge of his nose. "I'm *here*, aren't I? I've got a job, right? I mean, I'm starting to think I wouldn't mind working somewhere I could get tips, because I'm telling you, it sucks to not have any cash on hand, but I actually have a checking account and a savings account and I even paid off my ex-boyfriend's lease for two months, so he could keep the apartment if he could find a roommate—"

"Why'd you do that?" Cal asked, derailing a perfectly good rant about how Avery was *not*, under any circumstances, absolutely, positively, a fuckup who couldn't drive across country and relocate his entire life just because he deemed it should be done.

"Do what?"

"Pay your ex-boyfriend's rent."

Avery looked embarrassed. "Because. I mean, he was an asshole, and he wasn't particularly nice, but I sort of blindsided him. He said something snide one day—and he said something snide *every* day—but this day it apparently hit my button, and since I was the one who had all the money in order, I went through our finances and split them up without warning him. I mean, I made more money than him, and apparently he got embarrassed when he was out and shit."

Cal laughed. "You didn't *tell* him?"

Avery shrugged. God, how a perfectly nice conversation could get personal all of a sudden. "Well, he shouldn't have said . . . I mean, I know I'm not great to look at, but, you know—I don't need to pay someone to get laid."

Cal grunted. "Take off your glasses," he said abruptly.

He knew where this was going, but he complied anyway and blinked at Cal when he lost some of the best parts of Cal's strong, carved features. Avery was particularly fond of the shadows under the dark cheekbones, and the creases in the corner of his eyes that indicated he squinted through the weather a lot.

But he did catch Cal's almost soft smile.

"He was stupid," Cal said quietly. "You should have kicked him out."

Avery shrugged, pleased in spite of the fact that he was mostly sure it was bullshit. "I just couldn't leave him like that, not after two years, you know? I mean, yeah—cut my losses and get out of the relationship, but I had to make sure he was covered."

Cal nodded and then took Avery's fingers, where they gripped his strong black frames, and guided the glasses back onto his head. He lingered for a moment when his fingers brushed Avery's temples, and Avery knew *he* was the one smiling.

"That's sort of noble," Cal told him.

Avery's eyes grew wide. That there was his very favorite word. "That's . . . that's a really cool compliment," he said, delighted. "'Cause, you know—you and your brother? Same thing. I mean . . . that's my *hook* when I'm writing, right? That normal people can do noble things? That's why I write fan fiction, because the characters in the show, right?"

Cal shook his head. "I'm sorry, man. You totally lost me."

Avery's heart crashed to the table and writhed a little in the half a piece of pie left on his plate. "I'm sorry. That's why I go online and write my fanfic, you know? I don't like to bore people who—"

"You're not boring me!" Cal protested. "I just mean . . . I *literally* don't understand what that is."

"Oh!" Avery's heart crawled out of the pie, dusted itself off, and jumped back in his chest. "It's awesome. Let me explain."

Cal nodded, and then held up a finger. "I have to leave at midnight, though," he said seriously. "So maybe the short version."

"Yeah, okay. Why midnight?"

"'Cause the lady taking care of my grandfather and Keir goes home at twelve fifteen, whether I'm there or not."

Avery grunted. Well. So much for the importance of fan fiction. "Never mind," he said. "It'll seem sort of—"

Cal surprised him by putting a hand over his while he tried to scrape the last of the pie off his plate. "No, really." He looked around the hotel restaurant, and the big windows overlooking the bay. "I . . . I don't know. I'd just really like to hear something *new*, you know?"

Oh yeah. Avery could totally identify. "So see, it's like you watch the show, right? And you know the characters—they're these solid, strong archetypes, right? Gabe Hanford is like the classic American Romantic hero, and Max Fuhrman is the Gothic hero, and these two kinds of heroes, they have all the best intentions of the world, but there's this essential conflict. So people tune into that conflict, and they write stories of their own that feature that conflict. And yeah, sometimes the stories are romantic, but sometimes they simply home in on the mystery, and sometimes they project a scenario the writers would like to see happen, and sometimes they just get goofy and have characters crossover into another show or another movie, or even doing and *being* someone else, but still the conflict remains the same—"

"Oh!" Cal sat up excitedly and took a drink of his milk and coffee. "Wait—it's like . . ." He scowled, picking at his napkin like he'd find the right words there. "It's like tribe legends. Like there's legends of gods, right? And everybody knows the same gods, and in one story they'll be all kind and benevolent and shit, but in another story, they're angry and mean. So like, Bluejay. He's a trickster. In some stories, we like him, because he's tricking the gods to help the men. But in some stories, he's tricking the men to laugh at them because he's a mean little bastard. But he's always Bluejay, right?"

Avery was so happy he thought his butt cheeks might just propel him off his seat.

"*Exactly*! And just like with legends and mythology and stuff, people made up their own legends *all the time*. Like the Greek and Roman myths, right? So Homer did them first, and that's the *Iliad* and the *Odyssey*, and then Virgil was the aristocratic ass-kisser, and he wrote the *Aeneid*, and at the same time Ovid was laying *his* shit down and that was *Metamorphoses*, and the thing is, it's all the same gods, mostly, but it's who's telling the story that makes it totally different. And then we take that into *our* time, and you see that shit all the time on television and movies, because these heroes are part of our . . ." Avery floundered for the word for a minute. ". . . *our mythos*!" he crowed triumphantly. "We know the skeletons of who they are, so we can put flesh and eye color and hair color on them and dress them differently and move them to a place and a time we need them to be in and—"

"But doesn't that make it completely different?" Cal asked, following with what appeared to be total interest. "Because . . . like, with Bluejay. He's a trickster, right? But Uncle Nascha's tribe isn't the only one who has a trickster. The plains tribes have Coyote, right? So once you move the trickster from here to the plains, he becomes a different kind of animal. Coyote does different things. I've read those myths—Coyote, he's a little nicer than Bluejay. He's like . . . he's like an *angel*. There's a myth like the Christian one, where the Coyote is supposed to presage the reuniting of the tribes and shit. That's *huge*—"

Avery couldn't stop nodding. He'd *just* retrieved those books about Native American legends from his car, and now he wanted to read them *all*, cover to cover. "Right? But see, when fan fiction does that, when it becomes so much the fan fiction author's that it's no longer any part of the original script, well . . ." And he felt his shoulders deflate a little. "Well, that's when it gets muddy."

Cal cocked his head. "Muddy?"

"Yeah. There's like . . . *huge* bitter debates on the internet about whether or not something that starts as fan fiction can actually ever truly become something else. And see, I say *yes*. That if nobody can recognize it as the original thing, then it becomes *inspired by*, not *copied from*. But . . ." He shrugged again. "But, you know. There's people out there who might actually strangle me with a laptop power cord for daring to voice that in public."

Cal snorted softly, like Avery had cracked a joke.

Avery shook his head, because in the rabid little community circles he'd been traveling in during these past two years, this was a *very real* war. "I'm not kidding," he said. "Not even a little. Like, people would draw blood over this. No lie."

Again, that soft sound of disbelief. "You're fun, Avery, but you know some *fucked-up* people. I'm sayin'."

Avery grinned at him, feeling like a supernova at twelve o'clock on a very soggy night. "But I'm fun? Excellent. I'll take it. That's a win!" He waved his fists over his head in triumph, and Cal's lips pulled completely back, revealing a set of even white teeth, bold against the rusty brown of his skin.

Avery held his hand to his chest because, just like that, he could barely breathe.

Cal's smile faded, but didn't disappear completely. "What? What's that look?"

"I . . . God. You're . . . Damn. You are *really fucking beautiful* when you smile."

Cal bit his lower lip, like he was trying to keep the smile from escaping, but it kept tugging the corners of his mouth up anyway.

"That's . . ." He sat up and checked the wall clock. "Oh fuck! Damn it, Avery—I'm sorry. I've got to go."

"Aw . . . man. Sorry. I could talk all night. I, uhm . . ."

Cal paused in the act of standing and retrieving their plates. "Man, I, uhm . . ." He sighed and took a deep breath. "I really like talking with you, Avery. Same time, same place?"

Avery manfully refrained from another fist pump. "Yeah! Uh, you know, the convention ends the day after tomorrow. The day after that I'm writing my article, but the next day . . . Did you mean it? About taking me out on the boat? Because I'd love to. I saw the town this afternoon, and it was really pretty— I mean, I liked it. I'd love to see the land from the water, you know?"

Cal paused and his glance turned inward, like he was running through his own mental itinerary.

"Yeah. I mean, I'd like to take you. I'm off the night before. I totally meant what I said. I could take you home to say hi to Keir and . . ." Cal's brow wrinkled. "God. Yeah. Uhm—"

And Avery's heart was on top of the roller coaster again, threatening to drop and crash. "You regret asking, I get it—"

"No, no! It's not that! I just . . ." Cal rubbed his forehead with his palm in embarrassment. "Everybody who lives in my home has the violent cray-cray, Avery. I just, you know . . . don't want you to see me at my worst."

Avery blinked. Yes. Cal had real problems. Important to remember. "Well, you know. I'm good with Keir. Tell me what to expect from, uh—"

"Nascha, my great-uncle. He has Alzheimer's."

"Oh!" Avery nodded. "Okay. Well, my grandma had major dementia before she passed away. She was *not* a nice person, which she passed on to my dad, but I used to have to do my homework while she was going apeshit over the television. She had this conspiracy theory that said whenever the Dodgers lost, it was the fault of all the black people in LA."

Cal recoiled at the blatant racism, and Avery could have kicked himself. God, who wanted to hear that story, right?

"Did I mention she was mean as hell? And totally embarrassing, too. Man, we could *not* take her outside the house, because she would scream something at everyone in the neighborhood that *would* get the shit beaten out of me, because people assumed that if she was racist as all fuck, then I would have to be too. But anyway, if Nascha isn't that bad, I can totally take it."

And Avery saw Cal's smile again, but this time it was tender, and a little fond.

"Nah. Nascha's a good guy. I . . ." His face, broad, stoic, guarded, suddenly showed a vulnerability that made Avery rub his stomach in anxiety. "I miss how he used to be. But his heart is still good, you know? Even if all his memories fade away sometimes."

Avery nodded. "Then that's no worries. I'll crash on your couch, right? You can take me out in the morning, and drop me off at the hotel when you come to work. Maybe we can make a stop at the post office, because the bank *swears* I should have me a cash card by then, and if not, well, maybe some place I can wait tables or something for tips. Can we do that?"

Cal's vulnerability cloaked itself, and Avery was glad. Unless he had sort of a right to shore up that terrible sadness, he wasn't sure he could handle seeing Cal's heart that naked. Cal nodded, his perpetually even stare locked into place.

"Good. It's a deal. I'll see you tomorrow night if you're still up for hanging out."

"Another conversation like this one?" Really? Avery would totally *burn* his new bank card—if he had it—and drive his car off a cliff, as long as he could sit here and talk to Cal as the wind blew the trees outside in the ocean dark. "Man, you can't stop me from being here."

Cal's smile wasn't quite as spectacular this time, but Avery wasn't hurt at all. He would still be happy to see Avery the next day, and yes folks, that *was* V for "victory," there were no two ways about it!

CHAPTER ELEVEN

SNEAKING BITS OF SUNSHINE

C al could not remember looking forward to *anything* the way he looked forward to eating pie and drinking coffee with Avery for the next two nights.

Christmas as a kid had always been iffy—money had been thin even then, and he'd learned to not expect much, and to get excited over small things: a baseball glove, a hand-knitted sweater, a poem Nascha burnt into a piece of driftwood. After Keir came along, he was usually just happy nobody had gotten up and opened *all* the presents before anybody else woke up in the house.

Getting laid had been nice, but he hadn't been expecting it when it happened, and he never assumed it would happen after that, so he learned not to anticipate it, and make do with what he got. When he and George had started going at it about two years ago, Cal had sort of hoped it would happen, just because the physical release had kept him sane—but he hadn't yearned for it to happen.

He'd just started to look forward to high school graduation and all of those wonderful promises of scholarships and colleges when his parents had died, and then . . .

Well. That was the last thing he'd looked forward to in his whole life.

But he looked forward to coffee and pie with the scrawny, pale guy with the bug glasses, who wandered in at closing time and pretended to work on his computer until Cal clocked out. And for his part, Cal didn't wind down the clock until the last moment, either. In fact, he got his shit done early, just to go sit and talk.

On the second night, George had actually walked out a carafe of coffee. He'd spoken pleasantly to Cal, introduced himself to Avery, and walked away. A little awkward, yes, but Cal sort of took it as a blessing.

And in the meantime, he got to hear about Avery's progress in the land of fandom and conventions and writing—and, apparently, getting his shit together.

The last night of the convention, he approached table fifteen with mixed berry cobbler and their usual carafe of coffee, and Avery wasn't sitting square to his laptop, typing away anymore. Instead, he sat, chin on his fists next to a pile of empty Splenda packets, drawing pictures in the fake sugar on the Formica.

Northern Washington didn't have enough sunshine. It hurt to see the little bit of it taken away.

"What happened, Rescue Puppy?" Cal asked. "Someone steal your bone?"

Avery glanced up and smiled slightly.

"You ever feel like maybe the gods are laughing at you?" he asked, ignoring the "Rescue Puppy" gibe.

"No." Cal grimaced. "I think they're *fucking* with me."

A brief smile played with Avery's mobile mouth. "Yeah—I'd have to agree with that." He sat up and the smile deepened. "So my problems are still not that big. What's our pie?"

"Mixed berry, heavy on the ice cream. Seriously—why the, uhm, artwork?" Cal put the stuff on the table and slid into his spot in the booth. It was beginning to feel like there was a print for his ass right there on the vinyl.

Avery looked at his pattern in the Splenda, and gave an embarrassed shrug. "Well, for one thing, I need to change banks."

"Uh-oh . . ." Avery's fights with his bank had been epic and ugly. Fucking epically ugly. Fepugly.

Avery met his eyes through his thick glasses, and to Cal's horror, he looked like he'd been crying.

"See, the thing is, I told my parents I was leaving. And my dad, who has worked in the same bank for thirty years, told me I wouldn't make it past Crescent City, right? Because, you know. I didn't have a job where I wore a suit or punched a time clock, so I couldn't make it out of the state. I wasn't . . . I don't know, responsible enough, right?"

Cal nodded. Yeah. "I get it?"

"Oh bullshit!" Avery laughed bitterly. "You? You've been responsible for your whole life. Look at you—Nascha? Keir? You take care of them with all your heart. Me? I put myself through school, and make a living in my underwear. That's it. That's my accomplishment. So I'm going to make it here, and I've got a nest egg, and I'm going to make a life on my own, right?"

Cal just nodded, not taking the outburst personally. In fact, he was sort of warmed—but also increasingly concerned about Avery.

"So Gi-Gi left today, and the last thing she had me do, while she was watching, was call the bank. The bank told me that the card had arrived at its destination on Saturday—"

"But you called the post office—"

"On Saturday." Avery nodded bitterly. "Well, it turns out, my card arrived *at my parents' house* on Saturday because I don't know, back when I was eighteen I put them on my list of people to notify if I was hit by a bus."

"So, doesn't that mean—"

"Yeah, I know. So, after I talked to the bank, I called my mother. And she said she called up my apartment, and got 'that boy I lived with' to come pick up the card."

Cal lowered his head to the table and groaned. "Oh fuck no."

"So I call the bank again," Avery said, wiping under his eyes with his palm. "And there's nothing in the account anymore. And I call my editor from my last job, and *that* payment went through—and it's gone. And I call Billy and tell him that if he doesn't give me my fucking money, I'm calling the bank he works for and telling them about this, and he asks me who I think got him my pass codes, and then bragged about how good he was at giving head."

"Oh, Avery . . ."

Cal's poor little rescue puppy. He'd been hit by life's semi, and Cal hadn't even been there to scoop him off the road.

"I . . . I mean, Gi-Gi and Mr. G used their credit card for the hotel room. I'd prepaid it, but with their card as backup, I can stay the other week I'd paid for. They fronted me some grocery cash, and I've closed out the account and filed the paperwork for theft. They said they'd arrest Billy today, but that's still going to take weeks to sort out. If I can finish my article tomorrow, I can get them to send me a check—but I need something now."

"Do you have any skills?" Cal asked, thinking he must—he'd worked his way through college, right?

Avery shrugged and tried a game smile, before using his sweatshirt over the palm of his hand to wipe under his cheeks again. "I can make a mean cup of espresso!" he said brightly.

Oh thank God. "I can get you a job," Cal said with more assurance than he felt.

Avery blinked hard behind his glasses. God—after George's pity, Keir's aggression, and Nascha's pride, when was the last time Cal had been able to offer comfort to someone?

"Really?" he asked, eyes limpid as a faun's. "You could do that for me?"

"Yeah. The Stomping Grounds—it's a touristy little coffee shop on Main Street. They're always looking for help." He'd suggest going to help Derrick at the B&B, but Derrick and his new guy seemed to be doing fine there on their own.

Avery nodded. "They were already sort of on my radar. Think they'd hire me? I mean, I'm new to town, and all I got is my driver's license and . . ."

Cal nodded, and reached across the table to take his hand. It felt good—rawboned, and a little clammy from wiping Avery's face—but strong. Avery was strong—stronger than maybe anybody had ever guessed.

"Why did your mom do that?" Cal asked, because this was the part of the story that really bothered him. "Why did she give it to your ex-boyfriend?"

Avery shook his head and let go of Cal's hand so he could gesture. "It's the whole, you know, gay thing. I mean, they didn't kick me out of the house in the seventh grade or anything, but they just kept assuming . . . I don't know. That it was a mark of my immaturity, I guess. When I got older, got serious, I'd forget about being gay and bring home a girlfriend."

"So they gave your ex-boyfriend your money, why?"

"Because they didn't get the 'boyfriend' part, okay? I mean, I *called* him my boyfriend, and I introduced him as my boyfriend, and our fucking apartment barely had a kitchen much less a guest room, but they kept calling him my roommate."

"Well, that's fine, Avery—but didn't you *move out of state*?"

Avery swallowed and shook his head. "But they didn't think I could do that either. It was just . . . I don't know. Easier to believe he was my friend, and he'd get my card to me when I came crawling home with my tail between my legs." Avery leaned his chin on his hands again, his entire posture one of dejection. "You know. Just hard to take their goofy gay son seriously when he packed up everything he owns in a hybrid and says good-bye."

Cal was not seeing it. He wasn't seeing the goofy, he wasn't seeing the immature. Naïve? Well, yeah. But that was just . . . just *joy*. How could Avery take such joy in everything if nobody in his life took joy in *him*? Cal was starting to think that his naïvety took a special kind of strength. "But . . . didn't you tell your mom what she'd done?" he asked at last, still dumbfounded.

"Why?" Avery asked, drawing pictures in the fake sugar again.

"So she could, I don't know, send you money? I mean . . . *none* of this is your fault, right?"

Avery shrugged. "That's not the way they see it," he murmured. He straightened suddenly and wiped his eyes with the sleeve of his sweatshirt again. It would need washing, but Cal was starting to suspect Avery was rinsing his stuff out in the hotel bathtub and hanging it up on the shower curtain. The sleeves of what should have been a comfy blue hoodie were certainly looking a little stiff.

"How *do* they see it?"

Avery shook his head. "Goofy gay kid screws up, Cal. Are you not seeing the complete picture? I mean, you've sat and listened to me talking about fictional people *for days*. You go out and work your fingers to the bone because you have people who depend on you, and what am I doing while my life falls apart? I'm deeply invested in a *television show*. You gotta admit, it doesn't inspire confidence."

"My brother lives and *dies* by a television show," Cal snarled, feeling fierce and helpless. He'd felt like a trapped animal for *six years*—and the one person to show him a window out of the grim string of duties that made up his life was the "goofy gay kid" sitting across from him. It hurt something in Cal's heart to hear Avery reduce all that he was to something simple—something *small*. "You don't understand—in Native American culture, we live and die by our stories." Oh, how to explain, how to explain? Cal shoved his hands through his hair and then leaned forward on his elbows.

"We watch the gods in the stories explain things and fuck up their lives and our lives and we think, 'Yes, yes, they're gods, but then so are we sometimes, and we're humans, and so are the gods!'" Avery looked up, and Cal took a page from his book and used his hands to talk, to make this seem important.

"See, it's like Nascha told us some of the campfire stories, and Keir and me, we hold on to them. But we also have the white people stories, the TV stories, and you know what? The good ones are *the same stories*. You called them archetypes, but I call them gods. And the gods still fuck up and the humans still get to be gods—that's why you watch shows and write fiction about them. It's not stupid. It's not goofy kid things. You write articles and make the world a better place, and then you write fan fiction, and you find good things about human beings that give you the strength to make the world better. So . . . this *bullshit* about your parents just *giving up* because they can't take you seriously—that's *their* fucking loss."

And in the end, he didn't even have to *try* to talk with his hands, because he was pissed on Avery's behalf. His fist came down on the table with a crash, and Avery popped up in his seat and smiled at Cal like Cal brought the fucking sun to Seattle. Cal had to look behind him to make sure that kid wasn't looking at someone else.

"What?" he asked after a minute.

Avery shook his head. "You just make it really hard sometimes," he said, but he didn't sound like that was a bad thing, for "it" to be hard.

"Yeah, like how?"

"I . . . you know, keep reminding myself that there's a thousand and one reasons you want to waste your time on me, and, you know, none of those reasons are helping me forget I was ever stupid enough to fall in love with Billy the Fucking Douchebag."

Cal opened and closed his mouth, then tried *very hard* to put that together.

Couldn't.

"I am *so* not tracking."

Avery laughed a little and scrubbed his face with his hands. "I had this plan. I was going to come up here and start again, and be successful and cool, and maybe a little more attractive. But ... but you were just—" his voice dropped, became almost like wind "—so cool," he said, staring out their window. "So ... so wonderful. And I'm just a rescue puppy. Just ... I just keep getting more and more lost, and now, if you even look at me like that, it's going to be out of pity." He dropped his head and started playing with the Splenda again.

Oh. Cal swallowed, and his hands grew shaky and cold.

"I don't pity you," he said, his mouth dry. He took a drink of coffee, and that so did not help. Avery didn't even glance up.

"Right."

Cal mirrored his position, chin on fist, and then reached out with his mirror hand and started drawing patterns in the Splenda pile too.

Avery glanced up at him and shoved some of the fake sugar across the table, spreading the pile so they could both play.

Cal drew a sun, in big bold lines, and added glasses with finger-thick frames.

Avery snorted. "Cute."

"This is you," Cal said, not meeting his eyes. "I picked you up in the rain, and you were still all sunshiny. The only place in America that gets more rain than this part of Washington is Hawaii. The sunshine is like gold—not just the color, but the value. We *value* our sunshine."

Avery's hand stilled his own random sketching, and Cal risked a glance up. Those magnified eyes peered at him intensely. Avery erased the sun and drew a classically primitive bird, great wings outstretched.

"And this was you," Avery said. "Beautiful and noble and trying so hard to be free. And you picked me up and you could have eaten me. But you didn't. You dropped me off in a nest and fed me." He glanced up and smiled a little. "I sort of imprinted. I didn't want to see any other part of the nest unless you were there."

He looked down a little, and Cal's mouth dried up in a whole new way.

"Water," he whispered. He drew waves in his Splenda. "See, water is my freedom. But I think that's why I want you to come out with me so bad. Maybe if you come out on the boat with me, we can be free together."

Avery's finger stilled, and their eyes met, danced, an embrace of gazes, a moment of true communion.

"I came here to be free," he whispered, and Cal heard the throb of yearning.

"I . . . I don't remember what it feels like," he confessed, his chest raw, his eyes burning.

Their fingers hovered for a minute, and Avery's forefinger twitched in the Splenda.

Cal covered Avery's long bony fingers with his own sweating hand.

For a moment, the only clock in the vast world was the beating of both their hearts.

"I can't make promises," Cal said quietly. "Because I'm not really free."

"I can't make promises," Avery echoed. "Because I don't even have a real nest."

Cal spread his fingers and laced them with Avery's. "Until we can't," he said. It was how he'd existed so long as it was. He would do it, be Nascha's and Keir's support, be their caretaker, until he couldn't do it anymore.

"Yeah," Avery said. They paused for a moment, hands clasped, coffee cooling, ice cream melting, the active clatter of closing muted around them. "How long do you have? Tonight I mean."

Cal glanced at the clock and frowned. "I need to go home now, but..." He looked at Avery's face and chewed his lower lip. "Uhm, if you can wait, you know, tonight, I could shower, and check on everyone and see if Dottie can stay until the nurse shows up. I've got tomorrow afternoon off . . ." He grinned then. "I have tomorrow afternoon off."

Avery returned the grin and some of the subdued fear eased its electric grip on their chests. "If I can finish my article—"

"We could spend some time together."

"Would you show me the town?" Avery asked, sitting up excitedly.

"Yeah." Then Cal remembered who he was. "Would you mind if Keir came along? He doesn't get to go places often."

"Not a problem!" Avery said, nodding. Like getting along with Cal's difficult brother was some sort of special gift.

"Then it's a date." A genuine shaft of joy pierced Cal's chest, and he met Avery's eyes feeling painful hope fighting through the wound.

They looked at their twined hands again, and Avery was the one who released the clasp. He reached into his pocket and fumbled for his wallet, and before Cal could protest that the coffee and pie were free, he pulled out his hotel key cards.

Very carefully, he separated one and handed it to Cal. Then he grabbed a pen from next to his laptop and scribbled some numbers on a napkin.

"If you can't come tonight—if you can't leave them alone, or if they need you, call me. Don't worry about me falling asleep, okay? That's my cell, and that's my room number. Just . . ."

Cal reached out and cupped his pointed chin. He didn't have any stubble—really, he only had a few silky hairs trying to be a hipster's beard and failing.

"I won't leave you hanging. But if you get tired, lay down." He flushed. "It's, uhm, been a while since I did this with someone I liked. I might be better at it if I start slow."

Avery's smile, blinding and crooked, came out to brighten the late-night hum.

"Yeah," he said. "Yeah. Slow. Call me either way."

They stood then and walked toward the lobby, hands clasped. Cal saw George as he was passing the hallway to the kitchen, but his one-time antagonist/fuck buddy just nodded and smiled a little sadly.

Thanks, George.

They paused in the middle of the lobby and separated, Avery to the elevators, Cal to the parking lot. Avery hesitated, clinging for a moment.

"I promise, Avery. I won't leave you hanging."

Avery's chin quivered, and Cal was reminded that it had been something of a day for him, and then it firmed up.

Rescue Puppy was an unfair name, really. Avery could very much take care of himself.

He knew better than to speed in the dark and the drizzle, and better than to rocket into the house making a fuss. No, Cal was going to spend all of *his* recklessness on something less spectacular and more painful than a car accident or another fight with Keir.

But Keir was asleep—as he always was this time of night—so Cal kept it down as he came in. Nascha sat serenely in the recliner, watching *Inglourious Basterds*, which figured because the old man had a hard-on for Tarantino that wouldn't quit. Oddly enough, he was playing with some sort of tablet that Dottie had been bringing over for the last couple of days, and he seemed almost too engrossed to watch the movie. Dottie was stretched out on the couch, half dozing, but every now and then she'd emit a soft, hoarse chuckle of laughter.

They both looked up as Cal shut the door quietly behind him, and Dottie didn't make much of an effort to move.

"Hey, Cal," she said sleepily. "You're home early."

Cal chewed his lip and tried not to look at Nascha. "Actually, uhm . . ." He dug in his pocket for his tip money. One of the pluses of being so busy was that he'd made plenty of extra money over the last three nights—not *nearly* enough to cover his medical bills since he'd been laid up, but enough that taking a twenty out of the roll wasn't going to make them short on food in the next week. "I'd sort of like to go out tonight," he said, trying to make it casual. *I'd sort of like to get laid, really. In fact, I sort of met a boy I really like, and if the world was perfect, I'd sort of like to get laid a lot, but the world's not perfect so please take my twenty dollars and let me have my night.*

Nascha cocked his head and smiled smugly. "Go out? You have someone to go out with?"

"Avery," Cal said shortly. "You know, the guy we—"

"The guy you gave a ride to, that Keir thinks walks on water. Yes, Calladh—medication, remember?"

Cal took a deep breath. Yeah—meds. "So, Dottie, I can give you twenty now and twenty when I get home—but *only* if they get their meds, okay? The nurse is coming, but she hates driving in the rain and sometimes she gets here too late, so if you really can't do it, let me know and I'll be back before—"

"Cool your jets, cowboy," Dottie muttered. "I hear you. Extra money if I let them pump poison into their bodies. Hey, it's your family. *You've* got to live with your conscience!"

Yeah, well my conscience works better when I'm not terrified the two people left in my family might escape. "Okay," Cal said out loud. "So you stay the night, and then the nurse will be here in the morning. I'll be taking Keir out in the afternoon, so you probably don't need to—"

"No, no," Dottie said, her voice overly casual. She and Nascha made quick eye contact, and Nascha nodded. "I'll be happy to come over tomorrow. But that's real nice that you're going to take Keir out."

"Yeah, well, Avery wants the grand tour, and Keir sort of likes him."

"Well, that's good too. It's good he knows family is important to you."

Cal nodded and headed to the back of the tiny house. "We've talked a lot," he said. "He knows."

"Calladh," Nascha intoned, right before he got to the hallway.

"Uhm, yeah?" Oh God. *Please Nascha, please don't say anything that will make this awkward, or imply that this, in any way, means I want you to destroy our lives as we know it.*

"You have a good time with this boy. You work hard."

Cal's shoulders sagged with relief. "Thanks, Nascha. I'm gonna shower and take off, okay?"

"Check on your brother so I don't have to lie."

"Yeah, 'course."

Cal peered into Keir's room on his way to the bathroom. He was asleep on his back, his head tilted at an awkward angle, snoring loudly. His sweaty hair was plastered to his forehead, and he was wearing his flannel button-up shirt and white briefs. He'd kicked off his sleeping bag—which was what he liked to sleep in—and his arm had slid off his low, child-height bed and was resting on the floor next to his stuffed badger.

For a moment, he looked dear and vulnerable, and even though Cal knew better, his heart twisted in his chest. *Is this who you really are, Keir, or who we want you to be?*

But Cal was done with big questions for the night. He took another deep breath and went into the bathroom. He was about to scrub himself down—creases, crevasses, pits, and mysteries—and he wanted to do a really good job before those places came to light.

He walked out of the house not twenty minutes later, kissing Nascha gently on the cheek before he left. The old man tilted the screen of the tablet down over his lap, and Cal wondered what kind of totally depraved porn Nascha had to be watching to think it was bad enough to hide from *him*, and then he said good-night and drove back to the hotel.

He wasn't used to entering through the front door, knapsack hanging from his shoulder, and he was definitely not used to smiling shyly at the night valet who greeted him by name.

"Cal?"

"Yeah, uh . . . I've got a friend staying here. We were gonna visit."

He must not have put too much emphasis on any one thing, because Andre didn't even bat an eyelash. "Okay—have a good night. See you tomorrow?"

"Day off—but probably the next day, or the day after that." Because that's what Cal did. He worked. He couldn't imagine another way.

Avery had booked a room in a pretty nice section of the hotel, and Cal appreciated the view from the glass-sided elevator as it took him to the eighth floor. The sound was spread out before him, smaller islands silhouetted against the moonlit sky, and Cal wondered how someone could live *anywhere* but here.

From this angle, in the dark, it was almost as breathtaking as when you were inside it, in the light.

But that didn't stop him from turning away when the elevator bell dinged and wandering down the hallway looking for 8023.

And there it was. His breath hitched in his chest for a moment, and he imagined Avery, sleepy, bare-chested, snuggled under the covers. The thought made his stomach tighten, and his groin started a low, dull throbbing that seemed a little premature, but it was so delicious he wasn't going to try to stomp it down.

How long since he'd even *thought* about desire?

Oh hell—speaking of thinking, he hadn't remembered to call when he'd been at home. Hopefully Avery wouldn't hold it against him.

He took another deep breath and reminded himself that people did this every day. The gods didn't need to strike lightning or send prodigious fish in order to bless a union—people got naked and did the thing.

But it still felt momentous as he plied the key card and waited for the light by the handle to turn green.

And then he went in.

CHAPTER TWELVE

HAD NEVER KNOWN

A very had showered too, and rinsed all his private creases with lots of vigor.

Almost enough vigor to make himself hard, but then, as his cock started to throb against his thigh in the sluicing water, he realized that *omigod!* He wasn't sure if he had any condoms.

He must have, right?

He'd been planning on having sex again when he hit his new home—at least eventually. He'd even had daydreams of becoming king of the boy sluts, getting enough cock and ass to make Billy look like a virgin.

The thought made him laugh *now*, because his painful attachment to Cal only proved that he hadn't learned anything and he was getting too serious too soon for a guy who probably needed an Avery like Canada needed geese. (Not at all—to hear the locals talk, the fuckers were becoming public nuisances.)

And God knows, he'd been passing porn shops galore on the way up here—hadn't he thought to stop for prophylactics? Even once?

Apparently not. He started by sorting through his big suitcase, and then through some of his smaller boxes, and then through the little backpack he'd used as an overnight bag so he didn't have to haul *all* his shit into every hotel on the way up.

When the handle turned on the door, he was standing in the middle of the litter of his possessions on the hotel room floor, with a towel wrapped around his waist, *sweating* with urgency because he didn't have a fucking rubber.

He looked up at the dark blob entering the room and squinted.

"Cal?" he said hopefully.

"Rescue Puppy?" came the amused reply.

"I, uhm, I don't have any . . . uh . . . I didn't ask, but . . . you know . . . condoms? Lube?"

"All night service station?" Cal said, going through his overnight bag and putting what was probably a bottle and a box on the nightstand.

"Oh." Avery sat abruptly on the bed, conscious that the ruins of what was left of his life lay at his feet. "Good. Thank God. I . . . I mean, it would suck, to go through all of this and then have . . . you know."

"Yeah."

Cal remained standing, looking around the floor with sort of a bemused air. "You, uh, sure there's room for me?" he asked, and Avery's stomach rolled.

He was nervous. Cal was nervous.

Avery stood abruptly, still holding on to the towel, but determined to make him feel welcome.

"Here—take off your coat, and we can hang it up in the closet, okay? Nothing else is in there, it won't get anything wet. "

Cal put his stuff down in a semiempty spot near the dresser and shook the green Army surplus jacket off his shoulders. Avery took it from Cal's outstretched hand, and sort of wiggled past the nuclear furnace of his body in order to hang the thing up. It was there he ran into the classic dilemma: do something meaningful with his hands, or lose his towel.

He struggled with the towel and the clothes and the hanger, finally getting the jacket hung at the expense of having the towel held up by his chin pressing against his chest and dangling down his front, which was great, because it left his great white moon facing the guy he was trying to impress.

His mind-looping embarrassment sent a flush under his skin, heat rising from him like a cloud.

That quickly, Cal loomed over his bare back, digging a square chin into his shoulder.

"Here," he said softly. "The whole thing will go more quickly if you give me this."

He took the towel from Avery's chin press and threw it on the bed, and then plastered himself against the entire naked line of Avery's back.

"Nervous?" he whispered into Avery's ear.

"God, yes," Avery breathed.

"Good." Cal's hands smoothed along Avery's shoulders, and Avery couldn't help it. He tilted his head back against Cal's temple.

"Good?"

"My hands are shaking, Rescue Puppy," Cal said, licking Avery's ear between words. "Neither of us had condoms. Connect the dots here—this matters to us."

"Yes," Avery sighed, forgetting about his skinny white body and the stoop to his shoulders. The benefit of not wearing his glasses was that when he turned in the circle of Cal's arms, there was nothing to stop him from rubbing up, cheek to cheek. "I guess I can't have the other kind of sex."

Cal's lips against the corner of his mouth were sweet and soft. He licked a moment, and just when Avery opened to let him in, he pulled back just far enough to talk.

"I've had the other kind," he said, his breathing quickening. "I didn't kiss."

Avery closed his eyes, parted his lips, and took over.

He *needed* to sweep inside Cal's mouth, *needed* to taste what was in there. Cal opened for him and groaned, backing up against the wall. His hands slid over Avery's bare skin, catching a little because Avery had been stressing and he was still humid with shower and sweat. Cal didn't seem to care.

He kissed back, tugging until Avery's naked body covered his own. Avery wobbled a little, off-balance—but Cal caught his hips and pulled him closer.

"I've got you," he murmured. "I've got you. Can you trust me to hold you?"

Avery looked him in the eyes, and saw this was important. Of course it was. Cal, who took care of his brother and his uncle, who had to ask permission for some time for himself—he would need to know he was taking care of things—taking care of *Avery*.

Avery didn't remember the last time he'd been taken care of—not like this. Stumbling from boyfriend to boyfriend, from relationship to relationship, at the mercy of the Billys of the world who thought they were something because of their looks or their cocks—had he ever counted on someone to pick him up when he fell?

But ever since he'd left LA, people had been doing just that.

Faith. It was all about faith.

"Yes," he said, knowing it was a gamble. "Uhm . . . for the record . . . I was tested after the breakup, so . . . uhm . . . negative."

"I haven't been," Cal said. "Condoms."

"'Kay."

And just for that moment, Cal held him and they stared into each other's eyes, breathing in sort of a rushed tandem. Cal broke the tableaux by reaching under Avery's thighs to hoist him up, and Avery hung on, kissing him all the way. He tasted like the smell of the water and the trees, like sky and wood smoke and the moon on the water. And he held Avery firm, not faltering, making it to the bed and laying him down on top of the cover before pulling away and stripping off in record time.

He left his jeans and sweater in a pile on top of his sneakers and socks, and Avery liked that about him. The rest of the room was chaos, and Cal was not going to worry about the small stuff.

Good.

There was nothing small about Cal. Even without his glasses, Avery could see that.

"What?" Cal asked, smirking.

"Nothing," Avery said, propping himself up on his elbows. "Nothing at all."

"Nothing?"

Avery reached out and stroked Cal's stomach, almost afraid to touch the elephant cock in the room. "Well, maybe something."

Avery's hand slid from stomach to chest as Cal sank to his knees.

Avery turned on his side and propped his head up on his hand. "I just . . . I mean, my douche bag unfaithful embezzling boyfriend was a total jerk because he had a big one. And, uhm, it wasn't *that* big."

Cal rolled his eyes. "Do you want to take a picture and send it to him?"

Avery shook his head, still giddy. "No," he said. He could feel his smile turning shy. "Right now, it's all mine. Don't want to share."

"Good," Cal whispered, and drew close enough to kiss.

Avery spread his hand against Cal's cheek and brought him closer, and then slid his fingers through Cal's still damp hair. Cal continued his relaxed plunder of Avery's mouth, and Avery kept kissing, just kiss after kiss, drugging, bubbling wine kisses, heady and sweet.

Cal used his position to run his hand over Avery's body with a sort of dedicated fervor, like he couldn't remember the last time he'd touched someone skin to skin. Neck, shoulders, biceps, forearms, pecs, ribs, tender abdomen, all of it got the gliding rasp of a hard and callused palm.

The third or fourth time he smoothed that hand across Avery's nipples and his calluses caught, Avery let out a gasp and bucked his hips.

Cal put his lips next to Avery's ear and whispered, "Greedy."

"Yes," Avery moaned. He pulled back and tried to control his breathing. "Sorry."

"Why sorry?" Cal chuckled, bumping his nose along Avery's jaw, then licking down the tender line of his neck.

"Not attractive!" Oh God. He was nibbling right below Avery's Adam's apple, and lower, across his pec . . . would he . . . oh God, please? *Please, Cal, suck on my nipple, bite it gently . . . a sharp nip of pain, the heat and wet of your mouth. Damn it, I need!*

Cal stopped and frowned up at him, his smooth chin brushing Avery's shell-pink nipple just enough to make Avery shudder. "Who said it's not attractive?"

Avery's cock was leaking against his abdomen, and he bucked his hips some more. "Cal!" he whined.

"No, seriously, who— Wait. Don't answer that."

"*Cal!*"

"We're not going to mention his name when we're naked, okay?"

Avery was going to come, just from Cal's breath across his chest. "Okay," he squeaked.

"God, look at you," Cal said reverently, and very gently flicked his tongue out across ground zero-minus-ten. "It's like touching energy." He did it again.

"I'm going to come just from that!" Avery whined. No! So many things he wanted!

"You think there's something wrong with that?" Cal asked, and licked again.

"It's embarrassing."

Cal licked harder this time. "Beautiful," he said, and this time sucked on it, *hard*.

Avery's hips came off the mattress. "Augh! Cal! Not ready—"

Cal moved his head to the other nipple, and Avery stopped beating rhythms on the mattress next to him and tangled his hands in the smooth, coarse hair. He didn't want to tug too hard, didn't want to boss him around, but the terrible urgency, the need—

Cal nibbled, just a tad, and Avery gasped, his cock flopping across his stomach with a wet splat of pre-cum.

"I love it," Cal said, voice thick with wonder. "Love being needed. Love feeling you vibrate with touch. Like you need me."

"Need—!" Avery hated needing—he was supposed to be strong. Everything he'd done to prove he was independent, and here he was, begging for a man's touch? Oh Jesus, the ways this man could hurt him!

But Cal didn't.

He locked his lips over Avery's nipple and pulled, licking as he did. Avery groaned and spread his legs, bracing his feet against the mattress. Even though his nipples were aching with the attention, there were other parts of his body that were aching without it.

"I can take care of that," Cal said with a smile. He sounded proud, surprised, like he'd doubted his capacity for care. Avery wanted to tell him he should never doubt himself, but Cal dropped his head for a quick kiss on the head of Avery's cock, and he couldn't.

He could only gasp and moan and wiggle.

Cal grinned up at him. "Look at you. All this enthusiasm. I could lick you all day!"

Avery let out a whimper and bucked his hips. "Cal—like . . . like *now*!"

Cal shook his head, brown eyes grave, and slid his hand up to Avery's chest, where he pushed down. "Hold my hand," he commanded. "Hold it. Make all the noise you want, but relax your hips and hold on for the ride."

Avery clasped that wide, scarred, strong hand, and Cal bent his head, opened his mouth, and swallowed.

Oh . . . oh God. Avery moaned and focused on Cal's fingers, twining with his own. That mouth, so hot. His tongue rasped across the head, then skirted the ridge of the crown, and Avery pushed his hips into the bed and saw stars.

And Cal kept sucking, making love to Avery's cock like it was the center of his existence. Avery had to hold on to that hand or he'd rocket right off the bed and into outer space.

Cal kept up the pressure of his mouth, but he let some spit dribble through, and Avery felt a finger scoop through the spit and knew where it was heading.

"I'll scream," he promised. "You put anything there, and I'm loud and— *Ahhh!*"

Oh God. How long? Months? More than that. Since anyone (Billy) had paid any attention to his sensitive, needy orifice? Oh God . . . "Tight!" he squeaked.

"Pass me the lube," Cal ordered.

Avery let go of Cal's hand long enough to fumble for the supplies Cal had left on the nightstand, and dropped them on his own chest so Cal could grab.

"I'm gonna let go now." Avery's cock slide out of his mouth as he spoke, and Avery shuddered as it cooled in the air. "Press your hands into the bed, okay?"

"Nungh!"

Cal shifted, scooting belly first onto the bed between Avery's spread thighs, and Avery did what Cal had said, fisting the sheets on either side, fighting not to just buck his hips and come from his cock bouncing on his own stomach. He wanted so badly to impress Cal, he just lay there, oscillating with need.

"I'm gonna make you come," Cal whispered, his breath fanning Avery's sensitized crown, his heat filling the entire space of Avery's lower body with a thunderstorm of promise. "I'm going to make you come, and then I'm going to fuck you, and if you'll be too sore after you come you'd better tell me now."

Avery could take the tenderness of too much orgasm. He could take anything Cal had to give him.

"Please . . ." Not strong. He'd beg.

Cal fumbled with the lube, and then two fingers, and the glorious, amazing stretch, and Cal's mouth on his cock and . . .

"*Oh my God*!"

The entire top half of his body tried to arch off the bed, and only Cal's determined shoulders kept his knees from clenching and squashing Cal like a bug.

He poured his entire soul into his come, allowing Cal to see him naked and needy, ridding himself of embarrassment and inhibitions like he'd shed his past. He journeyed, in this climax, from the boy who was afraid to need, to the man who trusted he could.

His body was still shaking, mind still drifty, every nerve ending still on high alert, when Cal sheathed himself and added more lube, then lunged up the bed and positioned himself . . .

"You ready?"

Cal, inside him?

"Please," he breathed, entire body floating in the certainty that he could take Cal's cock in nothing but pleasure.

Cal was bigger than two fingers, and the stretch and ache snapped Avery out of his postorgasmic drift. He was abruptly *awake*, Cal's body invading his, Cal's arms supporting his thighs, his eyes boring into Avery's.

"Oh God!" His heart started pounding again, as his body ratcheted up to the top of the roller coaster again.

"Yes?" Cal asked, pushing forward slowly. A trickle of cum tracked from the corner of his mouth down the side of his chin, and Avery fisted the comforter on either side of him again.

"Yes . . . God, but . . . oh man . . ." He couldn't ground himself, the pleasure, the pain, the tenderness all at war inside him.

"Grab your nipples," Cal ordered, and Avery did, pinching so hard they hurt.

With the pain came endorphins, flooding his body with calm, and he took a deep breath just as Cal thrust all the way in.

"Ooh . . ."

They both made that sound. Beautiful, absolutely beautiful, the feeling of Cal seated deeply home in his body.

Cal fell forward, kissing his forehead, his lips, his chin.

"You good?" he asked, and Avery nodded.

"So good."

"Gonna move now."

"Yeah."

Cal rocked back and thrust forward, and "Yeah," became Avery's refrain. "Yeah, yeah, yeah, yeah, yeah, yeah . . ."

Cal chuckled and then kissed him, probably to shut him up, but Cal's taste—Avery's taste too, thrust back in his mouth—and the warmth and the possession, only made all the words and the joy in Avery's chest hum.

"You're never quiet," Cal whispered against his cheek.

"No . . . God . . . keep moving . . ."

"I love all your noises."

"I love . . ." He stopped, Cal stopped, and time stopped.

Too early. Too early. Not after a week and one orgasm, you didn't say you loved someone, but his heart was swelling and his *ass* was swelling, and he thought if he couldn't touch Cal he'd die.

"This," he finished rawly. "I love this. Don't stop moving. Keep moving."

Cal closed his eyes, his face as naked as Avery felt, and kept that steady rocking, but harder. Harder, and faster, and oh *fuck*, he hit Avery's gland just . . . just fucking *there*, and Avery saw an explosion of magnesium sparks behind his eyes. He cried out, and Cal banged that again.

And again.

Cal sat up on his knees, hauled at Avery's thighs and lifted his ass right off the bed, and started to hammer at him like the holy awesome god of fuck.

Avery ran out of words; all he could make were noises, helpless, squeaking noises, his arms too weak to even flail, and Cal started grumbling orders.

"You gonna?"

"Oh, oh, God . . ."

"C'mon, Avery, I told you . . ."

"Oh . . . God . . ."

"Come on, I wanna feel it . . ."

Fucking. For a moment it had been making love, but making love hurt, and now it was fucking, and Avery wasn't sure which one he'd needed more. Now he was getting the physical one, the pounding one, the exquisite border between pleasure and pain. Cal pummeled away in him until sweat ran freely from the both of them and Avery was reduced to mewling sex sounds, as lost in the frenzy as a man could be and still keep his soul.

Then Cal hit that spot again, and even his soul floated free.

His cock dribbled a weak droplet on his stomach and his entire body convulsed, his torso coming off the bed again. This time, Cal fell forward, groaning, pinning Avery to the bed as he came into the condom. His hips thrust randomly as he rutted through the last of his orgasm.

Avery couldn't stop shaking.

Cal wrapped his arms around Avery's shoulders and rolled to his side. His cock slid out, and Avery shuddered one more time, but Cal stayed steady, holding their sweating bodies together until the air conditioning dried them off, the tremors of completion barely faded.

Cal kissed his temple, a soft laugh puffing against Avery's face.

"Wow, Rescue Puppy—I feel like . . . like I *discovered* something. Like I picked you up on the side of the road looking all sad and shit, and you were . . . like secret sex gold or something!"

Avery laughed weakly. "That would be all you," he panted. "I swear, I was planning to go write after you came, rolled over, and went to sleep."

Cal laughed too. "Gonna go write now?"

"Can't brain words. No."

"Good," he murmured, nuzzling Avery's ear. "This is the way it should be."

"Is it always this way for you?" Avery asked, feeling a little sad. This had been a revelation for him—sex that consumed him, made him fearless and stupid, made him almost confess to things he shouldn't feel yet.

"No," Cal whispered. "No. Haven't had sex like this in my whole life."

"Thank God," Avery murmured. "Thought it was just me."

The last of the shivers passed, and he melted, boneless, into the comforter. Cal moved, got rid of the condom and cleaned Avery off, dropping the cloth next to the light. Avery stumbled to his feet for a moment, and Cal pulled down the covers and then, oh wonder of wonders, they both slid in together. Cal reached over to turn out the light—and set the alarm almost criminally early.

"Oh God—that's awful," Avery muttered. "I'm so sorry . . ."

"Don't be," Cal told him, laughing softly. "In fact, if you wake up in the middle of the night and want another go? Poke me with that thing, will you?"

That woke Avery up. "Yeah?" He felt his lips part, and knew his eyes had widened in the darkness.

Cal laughed for real this time. "Lemme guess. Skinny guy always bottoms?"

Avery hid his face against Cal's shoulder. "No one's ever wanted me to top before."

Cal whispered into the cave of their bodies. "I would *love* to have your cock inside me."

"Oh," Avery moaned. His manhood gave a quiet throb and went back to sleep. "Hell. We're gonna have to do that. But . . ."

"Not tonight," Cal supplied. "Yeah. It's been a good night, Avery."

"Yeah, Cal. Hey—what's that short for? Calvin?"

"Calladh," Cal murmured, surprising him. He was falling asleep, Avery could hear it. "Scottish, like my father."

Avery cupped his cheek in the darkness then, and Cal covered his hand. His breathing evened out only moments later, and Avery followed him into sleep.

CHAPTER THIRTEEN

FREELY CASTING NETS

The water didn't fight Cal the next morning. The fish swam into the net, accepted their fate and the judgment of the skimming net in peace, and Cal was able to come in early and pitch a full dory of perfectly legal fish in the back of his truck.

He took a minute to go in and check on Nascha and Keir. It was a nurse day, and she had come and gone. Predictably, they were watching television while waiting for Dottie to come by.

"So, Keir," Cal said, hoping this would be a good thing, "I don't work at the hotel today."

"Can we go somewhere?" Keir looked up from his big plastic bowl of fake Lucky Charms cereal with eagerness in his eyes. Usually, when Cal had time, he took them to Olympic National Park, or on a ferry ride across the sound, or once, when he'd caught a particularly nice haul during salmon season, into Victoria to tour the Butchart Gardens, because his mother had talked about them with a particular fondness.

But it had been a long time since they'd had the money—or Cal the time, or even the health—to take his family anywhere, and he missed it.

"Just to town and for a drive around the park," he said. "But, uhm, Avery might come with us."

Keir's smile was so sweet, so pure—God, it was hard to remember he was a little psycho in the making. "Avery's nice. He knows about *Avatar*. Do you think he'll talk about *Avatar* with me?"

Cal smiled back, wondering if he'd always been able to breathe like this. It felt like no, he hadn't, not in a long time.

"I think he's counting on it," Cal said, thinking he probably was. "He likes television shows."

"Does he watch *Wolf's Landing*?" Keir asked, eyes wide, and Cal felt a pang. He hadn't even seen Keir enough to mention this.

"Yeah—actually, that's why he's here. To go to the convention at the hotel."

"Oh." Keir's whole posture fell. "He'll have to leave, then."

"No—he's going to stay, get a job. Move here. Everything."

"Ooh . . ." Keir's grin split his face. "So he can come visit me and Nascha when we go to the places."

Cal stared at Nascha who looked blandly at the television. "What places?" he asked, wondering if Nascha had actually completely lost his wrinkled old Native-spirited mind.

"I don't know what he's saying, Calladh," Nascha said, his voice deceptively mild. "I have Alzheimer's, remember? I can't always remember what I say one day to the next." He looked meaningfully at Keir who nodded and smiled, all mischief, and shoved another spoonful of sugar and preservatives into his mouth.

For a moment, Cal felt the earth shift under his feet. Something . . . the old man was planning something. That quickly, Cal remembered Nascha's gambling days, and the smug, self-satisfied look he'd had when he stumbled home, exhausted, half-stoned, and with a pocketful of money. The last time he'd done it had been when Cal was trying to cover funeral expenses and he'd almost lost the house.

Until this moment, viewing those memories through grown-up eyes, Cal had never realized that being a cardsharp didn't necessarily make Nascha the most trustworthy of people.

And he was apparently not over his past.

"What did you do?" Cal asked, suspicion swamping him like a black wave.

At that moment, the television flickered, and Keir snapped, "*Avatar's* on, Cal. It's time for you to go. Dottie's here. You need to go drop off your fish, and get Avery. And come back and take me somewhere. Can we go to Olympic Park? I want to visit the river."

"We'll go through town first," Cal said, watching Dottie swing through the door looking innocent as all hell. "Nascha, is there something I don't know about?"

"Lots of things, Cal—but nothing is wrong, it's all good."

"You going?" Dottie asked. "Has everyone had their poison?"

Cal nodded. "Yeah. Everyone's med-ed up and good to go. I'll be back to pick up Keir, and then—"

"You staying out again tonight?" Keir asked. "Nascha was glad you went last night. He said you needed to get laid more than any man in history. Did you get laid? Was it good? Was it with Avery? He's skinny. Skinny men have big balls, like rats and gerbils—that's what Nascha says."

"Oh dear God."

"So," Dottie said sweetly. "You staying out tonight?"

"I don't have the extra ca—"

"On the house. Keir's right—you look damned happy today. Feed Keir, drop him back off, and I'll be happy to sleep on your couch again."

Cal swallowed. On the one hand, there was more fish stench in this room than in the back of his truck. *Something* was going on, and he should be terrified.

On the other hand, Avery had his hotel room for only a few more nights, and then he'd have a job and hopefully a shitty apartment. Cal desperately wanted some more precious, private moments with Avery before they both became consumed with real life again.

He didn't want Avery in a shitty apartment. He wanted Avery with *him*. The entire night before he'd dreamed of asking Avery to move in with him, and he'd awakened himself every time with the reminder that he slept in a queen-sized bed in a room so small there was only two feet of clearance on one side. It had been his parents' room—he and Keir slept in bunk beds until they'd died. Avery hadn't had a whole lot of stuff, but he'd had *some*, and *some* was more than this claustrophobic little house could take right now. *Besides* that, he knew that Avery's job depended on solid wi-fi, and the only reason Dottie could use her tablet was that she carried her own service with her. This place was seventy years old—there was barely sophisticated enough wiring for the *television* much less a router and a service.

In addition to being downright *creepy* on such short notice, asking Avery to move in with him would be damned impractical for Avery himself.

But that didn't mean Cal hadn't dreamed of it.

He ran into his room and shoved his last pair of clean jeans and last clean T-shirt and sweatshirt into his bag. He had to leave now or he wouldn't be able to sell the fish—Smith might look like a train wreck but he ran a tight ship—and he wanted to shower before he and Avery pretended he had a normal life like a normal man and could actually hold down a relationship.

"I'll be back in an hour or two. Keir, be ready, have your shoes on, okay?"

"Two?" Dottie said curiously. "It's five miles away."

Cal scrambled for words, when it would have been perfectly fine to say, "I'm gonna shower there!" but he couldn't. He had hopes, damn it, of him and Avery going fast and hard, and then having a day, and then doing it slowly and deliciously, and . . .

And of holding Avery, and feeling his wonder, fluttering right there at Cal's chest. Like a bird in flight, setting Cal free of every fear and worry.

Yeah.

"I'm . . . uhm . . . shower. Gonna . . . back. Hour. Back in an hour. Gotta go. Bye!"

He tore ass out of the house then, not looking back, and later he'd hate himself for that. So much he missed, in his endless loop of work and work and pay the bills and shoulder the world. So much he didn't see.

But the biggest thing he didn't see was that the things he didn't know about were for his own good, and that, perhaps, would hurt most of all.

Smith didn't give him shit about the fish, so he was soon up at room 8023, knocking hesitantly on the door before he used the key he'd kept from the night before. He walked in to find Avery hunched over his computer, earbuds in, so deeply inside his own head that he didn't see Cal enter. He was wearing a pair of sweats with no shirt, and had wrapped a towel that he had obviously brought with him around his shoulders to ward off the hotel chill. His hair looked like birds had slept there. A discount bucket of trail mix sat on top of the hotel desk—it hadn't been there the night before, and Cal grimaced seeing that it was half-empty now.

Rescue Puppy indeed. He went to the minifridge to see if Avery had stocked anything with actual food value and was pleased to discover a full package of bagels, with a small tub of cream cheese, and some sliced ham.

He had finished making the bagel sandwich and placed it on a stack of bathroom tissue since there weren't any napkins, when Avery sang, "Try to catch up motherfucker!" at the top of his lungs.

Cal startled, barely hanging on to the sandwich, and Avery *finally* saw him and stood up in startlement. The earbuds tugged him back, and he sat down abruptly in the bad hotel chair and went over backwards, onto the pile of boxes and blankets stacked behind him. His laptop threatened to get jerked off the counter, but Cal rescued it, pulling the headset cord out at the last second while maintaining a grip on the sandwich, and trying not to wet himself laughing.

"Ohmigod!" he said, leaning over Avery and making sure he could catch his breath.

Avery just lay there, mouth opening and closing like a landed fish, and stared up at Cal like he was trying to put his brain back together from the inside.

"Avery, seriously, man, are you okay?"

"Fine," Avery croaked. "All bones and muscles accounted for. What are you doing here?"

"We, uh, had a date?" Cal's heart sank, and then Avery blinked and frowned.

"What time is it?"

"Two. I know I'm a little early but—"

Avery's legs started kicking over the edge of the chair and Cal set the bagel down on the desk to try to help him up.

"Jesus, Avery calm dow—"

"But *I'm* the one who's late! I'm sorry! I was just on a roll, and I wanted to get that article in, and I *did*, I'd just submitted it and I looked up and it's two o'clock and . . ." Avery rolled to his feet and righted the chair, somehow finding the spaces between the boxes so he could move around. He sent Cal a sort of anxious, beleaguered smile and scrubbed his face with his hands. "I'm sorry. I get . . . caught up, you know? Especially today, because I made a promise, and I wanted to get my work done and keep the promise and . . ."

He'd been asleep when Cal's alarm had gotten him up that morning. Cal had dressed quietly, not showering because why would the fish and the birds care about the smell of semen on his skin, and then kissed Avery's cheek.

"I'll be back around two."

"Promise?"

"Yeah, Rescue Puppy. Not leaving you."

Avery's chuckle had been low and dirty. "'Cause I'm a secret golden sex bomb, right?"

"You know it."

"It's okay," Cal said now gently, knowing how desperate Avery had been because it was how desperate *he* had been. "We've got time. Here, you eat, I'll go shower, and then you can jump in when you're done eating."

Avery blinked at the bagel on the desk. "You cooked for me?"

"It was more like I assembled for you," Cal answered honestly. "Cooking would imply a stove."

Avery's lip twitched. "It would also require caring. Which you did. And I'm so grateful. It's a deal. Go shower, I'll eat, and join you in a minute, okay?"

Cal sighed. "Maybe not *join* me, join me. My brother is—"

"Waiting. I get it."

Cal touched his cheek gently. "I wish you did. But you try. That's important."

He abandoned all thoughts of a quickie then, because Avery needed to eat and to reassemble his connection with reality inside his head.

Avery gave a few garbled sentences with his mouth full then, and Cal laughed. "What? We're not *that* short on time."

"I . . . just . . . you know . . ." He blushed, which charmed Cal completely. "You're not going to be able to stay the night again, are you?"

Cal smiled very slightly. "If I did, you'd have to wake up extra early, you know that right? I mean, we wake up at my house and practically roll over and into the boat. Here—"

"I don't care," Avery said with conviction. He shifted uncomfortably. "I . . . I *forgot* how good it could be. You know?" He looked away. "Just . . . to have someone's complete attention."

Cal bit his lip. "Yeah," he said. "Yeah."

Avery turned back and grinned. "Okay. So, go shower. I may or may not try to climb in with you when I'm done with my breakfast."

"Avery, you're killing me!" Cal groaned. "God, *I* eat better than that." He shook his head and made for the shower, because odds were pretty good they'd have to take Avery to eat after they got Keir. No *wonder* he was so skinny. Cal grinned to himself in the impersonal hotel bathroom as he stripped down. But then, counting his ribs was pretty sexy. Cal would have to see if he got beyond Avery's nipple this time. He was pretty sure there were an extra two ribs on the bottom, because *nobody* could be skinny enough for them to stick out that bad otherwise, right? Because seeing Avery like that had been a revelation—he'd been wondering what Avery's bad points were, and he thought he could pinpoint one right then.

Avery got lost in his work.

That was good to know, because if they ever lived together, Cal would have to make him a schedule and make sure he looked up from his computer sometimes and ate and exercised and took time out from what was in his head to make love once in a while.

Like Cal had planned to do today, actually, but he'd gotten that sudden moment of cold feet, watching Avery stare at the bagel like he'd forgotten what food was.

He was such a coward.

He had more than enough time for the quick 'n' dirty he'd planned when he'd run out of his house, but he'd been caught unaware.

Avery had been so vulnerable—and so unconsciously in need of care. Cal had been assailed by the terrible press against his chest that had followed him for the last six years. He was not enough. He and Avery were together until they couldn't anymore. How hard could it be to hide the fact that Cal wasn't enough? How rough a gig was it to hide his complete inability to take care of people—to nurture them, in the way Avery screamed to be nurtured—until Avery and his bright and shiny new life in this old place became a thing of their own?

The thought made Cal's chest ache.

C'mon, Cal. You have a day, two. Maybe three or four nights together. Maybe a week. You have two jobs and people who can't be left alone. How long can this last? Enjoy it.

And he'd about resolved to do just that when the shower curtain slid open and Avery, pale and string-bean thin, stepped into the shower.

He very carefully did not make eye contact with Cal.

"This is a surprise," Cal said, slicking water back through his hair and blinking.

"I, uh . . . I wanted to make a better impression," Avery mumbled. "But it's harder in the daylight. I, uh, don't usually do affairs or one nighters or—"

"Affair," Cal whispered, wrapping his arms around Avery's thin shoulders and pulling him flush. The water covered both of them, and Cal reached for Avery's shampoo on the side of the tub. "Affairs mean something, right? Whenever they end."

"Yeah," Avery said, tilting his head back as Cal lathered up his hair. "Yeah, okay. Affair. Except that sounds like we're both married. Maybe just . . . you know. A relationship."

"I can be your rebound guy!" Cal said brightly, hating that idea.

"Not bouncing," Avery said promptly. "Not passing through."

Cal sighed. How often was he going to have a chance to call someone his boyfriend?

"Then a relationship. However long it is."

"Good," Avery mumbled, probably trying to keep the soap out of his mouth. "Good. Then whosis can stop being my last boyfriend, and I don't have to talk about him anymore."

"Unless you're pressing charges," Cal grunted, still hating him.

"Yeah, sure."

And like that, Cal knew he wouldn't. Because he was leaving that guy—and that life— behind him, and he meant it. Avery had that sort of principle. It's why he watched that damned show.

Cal made sure all the soap was out of Avery's hair and then grabbed some bodywash and the cloth. He soaped Avery's narrow chest and under his arms, turning slightly so he could lick some of the water off Avery's ear.

"I love that you don't mean that," he said softly. "I love that you're not vindictive—"

"I was," Avery confessed glumly. "That's how we got here, I think. I used my asshole power for evil, and this is what happened."

"And I love that you learned from your mistakes," Cal said, thinking of George. "I want to be like you." He moved the cloth to Avery's groin then, and Avery groaned.

"I just want you," he confessed nakedly. "Just . . . just this . . ."

Cal's cock had been growing gradually harder since Avery had gotten in the shower, and he pressed it up against Avery's backside. "I like this," he said honestly. "I want as much as we can do."

Avery ground back into him. "I want to take care of you," he said, and spots danced in front of Cal's eyes. Avery slid out of his grasp then and grabbed a towel from outside the shower, which he threw at their feet.

Then he sank to his knees, raised his face—squinting a little against the spray—and took Cal's cock in his hand.

"Oh . . . oh God . . ."

Take care of him? Avery was going to take care of *him*?

His hand on Cal was warm, squeezing firmly, and as Cal fumbled a shaking hand for the rail on the side of the shower, Avery opened his mouth and stroked the shaft, engulfing the bell with a soft tongue and palate just as his fist reached the crown.

Cal couldn't close his eyes.

He wanted to, because the pleasure weakened his knees, wobbled his senses, scattered his brain, but Avery was looking up at him, without glasses, hazel eyes squinting against the water. He kept stroking with his hand and swirling his tongue around the head, and he did this thing with his little finger, extended it, made sure it brushed Cal's balls on every backstroke.

Cal couldn't look away.

He turned off the shower, and the minute the water stopped spraying in his face, Avery ducked his head. He moved Cal's shaft to the side so he could delicately pull Cal's balls, one at a time, into his mouth.

Cal moaned. "Oh . . . oh yeah . . ."

Avery smoothed his free hand down the back of Cal's thigh and pushed a little. Cal lifted his foot and propped it on the edge of the tub, and Avery kneaded his slick butt cheeks with one hand. Cal scrambled for a moment—he'd seen conditioner in the soap dish, and he since they were in the tub, he wanted . . .

He reached for Avery's hand and squirted a dollop of conditioner in it, and Avery took the hint.

He spread the conditioner around his hand and then slid his fingers down Cal's crease to find his asshole.

And in that abrupt way he had sometimes, thrust his first finger in.

Cal squeezed his eyes shut and leaned his head back against the shower stall. He wanted to thrust his hips and take over, but the tub was slippery. He had to trust this boy he'd met a week ago to give him what he needed, to suck his cock hard into the cave of his mouth, to thrust his finger into Cal's ass again and again and—oh God. Oh God, it was better than fantasies, because it was real, and it was better than George, taking him up against the lockers because it was *Avery*, and because he was trying to give to Cal, trying to care for him, in a way that had nothing to do with selfishness and everything to do with taking pleasure from someone else's enjoyment.

Cal knotted his hand in Avery's hair and mewled, trying to warn. "Come . . . coming . . . Aver—"

Avery jerked his head back, and Cal looked down just in time to see him close his mouth and eyes.

Oh God . . . he wanted Cal to . . . to . . .

Cal squeezed his eyes shut and came. He leaned back against the tub and opened his eyes, saw the white and the clear of it across Avery's cheek, his eyelashes, his slicked-back hair.

He'd dropped the washcloth when Avery had first knelt in front of him, and now he put his hand against Avery's cheek. "Hand me the cloth," he whispered hoarsely. "I'll clean you off."

Avery nodded and felt along the bottom of the tub and then handed it up to Cal. Tenderly, Cal washed him off, careful around his eyes and his mouth, and for that moment, all he could hear was their harsh breathing echoing off the tiles.

"Let me help you up," he rasped, and Avery wiped his eyes one last time with the palm of his hand, and then reached for Cal's. Carefully—the slickness of the tub was a danger to them both—Cal helped hoist him up, and when he had his feet, he pulled him into a rough, needy hug.

"You're shaking," Avery said, full of wonder.

"Yeah." Cal didn't explain more than that—he didn't think he could. Instead, he just clung to him, their bodies cooling in the shower, Avery's semi growing flaccid against Cal's thigh.

They both shivered hard at the same time, and Cal buried his face against Avery's dripping hair. "You're not . . . I mean, I shoulda—"

"No," Avery said thoughtfully, stroking Cal's neck. "No. Avery got a bagel, Cal got a blowjob—we're good."

Cal tried to laugh. Couldn't. In fact, Avery was the one who stepped gingerly from the tub and wrapped a towel around his shoulders and helped him over the edge to the bathroom floor. Cal reached feebly for the clothes he'd pulled from his knapsack and put on the counter, but Avery tugged at his hand until he found himself outside of the humid bathroom and sitting his bare ass on the bed.

Avery sat next to him, a towel around his waist, and leaned his wet head on Cal's shoulder.

"We can dry off," he said, like that explained what they were doing there.

"Okay." Cal wrapped his arm around Avery's shoulders and shivered again. This . . . this was unexpected. This feeling of need. Of melancholy joy. "I'm . . . I'm sorry, I'm not usually so out of it after."

"Yeah, no. I get it."

"I . . . I mean, usually I'm done, and running out the door for a shift." George's cum running down his ass, because he didn't care about safety or condoms, or even lube most times. When he bent over for George it was because he was lost, drowning after six years of treading water, and George was a spar, a piece of driftwood that bore him up before it disintegrated.

Avery just . . . just held him, took his weight for a while. Kept him warm in the frigid waters of the sound.

It wasn't until this moment here that Cal realized how close he'd been to going under. The thought made him swallow, and he tightened his hold around Avery's shoulders almost convulsively.

"Cal?" Avery whispered.

"Yeah?"

"I don't know if we can have a quickie."

Cal thought he was laughing, but his eyes burned, and he hugged Avery one more time.

"Definitely not an affair," he mumbled.

Five more seconds, sitting in the fractured peace. Ten more seconds. A minute. God, five minutes.

Cal could get used to not fighting for his life anymore.

That was the only thought that propelled him up to get back in the water.

CHAPTER FOURTEEN

SHIPS AND PORTS AND DORIES

C al was either really confident in the open-mindedness of his hometown, or really oblivious, because as they walked the weathered boards of the tourist blocks of Bluewater Bay, he had no problem being inside Avery's physical space.

A hand at Avery's back, one on his elbow, a quiet word in Avery's ear—he was all over that shit.

Given that Avery had been introduced as "my friend Avery" for the last two years whether it was a corporate dinner or a family picnic, Avery found Cal's blatant possession to be sort of beautiful. Not the rebound guy. Not an affair. A relationship—however long it would last.

"C'mere," Cal commanded, grabbing his hand. "Keir—did you want candy?"

"Yes—can we get candy?"

Cal nodded and glanced inside. "But August is there. You need to be nice to her."

Keir's eyes narrowed. "August is a girl," he said, mouth hard.

"She is, but she's a nice girl. And this is *her* place, where *she* works. You need to be nice to her or no candy."

Avery suddenly saw why Cal was afraid for what his little brother would do.

"She's a girl—girls are mean. I'm not going to let her be *mean* to me!"

"Then we won't get candy." Cal sounded very matter-of-fact, and Avery wondered that he would doubt his ability to work with his brother. Had nobody told him that people with any sort of communication difficulty were a challenge? Just rising to meet the challenge could be exhausting, but Cal was doing it.

"Fine," Keir conceded, still glaring through the window. "But I don't like chocolate."

"I know."

"I don't like nuts."

"No nuts."

"I don't like ice cream."

"Yes, you do, now tell us what you do want."

"I want sour candy."

"Okay. Let's go in and get some lemon sours."

Keir smoothed his bangs out of his eyes and regarded him with suspicion, which he often did when Cal conceded a point. Avery found himself wondering how often and how bitterly they must have fought when Cal was younger. How hard won was Cal's patience now?

"Lemon sours are my favorite."

"I know."

"I like cherry too, but lemon is my favorite."

"I know."

"What's your favorite, Cal?"

"I kn—"

Avery didn't bother to hide his smile when Cal stopped his by-rote response and struggled to answer the question.

"Uhm, those chocolate-covered espresso beans," Cal said, like he was remembering.

"Really?" Avery asked, smiling. "I *love* those!"

"I'll bet you do," Cal grumbled. "You could vibrate for *hours* on just one bean!"

"Yeah, I know, they're *awesome!*"

Cal laughed, and then led the way into Sugartropic Chocodelic—which was one of those standard candy-by-the-barrel places. Cal nodded to the girl standing behind the counter. She was reading a copy of *Gravity's Rainbow* and toying with the gauges the size of a quarter stretching out her earlobe.

"August," he said casually.

"Calladh," she grunted. She had a baseball hat on over buzz-cut hair, spectacular eye makeup on to highlight a giant pair of brown eyes, and some lush red lipstick to make her full lips even fuller. Neck tattoos, blunt-cut nails, and a white tube-top under a racer-back tank added to the ensemble.

Cal didn't even seem to notice.

"Keir wants the usual."

August grunted and gestured with her chin to a barrel full of prewrapped lemon drops. Keir looked suspiciously at August, and then he ran to the barrel excitedly. Suddenly his square, sturdy shoulders drooped.

"What?" Cal asked, perplexed. "They're your thing. Go get 'em."

Keir shook his head, clearly torn. "You like the beans. Nascha said we had to think of you too. You always think of us, but we need to think of you. He said it's not fair."

Cal blinked. Well, it wasn't, Avery thought, but it was what it was. Cal had seemed to accept it. "I promised you," Cal said, smiling. "You got excited. I'll get something at the coffee shop when Avery applies."

"But . . . but *you* wanted the coffee beans!" Keir's voice pitched perilously, and Avery remembered the meltdowns that had happened when he'd been a volunteer.

"I'll get them for him," Avery said rashly.

"Avery!" Cal hissed, because Avery had maybe enough money in his pocket not to starve in a week.

"No, it's okay!" Avery insisted. Blithely, he sauntered up to the counter with a packet of the beans and a five-dollar (oh God, let it not be more than that!) bill. If this was the only thing he bought today, it wouldn't be too foolish, right? "Get the lemon drops, Keir!"

Cal shot him a killing look, but they both knew he'd lost. Keir grabbed the lemon drops almost gleefully, and August behind the counter took the five-dollar bill impassively.

"That'll be six fifty," she said. "So no change." She hit the register, dropped the five in, and closed it with her hip.

Avery stared at her in surprise, and Keir came up next to him. "My turn. Lemon drops. Cal will pay." He glared at her, almost terrifyingly, but she didn't respond.

"Yah, I know," she said, gazing at Keir with a kind of softness. "Your brother always does."

Cal handed her a ten, and she shook her head. "Four fifty, Cal. Hasn't changed."

He narrowed his eyes. "I was making up the—"

"Yup. Know what you were doing. Stop it."

Cal's hiss of frustration made Avery edge away—right into Keir, who threw his arms about to gain his balance. His hand sailed through the air and clocked Avery on the chin, and Keir whirled.

"You got in my way!" he yelled, and Avery backpedaled.

"Yeah, you're right. My bad. Got in your way. So sorry!"

"Take your change, Cal," August said clearly, shoving a five in his hand. "Get him to the coffee shop. Let him see you eat the beans. Jesus fuck, have a nice day for once."

"C'mon, Keir," Cal muttered, and Avery could hear the desperation in his voice as he tried to talk his brother down. "Let's go out on the boardwalk and have our candy."

"Is Avery coming?"

"Yeah, he's following, right?" Cal looked over his shoulder nodding, and Avery nodded back.

"Thanks," he said quietly to August, turning to follow.

"We used to be tight in high school," she said, surprising him.

"Yeah?"

"Yeah. He was like . . . that jock that everyone loved? He was patient and nice to everyone and didn't make people feel like shit. And everyone knew about his brother."

Avery sort of stared at her until she blushed and looked away.

"I just . . . not once has he brought a guy by. I went away to college and came back, and . . ."

"He's still here."

"If you're looking for work like you said, they really might be hiring. Dean's a fuckin' trip, but you seem pretty cool."

Avery listened, collecting little pieces of Cal like pebbles. Cal hadn't even let him come into the house. He'd left Avery in the front seat of the idling truck while he'd run in to collect Keir, and Avery had an impression of a small ranch-style house with peeling gray paint, a sagging porch, a sagging roof, and a lawn that hadn't had more than moss in it for at least six years.

Probably exactly six years.

"Thanks," he said again. "I really do need that jo—"

"Avery!" Keir demanded from outside. It sounded like he'd shoved about half the lemon drops into his mouth.

"Coming!" he called, and he rapped the counter twice and waved in farewell.

"What'd August say?" Keir asked. "She's a girl. I don't trust girls even when they dress like boys."

Avery ignored *all* of the politically incorrect implications. He just didn't know where to start. "She told me the coffee shop really might be a good bet," he said to Cal.

"Okay, Keir. You lead the way," Cal said, but he lingered back, grabbing Avery's hand.

Avery clutched it convulsively, wishing for some sort of magical formula that could make a trip out with Keir, new person in tow, not a major trial.

"You knew her in high school?" Avery asked, wondering what she must have been like then.

"Yeah—she was in drama. Really nice. Probably the first person at school who figured out I was gay."

Avery snorted. "How'd she do that?"

"Well, she asked me to the Sadie Hawkins dance, and I told her I was gay."

Avery dropped his hand to slug him in the arm—but not too hard. "Jerk," he muttered, and Cal grinned at him. The grimness fell away, and the years, and Avery could see that handsome jock that August had seemed to love.

"If she was the first, who was the second?"

Cal chuckled evilly. "Cordry Chambers," he said with satisfaction. "I was quarterback, he was wide receiver."

Avery blushed, thinking about a young, sexually adventurous Cal. "Uhm, did he receive?"

"Oh yeah. And then he threw. And then we did it again."

Avery grinned through his blush, and decided he liked this happy, bantering Cal as much as the thoughtful Cal or the protective Cal.

But he wasn't sure what to do with the Cal who had been so very undone by a blowjob and a little bit of tenderness. He was pretty sure Cordry Chambers had never experienced those wide-palmed, scarred hands shaking in his hair.

"Sounds like I owe him," Avery said, because maybe he did.

"Yeah, but you can't pay him back the same way," Cal retorted. Their arms were swinging in counterpoint, and Avery grabbed Cal's hand as it swung back and squeezed before letting it go.

"Do I owe anyone special?" Cal asked, and Avery had to think to figure out what he meant.

He blushed again.

"Uhm . . . well . . . I was out in the eighth grade, but I was like . . . the asexual gay boy for all of high school."

Cal grunted in what sounded like disbelief.

They were passing an antique store, and Avery looked inside, wishing he had an eye for such things. He really didn't—probably doomed to IKEA furniture forever—but he loved the *feel* of the antique rocking chair with the ragdoll inside.

"I don't believe you," Cal stated clearly, his voice flat as he peered over Avery's shoulder.

Avery looked at him, feeling wistful. "Nobody took me seriously, you see," he said, trying to focus on Cal's face through the glare off his lenses. "The girls thought I was gay and that was adorable, and the dumb jocks thought all geeks were gay, and the actual gay guys were all chic and cool and . . ." He shrugged. "I mean, I petitioned for the GSA in junior high, right? So I got the club and we had it in high school too, and hurray! Gay people had the right to dance and . . . I went with my group of girls and we drank punch. For five years, I went to dances and drank punch."

"Ouch," Cal sympathized, and Avery shrugged. Together they moved from the antique store down past one of the larger shops that seemed to carry nothing but yarn.

"I mean, my college roommate taught me the art of the BJ, and then told me if I was a girl, he'd marry me." Avery kicked uselessly at the raw wood that made up the boardwalk. "And then he married a girl."

Cal choke-snorted and very nicely pretended not to notice that the sound made Avery trip. He continued on and tried to stay rooted in the present and the uneven footing and the sunny day.

"And my first real boyfriend was great," he said. Cal grabbed his hand again as they thumped over the walkway, and Avery laced his fingers and held on. "I thought it was true love always. But he met a closeted actor and decided he'd rather be that guy's dirty secret than my boyfriend, and I spent a year doing volunteer work and swearing off men in general."

"And then . . ." Cal sounded like he knew what was coming.

"And then I met Billy, and . . ." Avery sighed. "I mean, we were broke—he was waiting tables, I was just getting my reputation and people were starting to send me jobs. I was working, like, my last shift as a barista to make ends meet, and he showed up after interviewing for his umpteenth bank job. It . . . We were fun and snarky. And I told him about volunteering and he got all wide-eyed and I thought, 'Wow. He gets it. He wants to make the world a better place.'"

"Not so much?" Cal asked carefully.

"I think it was fashionable," Avery said with a sigh. "I think it was just what his crowd at college was saying, and, you know. I gave good blowjobs."

"How were his?" Cal asked, with that overbright sound in his voice that said he was tired of hearing about Avery's ex.

Avery thought about it. "I don't really remember," he said. "That's odd. I mean, it's been a while, but . . . I don't know. Nothing to make me come off the bed and scream."

Cal laughed, low and a little bit evil, and Avery blushed, abruptly tongue-tied. At that moment, Keir stopped in front of them and turned, pointing. "The Stomping Grounds—see? This is where Avery can work."

Keir opened the door, and he stood there, proud as the butler to the King of England and let Avery go through first. There was a bulletin board to the immediate left as he walked in, announcing slam poetry meetings, environmentalists clubs, LGBTQ community outreach, volunteer centers, and . . . well, pretty much everything Avery wanted to be a part of. He took a moment, smiling at the thumbtack mosaic, and turned to Cal and grinned.

"I think I found the wallpaper of my people," he said. For the first time since he'd gotten off the phone with his mom—and his bank—he felt some optimism about his own future.

"You looking for something?"

Avery turned and smiled at the fortyish blonde woman coming his way. She had the tanned skin of someone who enjoyed the outdoors and didn't mind the extra lines around the eyes that came with it. She also had full-sleeve tattoos, and a few on her cleavage—Avery wondered if he'd also have to get a few to work in this town.

"Uhm, yeah—and hopefully you're looking for me too. Cal says you have a job open?"

She stuck out a lean hand with trimmed nails. "I'm Tori, and we need a barista. You going to be sticking around long?"

Avery nodded. "New start, new job—new place to live eventually—you know, new me!"

Tori perused him up and down, and he pushed his glasses up his nose gamely. He'd worn a shirt that buttoned over his jeans today, and tried to remember how to act around people who weren't dressed up as *Wolf's Landing* characters—or virtual.

"Does the old you know anything about coffee?"

Avery grinned. "Five years—through college and until my job started paying—"

Tori frowned. "What's your job?"

"Well, I'm actually a freelance reporter. I, uh"—oh God—"had some financial relocation difficulties," he said, because Christ, how embarrassing, and Tori twisted her lips.

"I hear a story," she said with decision. "Will that story get in the way of you sticking around for a while?"

Avery shook his head. His resolve to maybe join the human race a little more hadn't faded. In fact, taking a look at this place, with the wood paneling and the little stage in the corner and the pictures of the Cascades framed on every available wall, made him even more resolved.

"I may not need full-time after a few months, but I'll definitely be part-time for a while," he said honestly. "God, I *missed* working outside of my apartment."

Tori nodded. "Fair enough. And speaking of apartments—if you work out in the first week or two, I might have a place for you. We've got a little apartment upstairs. You don't steal, don't insult anyone, and for Christ's sake don't spill anything on the customers, we'll see what we can do."

She stuck her hand out, and he took it. Keir and Cal were still backed up behind him in the brief hallway, and apparently, he had a job and maybe a line on a place to stay.

"Thanks," he said. "Uhm, Avery. Avery Kennedy. Do you need me to fill out any paperwork?"

"Yup. Find yourself a table—drinks on the house for you and your—" She glanced behind him for the first time, her thickly made-up eyes widening. "Your Cal. How you doin', sweetheart?"

Cal looked embarrassed. "Hi, Tori," he said. "I, uhm— We came in with Avery."

"Of course! Well, good, 'cause Dean's been run off ey's ass, and we don't want that kid to lose ey's shine, right?"

Cal blinked, like he was trying to get his head in a different space. "No, uhm, we don't want that," he said greenly. "We'll just find a table, okay?"

Tori ducked behind a small magazine stand just inside the hallway and came back with an application, some forms, and a pen. "Here, Avery. Go take your boys and sit down. When can you start?"

Avery's mind boggled for a minute, and Cal was the one who said, "The day after tomorrow. I can bring him for the first week."

Tori nodded. "Solid. Good to see he's in with good company since he's new in town. Get to work—I'll have some hot chocolate for you and Keir and a . . ." She trailed off and looked at Avery meaningfully.

"Something iced with milk and chocolate," he said promptly.

She grinned. "That shit doesn't come in small batches," she told him, and he thought he might be in love. Who cared if she was a she and in her forties? She understood "giant vat of caffeine and sugar," which meant she definitely spoke his language.

He, Cal, and Keir sat down in a table in the corner, and as he was arranging his papers on the table, he looked a question at Cal.

"Dean?"

Cal shrugged uncomfortably. "Uhm . . . genderfucked, I guess. Uhm . . . goes by, you know, that weird pronoun shit. And face-to-face, great! Fun, bouncy, hella fun to talk to. But . . ." He shifted uncomfortably. "I'm just *terrified* I'm gonna screw up the pronoun!"

Avery blinked, the "ey" making sense now. He grinned and shook his head. "I'm fucking doomed then," he said frankly. "But usually if you're making a good faith effort, people can be pretty forgiving. You know—the pronoun thing: it's all about respect."

Cal nodded. "God. Yeah. Let's hope. If you're gonna be working here, I've got to put on my big-boy boxers, yanno?"

Avery grinned. "I like those kind," he said, and got to work on his paperwork to the comforting sound of Cal's chuckle.

The giant vat of caffeine, milk, and sugar turned out to be an extra-large mocha caramel macchiato, and Avery sucked it down gratefully while filling out paperwork. Keir got a giant strawberry milkshake—and just in time too, because he'd been eyeing Tori with a terrifying squint. Cal had pulled out some shiny malachite rocks in a leather bag and set them in front of him while they were waiting, and arranging those in different patterns and asking Cal what they looked like had worked as a diversion. Avery wasn't allowed to play this game. Much of it consisted of one word questions and one word answers:

"Cal?"

"Train."

"Now?"

"Clouds."

"Now?"

"Wolf."

"Now?"

"Coffee beans."

Cal's answer didn't seem to matter—what mattered was that it changed. Avery watched them with half his attention, feeling, really *feeling* why Cal had been so excited about pie and coffee with a guy who liked to talk.

"Tori?" he said, handing her the paperwork when he was done.

"What, hon?"

"If I wasn't gay, would it be okay if I married you?"

She laughed happily. "Ah, men keep saying that, but nobody wants my ass. They really just want my coffee."

"Well, anyone who makes coffee this good deserves better," Avery said gallantly, and her throaty laugh pretty much sealed the deal.

A good town. A happy job. Some social activism.

A man by his side who was thinking about coming in and talking to him while he worked.

Maybe it was all worth it—the bank card, the broken car, the trip spent in a deserted gas station waiting for a serial killer—all of it, if he was going to land on his feet.

Optimism. Couldn't beat it with a stick, right?

Cal drove them through the national park after they left the coffee shop, and Keir kept up a running commentary about what wildlife called the area home.

Avery tuned him out, nodding and grunting for the most part, and looking about him in quiet wonder. There had been fog earlier before Cal had picked him up, but now in the purple afternoon shadows, the sky was Easter egg blue, the big snow-whipped clouds scudding across the sky.

The mountain dominated the view, of course, but in that direction, everything from the snowy top of the mountain to the trees that crowded its slopes seemed to sear an emerald slash across that neon blue sky.

To say *the scenery was beautiful* was to say the ocean was vast, or the sky without city lights was full of stars.

Any words Avery tried to use were desperately inadequate.

He pulled out his phone—one of a handful of things still working that he owned outright and could afford—and started to take pictures. He made Cal pull over while he took a picture of an old barn, just because he loved the shadows so much, and then he took a picture of a stream disappearing under the road, in a frolic of wildflowers just because *Jesus* could real places be that beautiful.

There he was, standing on the side of the road, taking a picture, when his phone rang.

"Billy?" Avery had almost forgotten Billy would still have his number.

"Jesus, Avery—you had me arrested?"

"Well, you weren't returning my calls. I just want my money back, dick-weed!"

"Oh, sure—I give you the money back and what?"

Avery remembered his words to Cal. "I, uh, don't press charges?" He wanted the money, yeah—but once Billy's actions were no longer in his life, Avery didn't want an excuse to keep Billy there.

"You just walked away from me!" Billy retorted.

Avery sighed. "You weren't listening," he said at last, but he didn't say it angry. "And you'd already started blowing your boss—"

"We weren't even sleeping together!"

"You and me, or you and your boss?" Jesus, Avery didn't even actually *care* which one, at this point.

"You and me, Avery. You just . . . You pulled your money from the account and told me I didn't respect you and . . . you broke up with me."

That wasn't the way Avery remembered it. But then, maybe that was the point.

"You don't respect me," Avery said, his lips quirking a little as he watched the sky turn purple and orange in the midst of the azure. Behind him, the rumble of the truck stopped, and he heard both doors slam. Apparently Cal and Keir had gotten bored with waiting while he cleared up his personal life. "But . . . it was both ways. I don't like LA, Billy. I don't like suits. I don't like banks."

"What *do* you like?"

Avery switched the phone to speaker and sent Billy a picture of Mt. Olympia, the sun reflecting off her west side, the purple shadows of the spring evening climbing over her slopes.

"That," he said softly.

"That doesn't pay the bills," Billy said bitterly.

"Nope," Avery said. "But it makes 'em worth paying. I took care of you, Billy. I paid your rent, bought your pretty clothes. You weren't a douche bag when we met. Why is it okay now?"

Billy grunted. "You were really cute in your barista's apron, you know?"

Avery sighed. "I was never going to wear a suit."

"No. No. Fuck. You closed out the bank account—I can't even wire the money to you."

"I've got a PayPal account. Send it that way; I'll call the fraud people."

"I don't have all of it."

"My car is in hock and when my hotel reservations go away, I'm crashing on a friend's couch."

"God. Fucking pathetic, Avery, you know that?"

"It wasn't until my douche bag ex-boyfriend stole my money, Billy. I'm hanging up now. You do what you gotta—"

"I'm sorry. I mean, I'll send back the money, but I'm sorry. You're right. This isn't who I ever wanted to be."

Avery sighed, and what felt like a cleansing mountain wind blew through him, sweeping away some of the dirt and the painful weight of believing the world really was that bad a place.

"Thank you, Bill—I'm sorry too."

For giving up on them, for embarrassing him in front of his friends, for being as contemptuous, in his way, of Billy, as Billy was of him.

"Don't thank me until you see how much money we've got left," Billy snapped. "Bye, Avery."

"Bye."

Cal and Keir had been waiting patiently, watching the sun set over the mountain while he talked. Once he hung up, Cal stepped behind him and wrapped his arms around Avery's waist. Avery leaned back into his chest and closed his eyes.

"You are such a better person than he is," Avery said, happy.

"You haven't seen me mean yet." Cal sounded very serious, and Avery took him seriously. Everyone had a mean side.

"I could probably forgive it," he said.

"God, I hope so."

Avery didn't have any doubts. At this point he could forgive anyone.

They took Keir home near dark. Cal had been planning to take them out to dinner, Avery knew, but the time had gotten away from them, and they'd had to shotgun a burger on the way home to get him his medication on time.

Avery was beginning to see, in exacting breadth and detail, how important Keir's medication was to Cal.

They pulled up in front of the battered house, and Avery slid down from the truck to let Keir out. Keir slid out and took a step past Avery, then elbowed him hard in the chest. "You made us late," he snarled. "Now I'm angry! Cal might not be able to leave me home because I'm angry!"

Avery gasped, trying hard to keep his breath, and watched with wide eyes as Keir stomped across the yard in Cal's wake as Cal sprinted toward the door.

He stood there for a minute, clearing the adrenaline from his bloodstream and making sure he didn't have any cracked ribs, and then followed them in.

"I don't want to take the yellow pill!" Keir yelled as he walked in. "I'll take the blue but not the yellow!"

"You take the blue pill!" Cal yelled back. "Take the blue pill, and then we'll see!"

Avery walked through the door straight into a small kitchen, with counters so close together a child could put a hand on either side and hang suspended. The cracked tile had been washed recently. Like the rest of the house, it was still too bare to be dirty and too old to be clean. Cal stood at the end of the counter, where the kitchen opened up into the living room, with a little pill calendar in one hand and holding out a handful of meds on his other palm.

Keir stood, barely six inches away, screaming in his face.

In the living room sat an elderly man, face seamed with wrinkles, shoulder-length hair an iron gray, gazing at the two of them resignedly, like he'd seen this scene before. On the couch across from him sat a stringy woman in her sixties, dyed-red hair piled atop her head, her arms crossed at her chest in apparent disgust.

"Keir," Cal said, obviously trying to rein his temper back in. "I didn't say you had to take the yellow pill. It was just in the box, okay—but you know you need the others." He swallowed, his chin set so firmly, Avery could see the twitch in his jaw. "Please," he said hoarsely. "It's been such a beautiful day. Don't you want to feel it again? Feel that peace? I like it when you're happy."

Keir grunted. "I don't want to sleep."

"I don't want you to," Cal said, and although his voice relaxed, Avery could see that pulse still pounding in his square jaw. Suddenly he wondered about Cal's teeth—how long could he keep grinding them like that?

Reluctantly Keir reached out and took the little palmful of pills—pointedly leaving the yellow one behind. He dry-swallowed the bundle, and stalked to the living room, slamming himself on the corner of the couch and crossing his arms.

Cal dropped the yellow pill in the calendar and set the calendar on the counter with a sigh. "Thanks, Keir," he said softly.

"Fuck off," Keir snapped. "Is *Avatar* on? I want to watch *Ava*—"

The old man—he must have been Cal's much-loved Uncle Nascha—hit a button on the remote control and BAM! The show was up, and Keir's posture relaxed into the couch.

Cal's shoulders slumped forward, his head drooping, and he brought his hand up in an unconscious gesture to knead what must have been hellific kinks out of his own neck.

"Sorry, Nascha," he said, his voice flat. "We were late."

"You were having a good time."

Cal raised his head and his lips tilted into the ghost of a smile. "We were. The park was really beautiful today—Avery took lots of pictures." For a moment nobody spoke, and the only sound was the muted voice of the television.

Nascha smiled hesitantly into the awkward quiet. "Your young man is here—would you like to introduce him?"

Cal swallowed and nodded. Something about his posture struck Avery as unbearably young. "Have you had *your* meds tonight, Nascha?"

"Yes, Calladh. I have. Odds are good I'll remember them tomorrow."

Cal's spine straightened ever so slightly, and Avery took a few steps toward the couch.

"Uhm, hi. Nascha? I've, uhm, heard a lot about you."

He ventured into the living room, and Nascha stood up stiffly from the recliner and extended a hand. "Whereas I have heard almost nothing about you. But you've given Cal something to look forward to, so that's been a blessing."

Avery darted a glance at Cal, who was taking reluctant steps to be part of their conversation. "He helped me out of a rough spot." Avery smiled sheepishly. "Or two. Today was pretty sweet—got a job, saw the sights. You live in a really pretty part of the world, mister, uhm—"

"Nascha," the old man confirmed. "You can call me Nascha. Did you boys eat dinner?"

"We got a burger on the way home," Cal said quickly. "Keir's eaten. No caffeine either so—"

"I didn't ask what you fed him, Cal. I just wanted to make sure you've eaten. Were you planning on staying tonight?" he asked, turning to Avery. "Or were you going back to the hotel?"

Avery looked at Cal, who shrugged. "We were going to head back to the hotel tonight—Cal was going to take me fishing in the morning. Uh, Cal left some clothes there when he showered anyway."

Cal grimaced. "This is my last clean pair of jeans. I'll need to start laundry when we get off the water tomorrow, before I take you back to the hotel."

Nascha nodded, and then turned to the woman sitting on the far end of the couch. "You good with that, Dottie?"

"Yeah, Nascha. You know. We talked about this. Good to meet you, Avery. You boys should head out while Keir's quiet. He won't notice you've left."

Avery watched as Cal jerked his attention to the angry figure in the corner. "Okay," he said hoarsely. "Thank you, Dottie. Thanks, Nascha. I work a short shift tomorrow night, so I can pick up some slack."

"Avery, would you like to come over for dinner tomorrow night?" Nascha asked smoothly. "Cal's room isn't big, but you could fit."

"Yes," Avery said, jumping on the invitation, regardless of how startled Cal looked. "I'd love to come over for dinner. I . . . uh, I'm in the hotel for another couple of nights though, and I'll need to do some work at the computer while I've got good wi-fi, but Tori said I could start the day after tomorrow, and it will be easier to walk there from here."

"I can pick you up afterward," Cal said, and Avery grinned quickly at him.

Good. "Good." They were locking their lives together. Cal's tiny house, his tiny family, it was expanding to fit. Avery felt like he had lungs in his back, and they had just exhaled. He relaxed a little too, just like Cal.

Until they couldn't, right? Well, they'd just proved they could, even in everyday life, even for just two days.

"So, we'll, uh, see you tomorrow," Cal said quietly, and then leaned forward and kissed Nascha on the cheek. Nascha smiled at him, a serene expression that did something odd to Avery's stomach.

"Nice to meet you," Avery said brightly, but he was grateful when Cal turned and grabbed his hand, pulling him out of the tiny house, with all of the odd currents that took the air from people's lungs at unexpected times.

His breath came easier when they stepped outside, and Avery was reminded that it was colder and damper in this part of the country. He shivered and pulled away from Cal so he could thrust his hands in the kangaroo pocket of his sweatshirt.

"Sorry about that," Cal said, sounding stiff and awkward.

"Sorry for what?"

Cal swallowed quickly and audibly. "Family drama," he said tersely, and they separated and hopped into the truck.

Cal started the engine and visibly fortified himself with a breath.

"You kissed Nascha on the cheek," Avery said after a minute, and Cal looked at him, surprised, before turning his attention back to the road.

"Yeah?"

"See, I told my parents I was leaving to move, and I got a handshake from my father and a pat on the cheek from my mom. I didn't get a hug and a kiss. But you kissed Nascha's cheek—"

"That's just my family," Cal said, sounding defensive.

"Yes. And it's good. It's . . . You love each other," Avery said, thinking Cal might hate this observation. He was so private.

"Yeah," Cal begrudged.

"It's nice," Avery said, hoping he sounded dignified. "It's . . . You come from good people."

Cal turned to him in the darkness of the cab and reached out, rubbing Avery's chest through his sweatshirt. Avery tried to hide a wince because the smart of Keir's elbow in that spot lingered.

"Yeah?" Cal asked, voice bitter. "Yeah. Let me see if that bruises. I'll let you know if I agree with you."

Avery grunted and grabbed his hand. "Drive, Cal," he commanded. "Morning is just around the corner."

The darkness between them dissipated as Cal turned into the driveway of the Global, and when he parked in a spot by the back edge, under the trees, Avery looked out beyond the windshield with a sense of wonder. The Global sat right on the water, and he could see glints of the waves through the thick vegetation.

There was something so liberating about being this close to the ocean.

"It's like all things are possible out there," Avery said, relaxing against the seat of the truck. His chest still ached—was probably bruised—but he just couldn't hold a grudge.

"Yeah," Cal said, his voice gaining some life. "Like . . . the waters are so calm, but you know there's amazing shit underneath the surface. Even that fucking fish that tried to kill me—that was his home."

Avery reached out and stroked the back of his hand as it rested on the steering wheel. "Your home," he said, understanding the sort of investment Cal had in being here. For Avery, it had been a whim, a hope to find a group of people who understood him. For Cal, this place was in his blood.

Cal turned his head then and smiled—against his will perhaps, but it was a smile. "Yours too now, Rescue Puppy. You'll get to see it up close and personal tomorrow."

"I hope I don't get in the way," Avery said seriously. "I'm, uhm, not coordinated."

"You can sit on the end of the boat," Cal told him. "It's just peaceful. I'll do all the work tomorrow, okay?"

"Yeah. And I'll do all the work tonight."

He heard Cal's sudden breath, felt the heat roll off his body, thought: *He needs someone to take care of him. How hard has it been since his parents died? How tired is he?*

"Uh . . ." Cal massaged the back of his neck again uncertainly. "I . . . I would like that."

Avery opened the truck door and swung out. He shut the door and walked around the cab, slipping briefly on the dirt shoulder in front of the curb. He recovered, brushing the moist earth and pine needles from his hands and then off completely on the back pockets of his jeans.

He came around to Cal's side, noting that Cal hadn't moved. Even a little.

The door was unlocked because any vehicle this old didn't have automatic anything, and Avery struggled with the old latch until Cal finally moved and opened the door—right into Avery's shoulder.

"Ouch!"

"Oh Lord—Rescue Puppy—really?"

Avery smiled up at him and offered his hand. Cal took it, kissing the back, and Avery said, "No, no—tonight I'm not Rescue Puppy. I'm Prince Avery. I rescue *you*."

Cal's lips quirked back, and Avery reached up with his other hand and, dodging the healing scratch marks and the remains of the black eye, traced a crease on his cheek.

"What?" Cal asked, voice husky. "All my battle scars?"

Avery shook his head no. "You've got a dimple, or a . . . a bracket or something. It . . ." His heart suddenly pounded in his throat. "It adds to the appeal," he said at last, simply.

"I look like my brother," Cal said bleakly. It was true: the resemblance was undeniable.

"That was a lot of medication," Avery said delicately.

"'Cause he's got *everything*." For the first time since they'd started their long talks in the Global, Avery heard the true extent of Cal's frustration. "Asperger's, OCD, ADHD, and probably some bipolar thrown in, but with everything else there, it's hard to spot. That's what the yellow pills are—and he *hates* them." Cal pressed the heels of his hands against his eyes. "There is *no place* for him. And . . ."

The look on his face was so naked, so longing for understanding, Avery's eyes burned.

"He's my family. Him and Nascha—they're my family. They're my *job*. But *God*, Avery, he hates girls—I mean, *violently*—and I don't know what to do with that, and the health care system sucks, and any place we can afford is *terrifying*, and in the meantime . . . Jesus . . . I dream . . . I wake up from these fucking dreams where he's done something awful and it's on my watch and . . ."

"Shh . . . shh . . ." Avery leaned into the truck, rested his head against Cal's chest, and wrapped arms around his waist. "Shh . . . you're doing the best you can. Nobody can ask for more . . ."

Cal clutched his shoulders then, and Avery held on, face buried against Cal's hard midriff, as Cal started to shake again. That was the cost—it must be—of someone laying down burdens they'd carried for so long.

Eventually the shaking stopped, and Avery stepped back to let Cal out of the truck. Cal pulled him along through the back of the hotel, the employee's entrance, apparently, because there were a couple of people by the door, feeding their nicotine habits, who nodded tersely at Cal and didn't question Avery as they went in.

They didn't say anything as they got into the elevator, mashed up against the back with a maid and her service cart, or afterwards as Avery was leading the way through the featureless halls to his room.

The minute the door closed behind them in the hotel, Cal whirled him around, held his face and kissed him hard.

Avery opened and responded, for a moment overwhelmed. Cal's hands, his mouth, were everywhere, and as Cal bore him against the bed and flat on his back, Avery almost let himself be swept under. All that strength, all that need, and Avery was so very good at being born on the stream of life and letting it carry him along.

Cal needed stronger than that.

Cal needed the guy who left his old life and was embracing his new one.

Avery cupped Cal's cheeks in his hands and pulled away for a minute. "My turn," he whispered. "Prince Avery, remember?"

Cal closed his eyes and nodded, his body a bowstring drawn tight. "I . . . I need . . ."

But Avery knew what he needed. He pulled Cal into another kiss, and rolled, so he was on top. Cal was shorter, but he probably outweighed Avery by thirty pounds in muscle—he could take it.

"You need this," Avery said, feeling like the alpha male in the books or in *Wolf's Landing*, the powerful leader he never had been in real life, but that Cal needed right here in bed.

Cal closed his eyes and raised his face to Avery's care. Avery could have ruled the world—instead, he kissed Cal again, tenderly, on the lips, the corner of the mouth, his ear, down his jaw.

Cal tried to take over, moved his head so he could possess Avery's mouth again, but Avery nipped him gently on the earlobe.

"Shh . . ."

He kissed down Cal's neck then, and licked along the edges of Cal's Henley T-shirt, noting the entire neck was about to unravel.

Making sure his knees were nowhere *near* Cal's groin (because he'd made that mistake before with Billy and he didn't want to do *that* again), he pushed up so he could shove at Cal's T-shirt and pull it over his head. Cal lifted off the bed and helped, and Avery was there again, worshiping his clay-colored skin. Dark and bold, adamant as earth, that was Calladh McCorkle. To have him yield, quiver in Avery's arms, destroyed Avery's heart, and remade it again, a stronger vessel.

Avery could please him.

Kisses down between his clavicles, down his body, until he licked under the waistband of Cal's jeans before unsnapping them. He rolled and gave Cal room to arch his hips up and shove his jeans down, which he did after kicking off his worn boots with a heave and a grunt. Avery paused for a second, on his side, eye level with Cal's shallow navel. He toyed with it for a moment and then looked up to meet Cal's brown eyes.

Cal reached down and threaded his fingers through Avery's long, curly hair, pulling it out of his eyes.

"You're pretty no-bullshit for a rescue puppy."

Avery lowered his head enough to kiss Cal's erection through the fabric of his boxers. "Tonight I'm Prince Avery," he reminded. "Tonight, I save you."

"Yeah," Cal conceded, his fingers tightening in Avery's hair and then releasing. "Yeah, okay."

Avery pulled down his underwear and looked at him for a moment while Cal kicked them off. "You're sort of awesome down here," he said, smiling crookedly.

Cal stroked his hair back from his eyes again. "I, uh . . . I mean, in high school, I was sort of a dick about, uh, my dick."

Avery grinned at him. "'Cause it's big and uncircumcised?"

"Yeah. And, you know, word got around. The gay pool was sort of small and everybody wanted a taste." Cal sounded embarrassed, but he didn't hide his eyes from Avery.

"I don't blame them," Avery teased, sticking out his tongue and licking the edge of the head, where it was peeking out from the hood of skin.

"Ooh . . ." Cal closed his eyes then, and leaned back against the pillow. "I'm just saying," he murmured. "I'm not like that now."

Avery licked up the length again, the ridge line, from his balls and the black, silky hair, to the end again, where the hood was pulling back, revealing the bulbous end.

"I know," Avery murmured, concentrating on his task. "And I'm not the shy geek who'd be afraid to talk to the good-looking jock. We grow up, Cal. It's okay."

He wrapped his pale fist around Cal's darker member and took him inside, relishing the fullness in the back of his throat and Cal's fingers tugging at his hair. He was powerful, and Cal was needy—they'd had to learn how to be that way, how to accept those things in themselves. Different paths to meet, right here, Cal's beautiful body at Avery's mercy, the taste of Cal's pre-cum bitter and salty on Avery's tongue.

Avery groaned and tightened his mouth, pulling back, sucking hard, and Cal's free hand pounded against the mattress. What followed was a careful, aggressive dance, between Avery needing Cal inside him and Cal's tolerance for pleasure. He groaned, he tangled his hand in Avery's hair and tugged, he bucked, but in the end, he submitted to Avery's mouth, to his hand, to his clever, clever fingers as he used his spit to lubricate his teasing finger at Cal's entrance.

Avery penetrated him to the second knuckle, and Cal spread his knees and planted his feet firmly on the mattress.

Avery leaned back from his blowjob long enough to say, "Grab the lube and the rubbers from the dressers, okay?"

He propped himself up on one elbow, his hand resting on Cal's stomach, and after Cal wiggled for a moment, Avery opened his hand and took the supplies.

"I'm not great at this," he confessed, looking at Cal for reassurance. "I . . . I'll just keep being Prince Avery, 'kay?"

"You're good at it," Cal whispered, cupping his cheek.

Avery grinned. "You're pretty easy to rescue, Cal." He squeezed gently. "Just grab hold and tug."

Cal's laughter choked off when Avery crawled between his splayed knees and started to tongue his salty entrance. He pulled his thighs up to his chest, reached down to his ass cheeks, and pulled them apart, leaving himself open and bare, and Avery couldn't resist the invitation. While he was licking, he wiggled out of his own jeans and tennis shoes and then sat up on his knees and shucked his shirt and sweatshirt.

The cool air made his nipples pucker tight almost immediately, but in a way that was good; his hands weren't sweating as he fumbled with the foil package, and he managed to roll the condom on without mishap. He dolloped the lube on his fingers and greased Cal up first and then himself, quickly and mechanically, because he was concentrating on doing it right and he wasn't trying to do it fancy.

Carefully he positioned himself and then, finally, he allowed himself eye contact, *human* contact, with the man holding his knees to his chest in mute appeal. A jagged, almost healed scar stood out in stark relief on his hairy shin, and for a moment, Avery was afraid. Cal had been hurt so very badly already.

"Yeah?" he asked, nodding his head, hoping.

"Yeah," Cal told him, nodding back.

Avery thrust in slowly, watching as Cal closed his eyes, checked his breathing, and raised his hips to urge Avery to go faster.

And then . . .

Avery's breath whooshed out of his lungs as he rested snugly in Cal's body. Cal started shaking, and the sound that came from his chest was too deep, too greedy to be a moan.

"C'mon," he begged hoarsely. "C'mon, Avery. Go."

Thrust, retreat, thrust, retreat, slowly, slowly, picking up speed, moderately, hitting hard when he surged inside, stroking thoroughly on the way out, then . . .

"*God*, Avery, you're *killing me*!"

Avery gave in to the power of being the fucker instead of the fuck-ee. Oh God, he wanted to just . . .

Fast. Hard. Needy. Heedless of what Cal was doing, Avery started to fuck him with all the power in his slight body, and Cal tilted his head back and howled.

"*Yes!*"

Avery wrapped his arms around Cal's thighs and heaved, holding his legs flush and opening the way to pound and pound and pound.

At one thrust, Cal let out an especially frenzied cry, and Avery hit that spot again, and then again, and then again. He was getting close, so close, and Cal's cock was flopping on his stomach, spitting pre-cum, but not the big O, not yet.

"Touch yourself," he ordered.

"Ah!"

"Grab yourself, damn it!" Avery snapped, because he wasn't enough. Sweat poured into his eyes, down his chest, and he was going to come *right now*, and he didn't want to unless Cal peaked first.

Cal wrapped his battered, earth-colored hand around his swollen, purple cock, and started to stroke himself off almost brutally. Avery kept up the pounding, feeling the muscles in the back of his own thighs tremble.

"C'mon, Cal," Avery urged. "I wanna see it. Wanna feel it. Let me see I did it right, 'kay? C'mon, damn it, *come*!"

Oh, God! Cal's internal muscles clamped down on Avery, the pleasure wringing a sweaty, desperate orgasm from his heaving body. He bucked, convulsed, his vision going white-blind with climax. He grunted and fell forward between Cal's legs, catching most of his weight on his elbows. Cal's semen was sticky and hot between their bodies, and Avery's own cum had filled the condom, was trapped around his cockhead, and for a moment Avery hated it. He wanted to be inside—all of the way.

Cal let out what sounded like a whimper, and Avery remembered this time wasn't about him. He kissed Cal's forehead, slick with sweat, and nuzzled his temple. His cock slid out of Cal's ass, and Avery rested a little bit of his weight on Cal's sturdy body, so they could kiss.

He closed his eyes when their lips touched, and in that moment, his entire body, not just his cock, was surrounded by the glory of Cal's skin.

Their breathing eased, and Avery rolled to the side, keeping his head pillowed on Cal's shoulder. Absently, he kept a light touch over Cal's ribs, soothing, calming, waiting for either sleep or conversation to begin.

Cal's sigh indicated it would probably be conversation.

"I need to stop calling you Rescue Puppy," he said, sounding reluctant. "Those were *not* rescue puppy moves."

Avery closed his eyes and smiled. "I sort of like Rescue Puppy," he mused. "'Cause . . . 'cause you cared enough to name me."

"Avery's not a good name?" Cal nuzzled his ear, licking along the shell.

"Was my *grandmother's* name," Avery said, feeling the disgust down to his toes. "Her maiden name. The racist grandmother who got me beat up a lot. Man, family legacies—I woulda rather had money."

Cal started laughing then, and it began as a low chuckle, sort of pleasant—Avery had made a joke. But as the laugh continued it began to wobble, like a top losing balance, and in a moment, Avery was on his side, pulling Cal to his chest while he came completely undone, flew free of his axis, disintegrated in Avery's arms.

The storm passed, and he fell asleep, face mashed against Avery's wet and salty chest, down to hiccups like an infant. Avery rolled out of bed and went to the bathroom to throw away the condom and get a washcloth. He caught his own eyes in the mirror. He'd lost his glasses somewhere along the way, and in the harsh light of the bathroom, he looked naked and thin—pathetic, the rescue puppy Cal had called him, and completely unable to face up to his own problems, much less help Cal with his.

He looked away and turned off the light.

In the room, he took his time and cleaned Cal off gently, and then yanked the comforter from underneath Cal so he could settle it over that muscular, earth-toned body. With his straight black hair pulled back from his face, Cal almost looked frozen in motion, and his dark eyelashes fanned his cheeks in an expression of peace.

Like the waters of the sound, what was underneath the calm had nothing to do with peace.

Cal broke the moment by seizing the covers and wrapping them tightly around his shoulders, curling up into a tight, child's cocoon. Avery took the hint and put on his boxers, turned out the lights, and slid into bed. When he was there, he plugged his phone into the charger and set the alarm for the same obnoxiously early time Cal had set the alarm for that morning.

He sidled up to Cal, listening to his breathing in the dark, and found that knotted, curled-up back. He ran his palms over the smooth skin under their blanket shelter, and felt the quivers that racked Cal's body at being touched. He kept rubbing, kept soothing, kept reassuring, until Cal's posture under the blankets relaxed, his shoulders easing back, his legs straightening.

Avery took advantage and scooted closer, until his front was mashed up against Cal's back, and he could slide an arm around Cal's waist. To his surprise, Cal put his big-palmed, scarred hand over Avery's hand and laced their fingers.

"You did good, Prince Avery," he murmured.

"That's okay," Avery said, feeling a little lost. "You can call me Rescue Puppy."

"Only when you need it," Cal replied. He rolled over then, sleepy and languorous, so he could enfold Avery against his chest.

Avery sighed into him. "Needed it," he whispered, his voice blending with Cal's heartbeat. "Just like you."

He fell asleep listening to Cal's breathing in the dark.

CHAPTER FIFTEEN

MONSTERS BENEATH THE DECK

A very, true to his word, huddled in the back corner of the dory, wrapped as snuggly as he could be in a hooded sweatshirt and an ancient denim jacket that he claimed was the warmest thing he owned. He'd managed to pull a black watch cap from his luggage, and Cal had provided an extra pair of gloves from his own kit. Avery was also wearing Keir's hip waders so he didn't catch complete pneumonia in the dank northeastern fog.

He looked around avidly, eyes seeming to record every nuance, from the shadowed bulk of the islands looming around them to the mountain range in the southeast, nothing but a hint, the breath of a giant, disturbing the mist.

He seemed particularly intrigued by the water the dory sat in, dark and lapping gently at the hull of the boat. He watched as Cal skimmed the purse seine, looking for fish that didn't belong there, that wouldn't sell, or were on the endangered list, and flipping them out before he hauled the catch into the boat. The first time Cal had actually hauled the net up over the side, Avery had clung to the seat, eyes huge, watching in terror as the surface of the water grew closer to the high sides of the dory like he fully expected Cal's everyday job to dump him ass over teakettle into the sound.

But the ancient practicality of the design held, the world's simplest ship, and Avery eventually relaxed, trusted in the dory, in Cal, and started looking over the side, asking quietly why this fish and not the other, what was wrong with the big fat salmon, and when they were in season, why green sturgeon were endangered, did rockfish get any uglier—everything.

Avery asked about everything.

Not obnoxiously. He kept his voice quiet, below the muffled fog, and asked things like prices, and who Cal could sell to, and why he needed the extra job. He asked about health insurance (they had been living off Medicare until the recent legislation) and about the dangers. Cal answered, simply, quietly, as though giving these details about his life were the most common thing on the planet. It wasn't until his last haul that the thought occurred to him.

"Avery, are you writing an article on me?"

"Well, you suggested it, but no. I'm just asking questions. If I *did* decide to write an article about fishing and environmentalism, would you mind if I quoted you?"

Cal grunted. "I . . . you know. Some stuff . . . Uncle Nascha, Keir, that's—"

"Personal, I know," Avery said soberly, nodding. The fog was starting to burn off, but that didn't mean Avery didn't have to clear the condensation off his lenses periodically. He did that now, eyes squinting nakedly through the mist. Cal wondered if he knew how sweet his eyes looked without the lenses, even when he was peering through the dark, trying to figure out why his phone was making that hideous sound, and what a man was doing in his bed. But all that sweetness hid a fine mind and some serious curiosity. Cal was beginning to realize why Avery was in such high demand as a journalist—he was genuinely interested in people, and in what he could do to make their lives better. "I wouldn't be personal with it. I'd talk about needing health insurance, and how hard you work, and how we like to think the fish just flops on our plates fully cooked, but that's not the case. Would that be okay?"

Cal shrugged. "I . . . I don't know. What if I can't keep doing it?" he asked, eyes moving restlessly over the chilled grayscape. It was almost time to start back—but the only real color he could see over the mound of fish and through the fog itself was the brown of Avery's eyes. "What if . . . what if I lose it? Nascha ends up in a shitty old-age home, my brother ends up in a prison for nutcases, I never get to fish again, and my home gets repo'd by the state and bought by the tribe? I mean . . . no hero in that story, right?"

Avery made a distressed sound, but Cal couldn't stand to look at him, not when his biggest fears were right there, drying in the air like the fucking flounders on top of the pile.

"You don't think the last six years makes you a hero?" Avery asked, hands fluttering a little before he grabbed the board seat beneath his ass.

"Not if I lose it now," Cal said bitterly. "God. I was hanging on, right? And then that goddamned fish, and I was on my ass with infection for weeks, and now . . . It was bad before, but I just have this running total of debts and interest in my mind. If I lose the house, Avery . . . How much of a hero am I gonna be if I let them get taken?"

"You'll be the hero that let them know you loved them for the last six years," Avery said, his voice swelling under the silence of the morning. "Cal, I left town *forever* and nobody knew and nobody cared. You are *vital* to them. Keir would give up lemon sours for you. I mean, my mom wouldn't even forward my mail."

Cal looked over at him again, remembered the inexpert, earnest way he'd taken Cal's body. The thought made Cal's stomach muscles flutter, because he'd never been fucked like that—nobody had ever taken so much time, so much care, to make sure Cal was going to be happy when it was over.

"How come?" Cal asked, thinking they should go back. He'd stopped at the hotel and filled the back of his truck with ice—they needed to get the fish in. "How come they just let you go?"

Avery thought about it, which was sort of warming. Nothing was glib with Avery, nothing just slid off his tongue like water. He was good with words, but that didn't mean he didn't value them.

"I didn't fight for them. The people in the computer, the people I met to interview—those people I'd fight for. The people in my real life . . . they sort of thought that was bullshit. So I didn't fight for them. But you—you think that shit's real."

Cal sighed. "Still. You should have someone fight for you."

"Like you're fighting for Keir and Nascha. Don't think it doesn't turn me on."

A half-broken laugh cracked from Cal's throat, breaking the tranquility of the morning. "Well, good for you—'cause you know it's gonna end us. I couldn't tell you when, but I can tell you—"

"Not yet," Avery said quietly. Sincerely. His voice barely carried over the boat. "You said until we can't. We still can."

Something in Cal eased, and the bitter laugh died in his chest. "Yeah. Okay. Ready to go back? We gotta shovel the fish from the dory into the truck and take it for sale. I figure you can help with that part, you think?"

"God, I would *love* to help."

And the fact that he sounded sincere about that? That's what pounded a spike in Cal's heart. Because he could love that sort of sincerity, he really fucking could.

Still, the fog had burned off the water by the time they made it back to the house, and as Cal piloted the dory into the garage, Avery looked overhead at the sagging roof and the cavern of the little home boat dock, and his face lit up.

"This is pretty cool," he said. "I mean, you have enough beach on either side—this would be a prime spot for a boat dock."

Cal nodded. "Yes and yes. Some guy's been offering Nascha money for years. He wants to buy for the tribe so they can start a business here. I guess Nascha used to know some people in the real estate game, but he gave that up when he came to live with my mom."

Avery thought about it. "Why'd he do that?"

"Nascha—he's . . ." Cal had to smile, thinking about it. "He's a mystery. I think he used to make his living gambling, you know? I always get the feeling his life was so much deeper than I ever guessed."

Avery grunted and looked down at the mound of fish threatening to topple on his feet.

"Do you have *any* idea how much I would have given to have someone like your Uncle Nascha in my corner? Jesus. I'm pretty jealous, you know that?"

Cal glanced at him and smiled. "Yeah?"

"Yeah."

He pulled the boat the last few feet into the port, killing the motor before it bumped on the dock. He clambered out and onto the wooden platform, then walked to where Avery still sat, looking distrustfully at the mountain of fish and the distance from the seat to the top of the dory.

"Just stand up, Avery," Cal said gently. "Stand up, and start from there."

Avery pushed his glasses up and grinned, so incredibly game that the spike in Cal's heart twisted just a little more. An athlete? No. But that wouldn't stop him.

He stood, waders firmly on the bottom, then put both hands on the edge of the boat, breathing harshly when it rocked slightly. Then, one foot placed carefully at a time, he stepped up on the bench. Cal reached out and grabbed one of his hands to keep it from flailing around his head. Avery tightened his grip there, and lifted his leg to get it over the side.

For a moment, Cal was afraid he'd spaz out and drag them both into the murky water at the edge of the dock, but then Avery shoved and Cal heaved and together they stumbled backward onto the platform of the dock.

Avery landed in Cal's arms, mashed up against his body, and he felt good and right, and suddenly getting the fish in wasn't as important as kissing him, smiling. He'd had company out on the water, and once again, the water had been his friend. The rush that came with his tongue in Avery's mouth felt pure and clean and fresh, like breeze and salt water, and Avery was just so *joyous* when they kissed.

Cal's heart, which had been as brittle as a rusty car frame, was starting to shore up, fill out, was feeling more and more sturdy, like the aluminum dory that had kept him and his family fed all these years.

But warmer. Pliable. Human.

Avery chuckled and pulled back, and Cal found himself blushing, which was absurd because they'd already had sex, but . . . well, Avery made it all new again.

And not once had he compared what they'd done in bed to that most hated of all benchmarks: Billy.

They separated, and Cal walked to the side door that led to the kitchen. "Stay out here for a minute—let me make sure it's all quiet, okay?" He stuck his head inside, and saw that Nascha and Keir were both in their appointed places, and that Dottie was sitting in there with them, doing something on her electronic tablet.

He pulled back out and nodded. "Good! We're good to go. Let me pull the truck around."

Avery made the work go quickly, which was a good thing, because Avery had more rescuing to endure today. Douche bag ex-boyfriend had come through with what Avery claimed to be about half of the money that'd been in his account. He'd sat down and done something weird with PayPal, and had then asked if Cal could take him to a bank.

A bank, and then to Clarke's, and then Avery could get his car out of hock, and he wouldn't be dependent on Cal anymore to drive him around.

On the one hand, *Yay!* because Cal really couldn't afford to spend much time squiring his Rescue Puppy around, and he'd be more independent.

On the other hand, *Oh*, because Rescue Puppy didn't need him anymore, and Cal had sort of enjoyed being forced into closeness.

Well, Cal had other days where he didn't work both jobs, right? There could be other trips to the park. And if Avery had an apartment of his own nearby, there could be quick visits, or maybe the odd date for dinner, or more late-night conversations.

It was so little to ask for, but Cal couldn't help himself. He saw more of what they *could* do, and less of what they *couldn't*. Dangerous thinking, that, but watching as Avery stood in the boat, legs spread, stalwartly shoveling fish up onto the dock so Cal could shovel it into the back of the truck, Cal couldn't stand *not* to think about what they could do.

It felt so very close to hope, Cal let his guard down a bit. He'd always count that as a mistake.

Later that day, while Cal negotiated with Smith, the douche bag, Avery leaned against the truck casually and played with his phone.

"I can't give you more than—" Smith was saying for the six hundredth time.

"Going market rate," Avery said, walking up from the truck.

Cal jumped and turned to see that he was wielding his phone in front of him like a sword.

"See," he said, looking at Cal excitedly, "we've got—what, how many pounds of rockfish? Sole? Flounder? Well, right here is the going market rate in Seattle for each one of them. It's a good ten cents a pound more than you're offering. So you need to offer him the going market rate, or he's taking his catch to the Marriott, where I know they'll offer going market rate, because I did a piece on them last year, and they sort of advertised that shit to the sky. So, given that we've got, what? Three hundred pounds of fucking fish here, that's an extra thirty dollars, right?"

Smith gaped at Avery, opening and closing his mouth and expelling fetid cigar breath with each gasp.

Cal gaped at Avery too, but hopefully he was a little more attractive about it.

"Going market rate . . ." Smith muttered, reaching out for Avery's phone.

Avery kept hold of the phone, but he got close enough for Smith to look at it.

"So, can we get rid of this mound of fish or not?" Avery asked, sounding irritated.

"Yeah . . . uhm . . . Mike! Luke! You guys get over here and unload this truck!" Smith started ordering around the muscle, and Cal turned to Avery in wonderment.

"How in the hell did you do that?" he asked, staring at the thing in Avery's hand like he'd never seen a cell phone before.

Avery shrugged. "I know it's been a while since you've been social, Cal, but seriously—I don't hardly use mine to talk at all."

Cal nodded, feeling dense. He'd just . . . tuned out all of the things he couldn't afford in the past six years. It hadn't ever occurred to him that if he'd been able to spend a little money, maybe he could afford the one that would help him the most.

Then he sighed. Hell, if he could afford a phone, Nascha and Keir wouldn't constantly have to borrow Dottie's tablet, would they? Of course, that had only started up in the past month, and it was starting to make him edgy as hell—maybe a phone wasn't such a great idea.

"That was really smart," he said, watching numbly as Smith walked into the back office to get Cal his cash. "I wonder . . ." How much money he could have gotten, how many bad business decisions he'd made, how much he'd screwed his family, just not being savvy enough to do more than throw Smith against the wall and scream, "Give me my fucking money!" in his face.

"What's wrong? I mean I'm sorry! I didn't mean to . . . uhm, offend your pride or, you know, violate the rule of the fisher people or . . ."

Cal just shook his head and sent a weary smile to his side. "It's not that," he said, his throat and jaw suddenly swollen and tight.

"What is—"

"Here's your cash, fairy," Smith sneered, thrusting the money and receipt into Cal's hand. "It's about time you got smart about it."

"I won't make that mistake again," Cal snapped, throwing his armor on in a hot second. Without looking to see if Avery was following, he stalked to the pickup and slammed the door.

Of course Avery was following him.

Cal started the car and revved the engine, then backed out of the delivery bay faster than was probably safe. Well, fuck it—he didn't hit anyone, and his reputation as a badass was intact.

"The bank, huh?" he grunted.

"Yeah, uh . . . if it's close, and you're pressed for time, I can walk to Clarke's."

Cal shook his head. "No," he said, trying to hold on to his dignity. "You kept me from being cheated, I can do the same."

Avery nodded, earnest and trusting, and Cal thought sourly that he should count himself lucky that Avery still thought he had something to offer besides a battered pickup and a twenty-foot dory.

Cal got out at the garage this time.

He'd hung out in the truck when Avery had gone into the bank. It was the same bank that held the mortgage to his house, and he had an openly superstitious belief that going inside would make them speed up the paperwork to get them evicted. Nascha had shown him the stay of execution—something about disability insurance that Cal, quite frankly, didn't follow—but that didn't mean Cal wanted to tempt fate. Avery hadn't questioned his desire to stay in the truck—had, in fact, told Cal to catch a nap.

Cal had leaned back, closed his eyes, and thought about all the stuff about the world that he didn't know and Avery did.

The irony of his "rescue puppy" was beginning to crush his chest in.

He was damned relieved when Avery hopped back in the truck, cash in hand, and asked for one more ride.

"You get business taken care of?" he asked—but he had no doubts, really. For all that he was made of ears, elbows, and optimism, Avery seemed to have his shit together in a way Cal could only envy.

"Well, I cleaned out my bank account and I have enough cash to get my car out of hock and pay back the Gs for their help. I'm *definitely* going to have to work at the Stomping Grounds for a while, but I'm actually looking forward to it. If Tori can let me hang out in that apartment . . ." Avery beamed at him. "I, uhm, you know. I bet it has a bed."

Some of the weight eased up off of Cal's chest. "Me too."

"Uhm, you know. You won't be working both jobs *every* day." Avery was studiously looking out the window and into the bright blue of the spring sky, now that the morning fog had burned off.

"No," Cal said, managing a smile. "And I have to eat sometimes."

"Oh yes," Avery said, nodding seriously. "You need to eat more. I can . . . Well, I can cook ramen noodles and chicken fingers mostly, but, you know. Peanut butter and jelly—you've had that, and it's been awesome."

Cal's smile strengthened. "I could live on it," he said, keeping his voice somber. But inside, he managed to forget how truly unprepared he was for real life, and remember that this thing—this temporary thing, this rescue-puppy thing—might just have a future.

Clarke's Auto Repair and Fortune Telling Service was open for business and almost bustling this day—there were at least four cars there that had nothing to do with Avery's beat-up hybrid. Cal and Avery walked purposefully into the office, and Avery chatted pleasantly with the squishy woman wearing gray sweats and a graying ponytail, who shuffled a well-worn deck of colorful cards as they talked.

She had a few other decks at her elbow, and as Avery asked about his hybrid, she eyed him meaningfully, and eventually put the worn deck in her hands in its box, and pulled out something brighter, with grotesque, pixilated pen and ink drawings on the front.

"So, you have the money and you can collect your car when it's ready?" she said, beginning her shuffle.

Avery eyed the cards. "Uhm, yeah. But you don't need to do a reading—I can just ask Clarke when he comes—"

"Nope. Reading is free," she said. "To the auto customers, anyway." She eyeballed Cal. "Or this one, who needs to know his future more than you, I think."

"Yeah?" Avery asked, glancing behind his shoulder as he leaned on the counter so he could grin at Cal. "Why?"

She peered back at Avery, and Cal shifted as he stood, because in spite of the fact that Mrs. Clarke wore frumpy, colorless clothes, her eyes were this really uncomfortable, stunning shade of green that looked like they came from a contact lens. Since she wore bifocals, Cal could only assume that was her natural color, and that her affinity with the cards in her hand came from the fact that she was a fey witch from outer space . . . or, uhm, something equally terrifying who could read your soul from a stack of laminated pictures.

"Because you're agile," she said, cutting the deck and pulling out a picture of a young man strolling off the cliff. "You're the fool, but you're not really walking blindly—you just have faith. You have faith that you'll find ground with your next step, and your next, and sure enough, ground comes up to meet you. So, no worries for you. You'll make a path, and it will be a good one, and that will be okay."

"Okay, so that's good to know," Avery said, still grinning. This whole thing obviously didn't freak him out like it was doing to Cal. Because this woman didn't even *know* Avery and . . . damn. "What about Cal?"

Mrs. Clarke shuffled the deck again without looking at the cards in her hands, and kept her gaze focused on Cal. She set the deck down, flicked the top of the deck twice, and cut it in the middle, then took the card from the top.

"Ten of swords," she said, and Cal gaped at what looked like the mother of bad omens. It showed a man, face down, with ten goddamned swords sticking out of his back. "Yeah," she said, nodding. "It's not a great card. It means too many burdens, too many bad things, and a bunch of shit and betrayal is about to go down."

Avery recoiled. "Jesus, does that card have any good things?"

Cal grunted. "Yeah. The guy lying facedown gets to sleep."

Mrs. Clarke raised her eyebrows, but her freaky green eyes looked compassionate. "And sometimes, after he takes a nap, he can get back up and start again. That's the deal with this card. So, do you want a whole reading now?"

"So I can see more dead guys with heavy-duty puncture wounds? I'm sorry, Mrs. C—we just need to get Avery's car back."

She shrugged. "Suit yourself. I've got the invoice right here. The car's done, all I need is the cash."

Cal grunted, and the price for once wasn't overinflated. Avery really *must* have the ground coming up to meet him if Clarke wasn't going to overcharge him just for being out of town.

"Awesome!" Avery started to pull out the money and fill out the paperwork, but Cal had a ticking clock in his head for the start of his shift at the Global, and he didn't want to leave Avery alone until he knew he had a running vehicle. He patted Avery's waist and said, "I'll be back in five," and then disappeared out back, to where the day's work sat in a patient, muddy line, waiting for Clarke's attention.

Clarke was running at his usual half speed, and Cal found him with his head under the hood of a Miata, swearing colorfully about how the car's intake manifold was a cocksucking whore.

"Yeah, but you still gotta screw her," Cal said after walking quietly up behind the guy.

Clarke straightened and almost nailed his head on the hood, then ducked gingerly out of the way. "What're you here for, buddy?"

"My friend, the one with the hybrid. Shouldn't you be sending this thing on to Holly's?" There was one other auto repair in town, the one that dealt with the cars belonging to most of the TV people. The Miata was just enough out of Clarke's range that he normally would have sent this model on.

"Yeah, but I've got a new diagnostic toy for this one," Clarke said proudly. "I wanted to give it a whirl, and I think it worked, because I'm just a little bit of tinkering away from making it happen." Clarke grinned at Cal through a beard long enough to braid, and ran his greasy hand over his bald head. "I'm telling you, kid, if your life ever gets sane enough to come help me here, you and me, we could make this place purr!"

Cal made a keening sound of pure fear. "Yeah, Clarke, but your wife . . ." He shuddered. "She's a real nice lady, but those cards . . ."

Clarke nodded earnestly. "Sort of see through your soul, right? I made her stop reading for me. If I'm gonna get so much as a hangnail, I want it to be a surprise."

"Amen," Cal agreed fervently. "So my friend's car—it's gonna last him?"

"Oh yeah," Clarke nodded. He pulled his ever-present red rag out from his back pocket and started to wipe his hands. "I mean, it *sounded* pretty awful, but it was mostly the alternator, and once we rebuilt that, it started right up. Didn't need to send it off to Holly's Haus of Imports or nothin'. All good."

"Fair enough. He could use a streak of shit going his way, you know?"

"Yeah, Cal. So could you."

Cal tried not to think about that card with the dead guy on it. "Yeah, well, I'm not counting on it. He's signing the paperwork now, okay? I gotta go work at the Global. If for some reason he can't make it, can Mrs. C give him a ride home?"

"Yeah, Cal. No worries. I'll take him for a little test drive before he leaves, deal?"

Clarke may overcharge out-of-towners, but so far he'd been nothing but straight with Cal. "Yeah, okay. Let me just go tell him."

"Cal!" Clarke called as Cal turned away.

"Yeah?"

"This guy—what's he to you?"

Cal's face heated. "Uh, b-uh-friend."

Clarke's scowl could even be seen behind his beard. "It's okay, you know. You get to have people."

"Uh, well, I already got people."

"A person, Cal. Nothing wrong with having a 'b-uh-friend.'"

"How long can he last?" Cal asked, hating the defeat in his voice. "He's really smart and—"

"So are you." Clarke sounded surprised.

"Yeah, but Avery's got a future. I've got a family."

He didn't stay to see the look on Clarke's face as he pretty much doomed him and Avery to time-gone-by. He was too busy keeping the grief off his own face, because his b-uh-friend was all happy now, and Cal didn't want to fuck that up by living in the time when Avery couldn't stand him anymore and broke it off.

He had enough of a problem living in the now.

When he got back into the office, Mrs. Clarke was giving Avery his car keys, and Cal stepped forward and took Avery's hand.

"Clarke said he'd take you for a test drive first—you need to take him up on it. I gotta go or I'm gonna be late, 'kay?"

Avery nodded. "Yeah, okay, but she said I could just—"

Cal's throat tightened. "Avery, could you please, just for me, watch out for your own ass for once? Take the test drive, okay?"

Avery nodded, looking perplexed at his intensity. "Yeah, okay. I'll, uh, see you at the Global later."

Cal flickered a smile. "I may not be able to stay late," he said gruffly, meaning *No sex tonight.*

Avery shrugged. "A conversation during your break. It's worth it."

It was, for Avery. For Avery, it was enough. Cal closed his eyes and dropped a kiss on his cheek, thinking he smelled unwashed, and like fish, but that was okay.

"See you tonight," he said quietly.

Avery's grin told him it was a sure thing.

And that grin—that promise—made the oddest difference as he drove to work and then showered and dressed. He was on time for once, but more than that—he wasn't *angry.* Yeah, sure, work sucked, and even when he wasn't fucking Cal against the lockers, George was sort of a petty tyrant who acted like the café at the Global was a five-star restaurant in France. Tips were still shitty and he still had a pile of bills he needed to keep paying off, the money in his pocket from the fish notwithstanding.

But Avery was going to be in that night. He would bring his laptop and work studiously, and whenever Cal walked by, he'd look up and smile.

Such a simple dream, Cal thought, as the bright spring day outside darkened to evening. Such a simple dream. Avery sauntered in around nine, looking freshly washed and earnest in another jeans/hoodie combo he'd probably washed in the hotel bathtub, and Cal's heart started to do jumping jacks in his chest. Avery grinned at him, shyly, and shoved his glasses up his nose, and Cal's world, which had been limited to burnt coffee and dead fish for the last few years, suddenly opened up to the sea and the sky and the sound, the places he'd always loved.

Happiness exploded in his chest like an alien bird taking flight.

He almost didn't recognize it, and the joy of it physically hurt, but he couldn't cage it or tether it or shoot it dead.

Oh, Rescue Puppy, I'm not sure I'll survive rescuing you.

The restaurant was pretty quiet actually, and Cal found himself running around hard, trying to clean up, stock up, be done early so he could . . .

He didn't want just coffee and pie tonight. He'd had two nights sleeping next to Avery, and a day to watch him explore something new. Cal didn't want to just sit and eat with him—he wanted to *touch* him.

He walked past the dessert tray and instead of grabbing two, he grabbed one, and the carafe of coffee, winking in the face of Avery's disappointed expression. He wanted more than pie. For once in his life he wasn't going to settle.

He set the pie and coffee down and bent at the waist to whisper in Avery's ear. "Up in your room in forty-five minutes. I won't have long."

He stepped back and smirked as Avery gasped and melted against the vinyl bench.

"Enjoy your pie," Cal added sweetly, and Avery's smack on his backside as he turned to saunter away wasn't entirely unexpected.

Fifteen minutes later he passed the table, and the coffee cup was empty and so was the plate—and Avery was gone.

His cock stiffened in his pants because . . . because . . . oh God—what could Avery do, all alone, in his hotel room, waiting for Cal?

Bussing tables isn't hard, but for the past two years Cal had thought of his time as a drudgery, time in purgatory, a necessary evil. Tonight, although he worked as hard as he ever did, the job was simply that: a job. He cleared tables, rolled silverware, even prepared kiddie menu and crayon kits as fast as he could so he could leave early, and when it was time to clock out, he actually thanked George for letting him go.

"Cal—" George called as Cal was hurrying away.

Cal turned. "What? What'd I forget?"

George shook his head. "Nothing. Man . . . I just . . . He looks at you like you're . . . whosit. Who's the Native American god who hung the moon and set the planets and . . ."

"It depends on which tribe," Cal said numbly, trying to figure out what George was getting at.

George huffed out in exasperation and pinched the bridge of his nose. "Okay. Let's go Greek, since that's what I got in school. He looks at you like you're Apollo. Like you're beautiful and gifted and . . ."

Cal stared at him, some of his excitement deflating. "George— you know who I am. I'm . . . nobody."

"Not to him," George said earnestly. "Just . . . I'm glad for you."

Cal smiled a little. "Until we can't," he said, and for once, it sounded like that wasn't a death sentence.

"That's most people who've been married for years," George agreed.

The entire trip in the elevator, his warped, stainless steel image staring back at himself in surprise, he felt like he was shedding the weight of six years: six years of worry, six years running a hamster wheel and never catching up, six years of being trapped by the people he loved most. He got to Avery's room and pulled out the key Avery had just left with him, trusting Cal like he trusted the rest of the world, and knocked on the door.

"I'm ready," Avery replied. His voice sounded strained and reedy, and for just a breath, Cal indulged himself with all of the things *ready* could possibly mean.

He opened the door and stepped quickly into the room, and Avery was lying on his stomach, a shiny track of lube down his cheek to his backside. He was fingering himself, making breathless little quivery moans as his fingers moved, and he sent Cal a beseeching look over his shoulder.

There were condoms on the dresser next to him.

That feeling of lightness, of freedom, possessed Cal completely, and he shed his clothes like a phoenix shed ashes. One step toward the bed, and one more, and then he was touching Avery, and sheathing his cock, and inside.

Inside Avery, that tight, willing body squeezing him tight, Avery's open need, his throaty moans, *that* was where Cal felt free.

In a tender, urgent, sweaty explosion of sex and want and cum, Cal spread his wings and flew.

CHAPTER SIXTEEN

STRANGE LAND, STRANGE CUSTOMS

"You tripped?" Cal asked.

"I tripped," Avery responded with dignity, when he'd pretty much checked that at the door today.

"With a full tray of coffees."

"Thank God they were in to-go cups."

"Hold still—I need to get that blister."

Avery closed his eyes and let Cal put more burn cream on his narrow chest, heedless of the fact that they were in the parking lot of the CVS. "This is *so* not sexy," he muttered. "I was going to pack tonight."

He'd worked his third shift as a barista that morning, and in spite of the burned fingers from the first two shifts, he was starting to feel re-acclimatized to the job. He didn't forget any orders, he was nice to all the customers—who were a rather eclectic mix of locals and TV people who interacted politely with the locals—and he remembered the difference between a macchiato, a latte, and a mocha, without any prompting at all.

But every time he thought he was getting the hang of it, his own . . . *Avery*-ness got in the way.

Today, he'd tripped, fallen flat on his face on the tray with the to-go cups, hopped up, brushed off the concern of *everybody* in the store, mopped up, and re-made the order in about ten adrenaline-infused minutes. And he'd kept working too, keeping his face on "bright smile" and ignoring the increasing throb and ache of his skin until Cal walked in.

Cal took one look at him and said, "Jesus, Rescue Puppy, how much of that coffee are you wearing?" and Avery had felt his chin crumple. Like a big freak wave, the embarrassment, the stress of the new job and still living in the hotel, and the motherfucking *pain* of scalding himself with about a gallon of espresso crashed over his head.

"I'm . . ." he tried. "I'm . . ." Oh fuck. He was a *man*, damn it, a grown man, and he'd moved up here and he had a new job and . . . "I'm not sure," he finished with dignity, biting his lower lip to keep from wobbling.

Cal looked at him in a panic, and then, with a sweet little expression of kindness, he held out his arms.

There, in front of the entire tech crew of *Wolf's Landing*, Avery rushed into his boyfriend's arms and cried. Then he realized his entire chest and stomach was scorched and hurt like a sonofabitch, so he backed up three inches, put his face against Cal's shoulder and cried some more.

"Cal, take him home," Tori said over the collective "Awwww . . ." of the busy shop.

"But . . . but . . . my shift isn't over until . . ." Avery choked, trying to stand up and whimpering in pain.

"You're not getting fired, Avery," Tori said with patience. "For one thing, you're renting out my loft and you need a way to pay for it. For another, everyone gets a bad day."

She'd given Cal some accident report paperwork for him to fill out, and told him that any trip to the doc was on her. Five minutes after Cal walked *in*, he ushered Avery out, stopping in the parking lot to take off Avery's shirt and get a look at the damage. Avery had ridden in the cab of the truck wearing a flannel shirt from Cal's truck over his shoulders, and had sat there, shivering, while Cal ran into the pharmacy to get him burn cream.

Cal had put the first bit on there in the parking lot, while Avery had babbled incomprehensibly about warps in the space-time continuum and invisible groundhogs until Cal had, with his burn-ointment-covered hands held behind him, shut Avery up with a kiss.

Avery had melted into the kiss like it was Valium.

When Cal pulled back, he'd asked how it had happened.

The story had come tumbling out, and that's where they were now, with Cal stepping back, wiping his fingers on Avery's already-soiled shirt. "Avery, man, relax. They like you at the Stomping Grounds, and you've got your car back, and a place to stay."

Avery groaned. "Aw, man—Cal, we left my car back behind the coffee shop—"

"Yeah, I know. Look, I'll tell you what. I've got some Vicodin in the glove compartment and got some Advil at the pharmacy. I'll take you to the hotel and dose you with some painkillers and some ice. You stay there, drink lots of fuckin' water, and I'll be by after work to pick you up."

"But check out time's tomorrow," Avery said, feeling miserable. God, he'd been looking forward to getting out of the hotel. He'd actually done laundry over the last week, and organized his few possessions—he was going to have an *apartment*, and even if it wasn't *the* apartment, it was a place in a place that he was truly learning to love. He could never remember wanting to go outside to smell the air before.

Here, he did, and the air smelled green and blue and sharp and real.

He wanted to be a part of that, and have that smell in his clothing, in his hair. Add the smell of Cal's cum on his skin, and he was the happiest man on the planet.

"Yeah, I know. Look, tonight, I'll take you home. Tomorrow, we'll do the car shuffle and get your shit to your apartment. I'll take the morning off fishing, you're off tomorrow morning anyway—and I know you've got an assignment and you need to write—"

"But . . . but you need to *fish*!" Avery said, feeling awful. God, Cal couldn't take more time off fishing. In the past week, as Cal had made a point of having Avery look up the going market price every morning before he took his haul into the Global, Avery had seen firsthand how important that money was. That cash went to gas, and to buy Nascha's and Keir's meds, and to pay—in person—the power bill before it got cut off.

Cal looked away, and Avery got a firsthand look at how really desperate things were.

"Man, one more day more or less isn't going to break us—not after last month," he said with deep resignation. "I'll go out early and see what I can get, okay?"

Avery nodded, and cupped Cal's cheek. "I don't want to be one more duty," he said seriously. "I mean . . . you know, this shit didn't happen when I was in SoCal!"

Cal's smile went crooked, and he tapped the edge of Avery's glasses. "No, baby. In SoCal you worked until your vision went bad, and you lived with a guy who was mean to you—"

"I was mean to him back!"

"Yeah, but you're not mean, so this relationship, it was *no bueno*, and nobody told you that."

"Gi-Gi did," Avery said staunchly.

"Well, Gi-Gi's great, but she's not here. You tell me I'm not fucking up, and I need to hear that. You need to hear to take care of yourself. That's what I'm doing. This is how we take care of you today. Tomorrow, maybe I need to hear more about how I'm not fucking up."

Avery nodded, eyes fixed on Cal's expressionless face, his lips a slashed line against his cheeks. Cal glanced up, and suddenly his eyes were open, almost limpid, and his mouth softened, became vulnerable.

"I do my best, Avery. A burn on your chest I can cope with."

Avery felt a bubble of uncertainty in his chest. "You're not fucking up," he reassured. "You can cope with the other stuff."

Cal kissed his temple, but he still looked troubled. "I . . . I think I'm failing them more ways than I can count. I'm . . . Keir needs things to do. Nascha is up to something, and I'm just like . . . I mean . . . for all I know he's trying to gamble online and he's going to end up losing the house." He shook his head. "All the stuff you know about the world outside this town, and I haven't had time to keep up." He sighed. "Let's get you back to the hotel."

The night before he'd seemed so . . . so powerful. Avery remembered the way he'd taken Avery's body, like a god. No uncertainty, no fear.

Apparently proof of Avery's mortality was enough to bring the fear back in big crashing waves. Avery couldn't think of a thing to make it go away—not when he was embarrassed and in pain.

Cal had gotten a couple of bottles of Gatorade and some trail mix when he'd gone into the CVS and he walked Avery up to his room and gave him the painkillers and set him up on the bed with a big batch of pillows and his laptop.

"You know, as spacey as I'm about to get, I may just end up watching porn, and that would be pretty damn unheroic of me," Avery said as Cal stalked around his room and started to fold his clothes and organize his stuff.

"You go ahead and watch porn," Cal said, making a neat stack of Avery's books and putting them back in the box that they'd come in. "Maybe you and I will get to act some of it out."

Avery hummed a little in his throat and settled himself back against the pillows. "You know, I've had more sex in the last two weeks than I had in like, the six months before that?" Probably not true in strictly numerical terms, but as far as every time with Cal being worth six to eight times of giving Billy a blowjob and then having him fall asleep while Avery brushed his teeth? Oh yeah. Cal had already beat Billy as a lover, probably by count of Avery's orgasms alone.

"Yeah, well, we've already established that your ex was a tool."

"He gave back the money though," Avery said, still a little in awe of that. Damn, if Avery had known he could get those kinds of results by confronting Billy and pushing for a result, he might not have broken up with him in the first place.

"He gave back *some* of the money," Cal growled, grabbing Avery's biggest suitcase and folding the clean batch of clothes on the corner of the bed into it. "And he did it because you were going to press charges."

Avery sighed. "You're so fucking honest—you'd cut off a finger before you took anything from me."

Cal stopped his folding and looked at Avery distrustfully. "You don't make that sound like a good thing."

"I just . . ." Avery shook his head. Fucking painkillers. "If I could work two jobs—"

"Which you're doing," Cal reminded him, because, yes, Avery had been trying to keep up with his freelance deadlines too.

"Yeah, but if I could work two jobs and not be pathetic about it, I'd give you some money so you could keep your house, and be happy Cal, with his family."

Cal grunted and finished his Tetris packing job in Avery's suitcase. "I love that you want to do that for me, Rescue Puppy, but right now, let's keep you from passing out."

So that wasn't a solution, Avery thought mournfully. In the hurt quiet, he noticed that the pain of the burn was conspicuously absent, and he moaned in luxury. "Passing out sounds like an *awesome* plan of action, do you know that?"

Cal straightened and came to kiss Avery's cheek, and check on his bare chest. Oh, oh damn—even Cal's breath made Avery's skin hurt. "Are my chest hairs still there?" he asked, feeling very free-floaty.

"You have chest hairs?"

"Apparently not anymore. I think they shriveled up and fell out after I scalded them to death."

Cal smiled enough to show teeth. Oh good! Where honest sentiment failed to take the worry from his eyes, Avery being goofy did it. Avery would be as goofy as he needed, just to see that smile. "Don't worry. You're still growing. You turn thirty, you can have a chest sweater. I'll enjoy that."

Avery giggled. "My dad has hair growing out his *ears*. You might not think that's so sexy."

"Yeah, well, we're gay. *That* shit we get to pluck."

Avery giggled some more. "See, my dad just thought it was a phase. How do you explain that you're never going to phase out who you keep falling in love with?" He wrinkled his nose. "Except losers. I think I finally phased losers out of my repertoire when I fell in love with you."

And like that, Cal's easy smile disappeared, and he straightened and went back to Avery's loose electronics and his external hard drives, which he wrapped up in the clean T-shirts and arranged back in the suitcase.

Avery closed his laptop and put it on the bed before he let it slide on the ground, and tried to figure out where he'd gone wrong.

"Oh," he said, his eyes at half-mast. "Oh. I'm sorry."

"Nothing to be sorry about," Cal said, stacking all of Avery's boxes and suitcases in a neat pile to the back of the room. He'd left a clean outfit, including a clean barista's apron, since Tori had given Avery two of them, out on the desk chair. Everything else Avery had was packed. Damn. All while Avery rambled on and ...

"I said the no-good, terrible, awful, very bad, shitty, frightening word," Avery said humbly. "And I pissed you off."

"You're drugged," Cal said, checking the refrigerator. He started making two bagel sandwiches, and Avery knew one of them was for himself. That made Avery feel good. Cal would eat his food and not be obligated to pay.

"Yeah, but the drugs just took the locks off," Avery confessed, thinking maybe the bagel would take the edge off of hallucinatory pain-med fugue state. "That fierce creature would have gotten out eventually."

Cal grunted and looked behind his shoulder. "Yeah, well, if you let those things out before they're full-grown, they can do a lot of damage."

"I didn't want to do damage," Avery mumbled, thinking he wasn't going to make it until sandwich time. "I just wanted to love you."

Cal sighed and brought him a sandwich. Avery took a dogged bite and knew immediately he wasn't going to be able to finish. The sandwich drooped to his lap, and he looked dolefully at Cal.

"And now you're going to run away," Avery said. "I terrified you. Fucking drugs."

Cal nudged his hand. "Eat, Rescue Puppy. I'm not running yet. In fact, I think we just covered that I'm taking you home."

Avery took another bite. "Because you feel sorry for me."

"Well, yeah—you've got burn blisters all over your chest. But that's not why I'm taking you home."

Avery swallowed and managed another bite. "Well, why are you?"

"'Cause I like to dream."

Avery tried to pull his brain out of the morass the painkillers had made of it.

"Dream of what? Pink ponies and rainbow farts?" He giggled, because apparently Vicodin revealed his inner twelve year old.

"I didn't dream of that shit when I was six," Cal said soberly, cramming a bite into his mouth.

"What'd you dream about?" Avery asked. "Flying? You told me you dreamed about flying."

"For a little while, once I figured out what they *should* be, I dreamed about having a little brother," Cal said, his voice husky for no reason Avery could imagine. "And I dreamed about having a dog."

"Good dreams," Avery said promptly. "I never had either one."

"I did. My little brother killed my dog."

Avery gasped and struggled to wake up. It wasn't working, and he whimpered, reaching for Cal's hand.

Cal grabbed his hand instead, hard, callused and insistent, and Avery squeezed tightly.

"What's your dream now?" he asked breathily, head a muddle of grief and hope.

"That someday I'll live with a guy with really thick glasses and the worst luck known to man."

Avery let out a little breath, and that hand, solid in his own, became the only real thing in the world.

"That's a good dream," he said, aching.

"I think so."

"God, I hope out it turns out better than the last one."

"Me too."

Avery fell asleep then, and didn't wake up until Cal came in after his shift with two giant to-go containers of hotel coffee and pie. When Avery's burns had been treated again and Cal had made sure he was awake and fully functional, he started hauling stuff down to Avery's car while Avery attended the business of checking out. It took Cal three full trips—one of them with Avery in tow—to move all of Avery's stuff out of the hotel room where he'd lived for the past two weeks. Of course, Cal's packing job was better than Avery's had ever been. When they were done, Avery waved a cheery good-bye to Kendra—whom he'd seen in the Stomping Grounds—and told her to come in for a free refill on him someday.

She looked at him dubiously. "Avery, all everyone could talk about when I went by this morning was how you'd boiled yourself in coffee. Maybe find a different way to say that, okay?"

Avery grimaced. "So, like, I'm *famous*?" he asked, because it was one thing to be this much of a clod in LA where a freakin' bajillion people didn't really give a shit how much of a loser you were, but it was finally starting to dawn on him that here, in a small town, he wasn't just going to be a goober on his own time.

Kendra nodded, totally confirming his worst nightmares. "Oh yeah. I mean, the tech crew of *Wolf's Landing* was starting a collection for you when I came in. They said you were the cast's favorite fanfic writer now that Kevin Hussain is writing for the show—"

Avery gaped. "They *know who I am*?"

He'd recognized the big-city haircuts and the slick clothes and asked them if they worked on the show. How was he supposed to know—

"Well *yeah*, Avery—they all recognized you from the panels. Remember? You came here to go to the convention? And your picture was with your bio on that piece you wrote. The whole town knows who you are now."

Avery blinked at her slowly, aware that Cal was standing at his shoulder at the registration desk, listening with interest.

"But . . . but . . . nobody at the shop said anything . . ." he sputtered.

Kendra shrugged, her blonde coif hardly moving it was so well shellacked. "Well, yeah—but nobody at the coffee shop asks if Dean's a he or a she, or if Tori swings both ways, either. We like our privacy here. The TV people respect that—it's why we love the show so much." Suddenly she looked over his shoulder and smiled genuinely. "Hey, Cal. You taking him home?"

"Well, to my house. He's moving into an apartment tomorrow."

Kendra smiled and held out her hand. "It was a pleasure to get to know you, Avery. I look forward to seeing you around town."

Avery shook her hand, feeling bemused. "Me too," he said. "Uhm, don't forget the coffee. My treat." He smiled, all teeth, to show he'd learned about not saying "on me," and she smiled back. He made a mental note to save a cookie for her kid. She'd been damned human to him when he'd first arrived, and he liked to reward that sort of niceness in the universe.

And then he was making his way through the slick and shiny darkened streets of Bluewater Bay in the early April night.

Cal drove considerately but the world was still a foggy, murky place, even if the landmarks were becoming more and more familiar. Still, he was relieved when Cal pulled the truck up to the disintegrating house on the water. He was awake and alert, but his chest was starting to ache again, and he really wanted some more painkillers until the swelling went down.

And he was going to have to sleep with his shirt off, because right now the chafing was making him nuts.

He swung out of the car, grabbing his backpack, which Cal had considerately packed with his toiletries and some clean clothes, and joined Cal walking across the nominal yard.

"Is everybody asleep?" he asked, thinking he didn't know much about this part of Cal's day.

Cal shook his head. "No. Dottie's here, keeping watch, and Nascha doesn't go to bed until I get home. Keir goes to bed at eleven thirty, every night, on the dot, and wakes up at seven in the morning. Even if he's awake, he lays there and waits for the clock to click to seven—my dad sat outside his room with a spanking paddle for a month, and followed through too, until Keir got used to the idea that he couldn't leave."

Avery sucked in a harsh breath. God. What Cal's family had gone through to keep Keir safe from the world—and the world safe from Keir. It was terrifying. No wonder Cal had such simple dreams—and he doubted they'd come true. No time in his heart for anything else.

"You don't talk about your parents much," Avery said as they drew near the porch. He knew that Cal's dad was Scottish and his mom was from the S'Klallam tribe, just like Nascha.

Cal stopped and turned toward him, his eyes fathomless in the dark.

"They were . . ." He smiled slightly. "Dad had a redheaded temper, you know? The world was his playground, and then something would set him off and he'd swear a blue streak. He wasn't violent—not really. He used the paddle on Keir because it was concrete, and he could be consistent, but he wasn't trying to bruise. He was just trying to set up consequences, you know?"

Avery's father had sort of randomly spanked whenever he was irritated. "That actually sounds sort of fair," he said, thinking about it.

Cal nodded. "And mom was . . ." His lips twisted. "She was serene. Even when Keir was at his worst, or Nascha paid the mortgage with gambling money. She'd just smile and say, 'We have food, a home, and each other.'" He shrugged. "And Dad would look at her and say, 'Yeah, honey. You're right.'" Cal looked out beyond the porch to where the stars were twinkling clearly between the great gray clouds. "I mean . . . it's so normal. They were so normal. Dad went out and fished every morning and worked for Clarke in the evenings. Mom baked bread for the local B&Bs. It's like . . . like they were the perfect parents, and then they were just . . ."

His voice faded, and Avery reached up and cupped his cheek.

"I'll stay," he said, smiling because he thought that was hopeful.

"Yeah, but I might drive you away."

Avery gasped and pulled back his hand. "Why would you—?"

"Why would I drag you down with me, baby? I'm going to be doing this for—"

"But so were they. *They* were happy. We could be too."

Cal shook his head. "Until we can't, okay?"

Avery sighed. Well, it was still a promise of sorts, right? His shoulders slumped, and his T-shirt rubbed his chest. He grimaced, and Cal wrapped a callused hand around the back of his neck.

"And right now we can. Let's get you inside. I've got the rest of the Vicodin. Let's dope you up. I figure that if I go out early, you can sleep until I get home and we can get you moved in, okay?"

Avery nodded, trying hard not to push.

Patience, right? Just because the past couple of weeks had rocked *Avery's* world didn't mean Cal wouldn't need more time to dream.

He followed Cal into the darkened house.

Nascha was sitting up, doing some sort of financial program on a tablet, and Dottie was looking over his shoulder. When Cal shut the door behind them, they both looked up guiltily, and Nascha handed the tablet almost surreptitiously to Dottie, who took it like a kid taking a passed note and sat down primly on the couch.

"Hello, Avery," Nascha said, his sonorous voice smoky in the lightless room.

"Heya, Nascha," Avery said, trying really hard to keep his good cheer intact. "I hope it's okay if I stay the night. I, uh . . ." Cal shifted, just enough to graze his chest, and his vision sort of grayed at the edges.

"He's hurt," Cal said shortly. "The burns will be better tomorrow, but right now he needs some pain meds and some more burn cream before he can function. I didn't want him alone."

Nascha nodded and smiled faintly. "Even Dottie heard about your fall, Avery. We're glad to see you're okay."

Avery groaned softly. "Oh *man!*" he muttered. "I don't *believe* this!"

"Nascha and I read your article this morning!" Dottie said brightly. "Keir even read your bio—which, by the way, you need to update."

Avery grunted. "Why?"

"Because it says you're living in LA, right? Aren't you moving to an apartment tomorrow?"

Avery smiled gamely. "Yeah. I'll remember that!"

That idea was actually sort of optimistic. Yeah, the whole town knew he was the guy who spilled coffee all over himself, but he was also the guy who wrote the article about the convention. He sort of had a town identity already, and it wasn't a bad one.

He actually belonged here, even before he moved into his apartment, and that was damned cool.

"C'mon, Mr. Fame and Fortune," Cal said dryly, handing him his Vicodin and some water. "Let me put you to bed."

"Do you need the couch?" Dottie asked. Avery choked on his water and every man in the room looked at her on sufferance. "Never mind," she returned sheepishly. "Jeez, Nascha—you didn't have to eyeball curse me, I was just asking!"

"We want Cal to keep bringing him here," Nascha said meaningfully. "He needs to feel welcome."

"I do; thank you, sir," Avery said, smiling. Cal took his cup and he floundered around for something to say. There was something he was missing—he could tell—but damn. The pain meds were kicking in that quickly, and although he wasn't tired, he wasn't feeling up to communicating with pretty much anyone but Cal.

Cal steered him through the tiny house, down the hall and past two closed doors and one half-open door that led to the bathroom.

All that, and a quick left, and they were . . .

Well, bedroom was sort of an exaggeration.

"Did they *build* the bed frame in the room?" Avery asked, trying to wrap his foggy mind around how it fit there.

"Well, I think they disassembled the frame, but since Dad actually did make it, he probably designed it to fit in tight places."

Avery pinched the bridge of his nose and then squinted at his new boyfriend under his glasses. "Of course, you would come from a big happy family of people who can make their own beds and engineer them to fit in impossibly tiny places with a matching dresser."

The workmanship was lovely. For one thing, the wood hadn't been perfect and smooth—it had been the curved outside of a great tree, and although the wood had been oiled and cut cleanly where it needed to be flat, the visible parts were still curved, oiled and sanded, but very clearly the original rose and cream color of the wood itself. The wood was fragrant still, and the fact that the dresser sat flush against the wall where the bed was pressed as well told Avery all he wanted about conservation of space.

"Where'd they keep their good clothes?" he asked, mind wandering to his parents' own bedroom. His father had a million suits, which vied with his mother's pretty satin dresses for priority in their walk-in closet.

"Keir's room," Cal said, his voice dropping in that expressionless way he had when Avery was about to find out something *really* heinous or uncomfortable about Cal's little brother. "We went to go through them after my folks died, so we'd have something to dress them in for the funeral, but Keir had taken scissors to them. We had to buy a dress for my mom, but we dressed dad in jeans and a flannel shirt. He was happier that way."

Avery's chest hurt in a whole new way that had nothing to do with Keir's elbow or the half a gallon of coffee he'd spilled on it.

"That's . . . nice," he said at last. "God, I wish I could have met them."

He was conscious of Cal's hands on his shoulders, helping him out of his T-shirt and then loosely taping gauze to his chest after he threw the oozy shirt into the hamper.

"If they'd lived, I don't know if we would have met," he said philosophically. "I would have gone out and gone to school and . . ." He trailed off and smiled, like he'd remembered all those late-night talks just like Avery had.

"You would have ended up back here," Avery said, feeling proud of himself.

"I would have," Cal told him, setting him down on the bed so he could untie Avery's shoes. By necessity he left the door open, because if he closed it, there wouldn't be enough room to kneel in front of Avery or move about the tiny room. "Or maybe I would have visited Southern California for a little while."

"We would have met," Avery said with confidence.

Cal smiled at him gently. "With you, I have no doubts. Now stand up for a minute and I'll take care of the jeans."

Cal threw those in the hamper too, and Avery sighed as Cal peeled back the covers so he could slide in between. Carefully, he scooted back so he was mashed up against the wall, and Cal would have room when he came to bed.

"Life's weird," he mumbled, letting the pain meds take over once again. "I just can't imagine a possibility without the last two weeks." He giggled a little. "But next time I'll try not to trip."

Cal grunted and wiggled his hips back so their thighs were touching but Avery's chest was left alone. "That makes no sense at all," he grumbled. "Sleep."

"Story of my day."

"Avery!"

"Fine, fine fine." Avery smiled even as he closed his eyes. "This feels like a real home. Like real life. I like this."

He was almost asleep before he heard Cal whisper, "Me too."

It was funny—okay, not funny—it was fucking brutal and ironic how sometimes, when you were at the height of that fuzzy feeling of well-being, life could really fuck with you.

Avery woke up around eight the next morning with a bleary recollection of Cal applying one last round of burn cream, and finishing it up with a warm kiss before he slipped into the foggy dark.

His chest felt *very* much better, and his blisters had all receded, and mostly, he just had to endure the peeling stage that most sunburn sufferers dealt with, and he'd be over the whole incident. He wiggled out of bed and grabbed his knapsack from the tiny space between the foot of the bed and the dresser and then made his way to the tiny bathroom. There was no tub, just a shower cubicle with a bench inside—probably for Nascha—a sink, and a commode.

Avery loved the coziness of it, the feeling that real people lived here, and he wasn't going to complain about space because really, the apartment he'd shared with Billy had been smaller, with fewer rooms. But he was starting to understand why Cal had kept showing up at his hotel room with condoms and a wistful expression on his face.

There would be *no* sex in this shower. Ever. Lives depended on it—probably Avery's life in particular. If he didn't impale himself on the prehistoric spigot, he'd crash through the loose (and loosely broken) shower doors, slip on the cracking tile, and fall through the dry-rot between the toilet and the sink.

He'd seen the cracks in the tile of the kitchen, and had felt drafts as he'd walked by the windows. The electrical system was old, the heater did nothing to keep away the spring chill, and looking at the roof from the outside was an exercise in faith.

Poor Cal.

What must it be like to come to this house every day, see all the things that needed fixing, and not have time to do any of it because you were so busy living check to check?

Avery came out of the bathroom with a few new bruises from banging his elbows on the sink and a new appreciation for the roominess of airplane toilets.

And a new coiling in his gut for how long Cal was going to be able to do this.

"Hi, Avery," Keir said from the hallway. He was just standing there, apparently waiting for Avery to come out.

"Hi. Uhm, did you want to, uhm, use the bathroom—"

"I was waiting for you to wake up. We can watch *Avatar* together. Nascha said you needed to get out of the bathroom first."

Avery smiled at him. "Nascha is a wise man. May I trouble you for a cup of coffee and some toast?"

Keir's eyes got really big, and he opened his mouth and bawled, "*Nascha! Nascha! He wants toast!*"

Avery tried not to reel back, because, well, loud, and Nascha walked sedately into the hallway, apparently not at all surprised.

"Keir, brother, go sit in the living room and watch television, okay? I'll get Avery some breakfast."

Keir nodded abruptly, but he did what Nascha said.

Avery followed Nascha back down the tiny hallway and into the kitchen, and Nascha gestured to a cheap Formica table. Avery sat, and watched as the old man pulled out a toaster and rifled the refrigerator, coming back with what looked to be prime supplies for a breakfast sandwich.

"Do you like bacon and jelly on your toast?" Nascha asked, smiling a little. "We don't get guests that often."

"That sounds awesome!" Avery didn't usually eat jelly on his toast, but he wouldn't turn Nascha down for the world.

After a few moments of silence, punctuated by the television on in the background, Nascha presented Avery with a neat plate, containing a breakfast sandwich, complete with precooked bacon, jelly, and a fried egg, yolk broken.

And coffee.

"You already ate?" Avery asked, and Nascha shrugged, sitting in the vinyl seat next to him and nursing his own coffee. The rest of the table was heaped with mail, *TV Guide*s, and fishing catalogs, so it was like eating in an oasis of clean.

"I've been getting up when Cal gets up and napping when Dottie gets here to watch Keir."

Avery nodded and took a bite, then closed his eyes and savored. Okay. Breakfast sandwich, jelly too. On the menu. "Why so early?" Because Cal's hours were awful.

"So I can remember to take my medication, and keep an eye on Keir." Nascha grunted. "It doesn't always work."

Avery nodded again, and looked at him carefully. It had occurred to Avery that Cal's situation here . . . it was so precarious. One more misfortune, one more monster fish, one blown tire, one more item on the medical roster, and Cal would have to live his worst nightmare and give the people he loved to a system that was an admitted national disgrace.

"But Cal probably appreciates the help," is what he said.

"Appreciates, but doesn't trust," Nascha said, looking at Avery seriously. "And he shouldn't. I wrote a note to myself last night to remind me you'd be here. I still almost called out to Owen, Cal's father, when I heard you in the shower."

Avery thought about it. "I can see that," he said through a full mouth. "I still have dreams that I'm back in high school and I forgot where gym class is."

Nascha laughed appreciatively. "That's because you don't feel ready to be grown-up," he said, sounding like the wise elder Avery had always wanted when he'd been walking batshit-crazy Granny Kennedy around the neighborhood.

"Yeah, well, that doesn't stop time from happening. You cope with it."

Nascha's smile was truly a thing of beauty. His face still creased, and his eyes were still rheumy, but that smile spoke of every hard-won perk aging had to offer.

"You're good for Cal. You need to stay in his life."

"Well, I'll try if he lets me," Avery said cheerfully, thinking he didn't really want to talk about the source of Cal's problems with, hello, one of the sources of Cal's problems.

"I'm being serious," Nascha said, grabbing Avery's arm with bony fingers. Avery looked at him in surprise. "Cal will have need of you— he's been alone in his own head for so very long."

Avery sighed and regarded Nascha soberly. On the one hand, it was nice to have some contact with Cal's family. On the other hand, his parents had cheerfully stayed the hell out of his personal life and he wasn't sure what to do with all this interest.

And he really didn't want to talk about Cal when Cal wasn't there.

"Cal is really private," he said softly. "I know he needs someone. But if he can't tell me that, I can't really do anything."

Nascha grunted. "Fair enough." Suddenly he stiffened and looked up. Somebody was on the porch, knocking on the door. Through the thin curtain on the window, Avery could make out a slender form with a baseball cap who was *definitely* not Cal.

"Cal?" called a female voice—probably August, who had visited Avery at the coffee shop. "Avery? Tori's waiting for me—I'm dropping off Avery's car like you asked, Cal."

"Oh!" Avery said, happy. "That's awesome. Here, Nascha—sit down, I'll get it."

He stood and went to open the door, aware that Keir had stood up in the living room and was bouncing anxiously on his toes. Uh-oh—Cal had told him frankly that Keir wasn't good around girls, and Avery had seen him firsthand be rude to August and dodgy around Tori.

"Here, August!" Avery called. "I'll come out there, okay?"

He rushed for the door, making it outside and slamming it shut. Behind him he felt a shudder and a thud as Keir's solid body hit the frame.

August had taken three steps back and was staring at Avery with big eyes.

"Oh my God!" All trace of the cool, hooded-eyed hipster was gone, and what was left was a terrified, vulnerable young woman. "Was that *Keir*?"

Avery nodded, heart thundering in his ears. Behind him, he could hear Nascha talking frantically, and then another thud and shaking from the fragile house. "He . . . you know."

"Doesn't like girls," August said, holding her hand to her chest in a decidedly female gesture of fear.

"I think you took him by surprise when you came over," he said, because Keir hadn't seemed this bad in public in town.

"I . . . God. That's gotten worse. I mean, it was bad when we were in high school but . . . Cal *lives* with that?"

Avery nodded. He did not add *In fear* because, well, *duh*! "Here, I'll take the keys—and tell Tori thank you for me, okay?"

"Yeah, no problem. Glad to see you're better." There was another thud behind him and August waved quickly and took off running for Tori's car, which was idling in the street in front of the house. Tori tore out of there, and Avery heard an echo of another engine, this one two stroke and puttering into the garage dock just as he turned to open the door.

He didn't count on Keir's determination.

That sturdy, fireplug body rushed him just as he opened the door, and all Avery could think of was Cal's fear, his hand-shaking nightmare, that his little brother would get out and hurt somebody. Instinctively he bent his knees and tried to block, but Keir elbowed him in the chest, shoving him aside, and Avery stumbled, his glasses flying to the side as he scrambled, looking for purchase. Before he went down, he stuck out a foot and caught Keir midstride, sending him sprawling down the stairs, where he landed in the mud and howled with rage.

"Keir! She's gone! She's not going to hurt you!"

Keir pushed himself up from the mud about the time that Avery caught his balance on the porch, and for a moment Avery thought he was going to continue out into the street and away, loose in the world while Avery struggled just to stay upright.

And that's when he turned to Avery with a look of confusion and unbridled rage, and Avery realized there were worse things than chasing Keir into the wild blue yonder.

Way worse things.

CHAPTER SEVENTEEN

NO GROUND RISING

C al heard the raised voices as he pulled the boat into the garage port, but he didn't really worry until he heard Avery scream, "No, Keir, no!"

Oh God.

Avery! Avery, who didn't know Keir, and who wasn't as strong and—

He heard the thud of bodies hitting the porch, and then hitting the mud, and Avery's gurgled shouts, and he didn't remember bolting through the house after that, past a frightened Nascha and into his front yard.

By the time he got there, Keir was sitting on Avery's chest, hitting him repeatedly with his bunched right fist. Avery had stopped struggling to get up and was just protecting his face, and for the first time in his life, protecting his little brother was not on Cal's priority list.

He got behind Keir and dragged him off Avery, then thrust his knee into that sturdy back and put him in a three-point restraint, every muscle strained against that strong, struggling body.

"Nascha!" he shouted. "Nascha! Call 911! Call the hospital in Seattle, the one we looked at! Tell them to expect him!"

"I'm calling, Cal," Nascha hollered through the open door, and there was a serenity, a resignation to his voice that Cal had never heard before, apparent even above Keir's outraged screams. "Is Avery okay?"

Cal looked quickly from his restraint on Keir to Avery, who was rolling over in the mud and pulling himself up on all fours.

"Avery?" Cal asked, fearing the answer for a moment.

"I'm fine," Avery lied, spitting blood through a bruised mouth. "Perfect. Awesome."

"Oh God," Cal muttered. "God, Avery."

"*I hate him!*" Keir screamed. "*He kept me from the girl!*" His muscular torso bucked under Cal's weight for a moment, and Cal was only vaguely aware of Avery hoisting himself up and over to the porch where he sat down and leaned his weight on his elbows, trying to get his bearings.

"You did good," Cal said over Keir. "God, Avery, I'm so sorry. You kept him from..." From what? Hurting someone? Because Avery sure didn't look *unhurt*. God, he was bleeding. *Bleeding*. The guy Cal had been calling Rescue Puppy had needed rescuing from *Cal's brother*. Cal's voice broke. "You did good," he said, feeling lost.

Thank God, thank God, for the fire department and the paramedics and for restraints on gurneys and injected sedatives, because that—all of that—happened, just as Cal realized he didn't have a clue what to do next.

The paramedics told Cal to follow them in the truck, and they'd given him the slip of paper with an address on it. Cal had glanced at the paper as the guy was talking, because he *thought* he knew where Keir was going. He wasn't stupid. He'd had a worst-case scenario planned with Keir's psych guy since they'd had to restrain Keir after their parents had died. But as he went to jump in the truck, he realized the address wasn't right.

"Hey, Nascha!" he called. "Where is this place?"

Nascha came out of the house with two packed suitcases that he handed to Cal. Cal looked at them in confusion—it was like they'd been waiting for this to happen, those two suitcases. Nascha had shoved Keir's badger—which he slept with every night—on the top of the second bag, like it had just needed to be added.

"It's only about a half an hour away," Nascha said, looking at Cal firmly. "Don't worry, Cal. He's already registered there. Make sure he's settled and give them his possessions. Then come home and take care of Avery."

Cal stashed the suitcases in the truck, and then stared at Avery, who came down off the porch to see him off. He'd been looked at by the paramedic, and had a butterfly bandage on the cleaned wound on his head, and some anesthetic balm for his split lips. His hooded sweatshirt was bloody, though, and so was the once-white T-shirt underneath it. He squinted at Cal from two blackened eyes and held a cold compress to his broken nose.

"God," he whispered. "I'm so sorry."

Avery nodded. "Me too—I didn't know what to—"

Cal shook his head and cupped the side of his neck. "Avery. Avery, I'm so sorry. This isn't your mess. This is mine. He was like . . . like a time bomb, and I kept thinking we had time and . . . Oh God. I'm sorry. He went off, and he hurt you—"

"But he didn't kill me," Avery said with a faint smile, holding Cal's hand. "Look—go check on him. I'll stay with Nascha and you can come back and tell us how he's doing, okay?"

Cal nodded, and brought him in for a very chaste, very tender kiss on his temple.

"Avery . . . Jesus. Stay safe, okay?"

"Cal, I—"

"Just . . . I'll be back." Cal kissed his temple again, and then pulled away, Avery's silky hair sliding against his callused palm as he did so. His eyes burned, and his throat swelled, and he longed to throw himself on Nascha's lap like a little kid, or in Avery's arms like a frightened man, but he did neither. He got into his truck and waved at them both and drove away.

Yeah, he thought it was the right thing to do then.

The shit that goes on when you're not paying attention—that'll fuck you up every time.

The hospital was nice—even Cal had to concede it was nice. The furnishings were up-to-date, it *didn't* smell like cigarette smoke and puke, and the grounds behind it stretched out in an extensive garden. There were no chain-link fences, no concrete aprons with butt-filled coffee cans, and no bored ghosts drifting through hallways looking perplexed and depressed.

The recreation room featured attendants actively participating with residents in things like Monopoly and Ping-Pong, and the residents seemed to be laughing in non-horror movie ways.

Cal looked around in a daze, not sure how Nascha thought they could afford this place, and when he found the woman at the registration desk, he felt a shudder of relief.

He gave her Keir's information, and the luggage Nascha had packed, and watched her look things up on a computer with so much ease that he got the feeling everything she needed to know had already been there.

"Uhm," Cal said, feeling dumb, "just out of curiosity, how much is a week here going to cost us?" Because he was thinking if they could afford a week, just a week, to calm Keir down, then they could have him moved to the shitty place, the place that made Cal dead to think about, but that would let him and Nascha keep the house.

"Oh don't worry, Mr. McCorkle—you're more than paid up. In fact, there's a trust in place here, backed up with your brother's social security checks, that will make sure Keir gets to stay here as long as he needs to."

Cal gaped at her. Money? They had the money to put Keir some place like *this*? How did that . . .?

Cal swallowed against a dry throat, and tried to keep the spots from dancing in front of his eyes. "Uhm . . . who's name is that in again?" he asked, his voice feeling distant and tinny in his own ears.

He didn't even need to hear her answer.

Avery's car was gone when he roared back to the house and slewed to a halt in the middle of the so-called yard. He left the truck sitting cockeyed on what used to be a lawn, the bumper less than three feet from the porch, and thundered inside the empty house.

The pile of mail—mostly stacks of late bills—had been cleaned off the table. What was left were the current—open—envelopes, in a neat stack, with the current balances, and one plain envelope next to them with his name scrawled across the top.

With shaking hands he went through the current bills first.

All of the balances were at zero.

He looked at the mortgage. It had been completely paid.

That was when his knees went weak and he sank into one of the cheap vinyl and aluminum chairs, not caring if it creaked or even if it chose this day to go out from under him. With spots dancing before his eyes, he reached for the plain white envelope.

Calladh—

Even in Nascha's uneven scrawl, he could hear the somber power of his full name.

Please don't blame Avery. He has no idea where he's just taken me, or that I plan to stay. I've left you the address—when your anger has faded, please come visit, and yell at me until it is gone completely. If I am lucky, I'll forget that day.

You could not do this much longer. It was killing you. I've loved the time I've lived with you and Keir, and watching you struggle, no man could doubt he was loved.

But if we loved you, we had to let you go.

I sold the house to the tribe for a shit-ton of money, Cal. Enough to pay for the good places for Keir and me. Enough to set you up anywhere you want, and let you find a path that has nothing to do with either of us. Dottie helped, and I was going to tell you the day you picked Avery up off the road. But you looked so happy—I couldn't do it then. I couldn't take that happiness away from you when it was so new—and you'd needed it for so long.

But Keir forced my hand, and I couldn't wait to tell you until you were ready to hear. It was time to go.

When your anger has faded, we hope you visit. We miss you. We especially miss your smile.

The details are listed below, including how to access the money in your account, and who your contact people are for visiting and such.

You have sixty days to move—and since they're building a small marina here, you'll have a lifetime slip for your father's boat. I knew that would be important.

You are loved, Calladh. By me, by Keir, by your young man. Please don't squander this chance to fly.

Nascha

Cal couldn't even look at the information at the bottom—his brain wasn't getting it. *Wouldn't* get it.

Gone?

Nascha and Keir were *gone*?

His home was *gone*?

He sat at the table and rearranged the order of the world, trying to take in breath while the long afternoon shadows stretched under the cloud cover and through the windows. He didn't even realize he was crying until Nascha's letter started to blur.

He shoved it away and stood up, taking a restless step through the kitchen, where his foot dislodged a cracked tile, and then another.

Cal looked around the little house, and saw it as Avery must have seen it—the tile disintegrating, the cabinets falling, the carpet worn to the floorboards, the big hole in the bathroom next to the toilet— and for a moment, he felt shame.

This was all he had? He'd worked his back to breaking, and now his family was gone, and all he had was this crumbling house and not even that for very long?

His footsteps echoed loudly, and for a moment, he felt like he did on the sound in his boat, under a barely dawn sky.

Like his was the only heartbeat under the sun.

The patter of nervous footsteps slammed that heartbeat into his chest, and the tentative knock on the door followed by the turning knob spun his mind and his heart in a whole other direction.

Don't blame Avery. He doesn't know what he's done.

"You took him away?" Cal asked, belatedly wiping his eyes with his palms.

Avery squinted at him unhappily from behind those thick glasses, one foot in the doorway and one foot out. The glasses themselves sported a piece of tape at the hinge—they'd probably gotten broken during the fight—and Cal fought with himself not to reach out and beg for the human comfort he needed more than anything right now.

You let your family go.

On this thought, his arm collapsed limply at his side.

"He . . . he just said . . . he said he had a plan for this," Avery said uncertainly. "He . . . he had suitcases packed and everything. He . . . uhm . . . he told me I shouldn't come back. Not tonight. He said you'd be pissed. But . . . but *Cal*—man, your little brother—"

"He was right," Cal said, feeling brutal, shaking with adrenaline and anger, most of it not directed at Avery, but holy fuck, he was *right here*, wasn't he? "You shouldn't have come back."

Augh! That fucking confusion! That hurt! Oh *Jesus*, Rescue Puppy, couldn't you, just this once, take the initiative?

I need!

I need to be left alone!

Avery squinted, scrutinizing his face in the bad light, and a suddenly adult expression hardened his features.

He took the final step inside the house and shut the door behind him.

"You need me," he said with certainty.

"I—"

I couldn't take care of them. I failed.

"You need me," Avery said, his voice breaking. "You . . . you need *somebody*, Cal—"

"I don't *get* anybody!" Cal snarled, the savagery taking him by surprise. "Don't you see? That . . . that wily old man had me running around in circles, and the whole time he'd planned to . . . to just *leave* me. Leave me with nothing!"

Some of Avery's certainty faded in the face of Cal's fury.

"But you don't have nothing," he said, voice cracking. "You've got me."

Cal closed his eyes, wanting to throw himself into Avery's arms more than he'd ever wanted anything in his life.

"You'll just go too," he said, his voice choked.

"But Cal—I'm *right here*!"

Cal's skin hurt. If someone touched him right now—if *Avery* touched him right now—he'd fly apart and never find himself again.

"Just go," he whispered. "Just go."

"No," Avery said, taking another step closer. Cal remembered that night, that inexpert night, when Avery topped and Cal had been able to give himself over to another person and trust that the universe would take care of him. That was the Avery he was trying to be.

"I said *go*!" Cal shouted. *I'm not worthy of that Avery!* "Go, Rescue Puppy—nobody needs you and I certainly can't *help* you. Look around!" He gestured wildly at the destruction of his parents' hopes, of the home he'd remembered with such joy. "It's over. Anything I had to offer you—it's over!" And, God help him, he knew everything from Avery's past, every hurt, every wound, every knife that had ever been stuck, and he twisted the first one he found. "Unless you just want the fucking money. Right? That's your sticking point— Well, guess what. I'm fucking *loaded*. Is that the Cal you want? The guy who's going to pay your way—"

"*Stop!*" Avery snarled. Tears slicked down his face, and his glasses steamed. *Oh God, Rescue Puppy—now you get to see the worst of me. The Cal who yelled at Keir, who called Nascha "old man" like he hadn't given his youth to be with us. Now you get to see me ugly, and maybe it will drive you away too.* "You think I don't have this inside me?" Avery said, chest shaking. "You think I don't know where the bad shit comes from? I've dished it out, Cal—I told you that. But I'm not going to now."

"Don't even—" *Don't even compare yourself to the monster I am right now.* "Why not— Can't defend yourself?"

"If—" Avery's voice cracked, and his throat worked. "If you get past the ugly, Cal, I'll be waiting."

His battered face twisted like he was fighting himself not to come rushing to Cal's side, and Cal thought dispassionately that he'd had a rough couple of days. But that wasn't Cal's concern right now. Nothing was Cal's concern. The things that he thought were his concern had just resolved themselves without him. Who was he without his burdens? Who was he without his family? How could he help Avery when he couldn't help himself?

"Just go!" he shouted, closing his eyes and sinking onto the cracked tile floor. "God, Avery, just fucking go!"

He heard the door shut, but he didn't see it. He was sunk there, in the rubble, in his misery, crying like he hadn't cried since his parents died and left him the man of the house.

Three days after Cal screamed at Avery, kicked his Rescue Puppy and sent him away, Cal found himself at the Eagle Pines Senior Center, glaring at a particularly uncontrite Nascha.

"What?" Nascha said innocuously. "You expected to find me behind glass, like in a prison movie?"

"You . . . old man . . . what you did to me . . ." Cal fought against gesticulating madly, thinking with a horrible pang that it was the sort of thing Avery would do. Three days. The first day he'd barely managed to pull himself together enough to call in sick to the Global.

The second day he'd gone through the house and realized that the only thing left besides his own clothes was the furniture. He'd boxed up the dishes, and the pictures, and the extra blankets and towels, and then just stood and stared into what had once been his parents' bedroom.

It would take him maybe two hours to pack that up, and he had nowhere to go.

The day before, he'd gone searching for apartments, but most of them had been taken by TV people. He'd found a house though, something that had been built by vacationers years ago, but had been kept up and redecorated. It stood right on the water, with wood paneling, and big picture windows. He'd looked through the front window and saw the sound, the ocean and the islands he'd seen his entire life, and thought, *Avery will love that view.*

His entire body had shocked then, tingling, growing cold and clammy, like his heart was one big pinched nerve, as he remembered that he'd told Avery to go.

And Avery had gone.

He'd mumbled something to the real-estate woman, and barely remembered tucking her card in his wallet, and then he'd driven back home.

To the home that wasn't his home anymore because all that was there were his clothes and the big television that nobody was watching anymore.

That morning he'd emptied the rotting fish out of the dory (since he'd forgotten to unload them on that horrible day his life detonated) and, when he was done hosing it out, took the boat out on the sound.

He didn't fish—didn't need to.

He just sat there, in the midafternoon sunshine, and turned his face to the sky.

The quiet settled into his bones. Just Cal, a part of the sea and the wind. What was left when the sea and the wind had swept him away?

But they didn't. The waves rolled, the wind blew, and Cal was still there.

Unbidden, he remembered when Avery had been there, sitting at the end of the dory, asking quiet questions, worming under Cal's skin, becoming a part of his heart.

Cal wasn't alone here, under the sky and on the sea.

Avery was there too.

He stayed there, breathing in the air of the sound, the pine trees, the sweet wind and the coming rain, and tried to picture his future.

For six years he'd labored to keep his family together, and now his family was nothing—less than the wind in his face and the sun in his eyes. He'd woken that morning in a cold sweat, the sky still dark overhead, sure that he'd left some crucial task undone, had forgotten somebody's medicine, had neglected to pay a bill, had let the mortgage lapse or forgotten to go to his second job or slept through his alarm and wouldn't be able to fish this day or . . .

Oh no! He'd have to tell Avery that he'd be gone, or he'd fucked up, or he'd lost a job, or he needed to find his brother, or that Nascha couldn't be left alone or . . .

And then all those things melted away.

The relief left him breathless, shaky, almost in tears again as he tried to imagine his life without those things.

He'd have to tell Avery that . . .

But Avery was gone too.

And now, he was out on the sound, and picturing his life as it would be in a week, or a month, or a year, and that refrain, started over late nights at coffee, made more secure over later nights in bed, wouldn't leave him alone.

I have to tell Avery . . .

Avery would have an idea . . .

Maybe Avery could help . . .

Cal knew who he had to talk to before he talked to Avery.

And here he was, Nascha stretched out on a comfortable recliner like he'd lived in this high-class nursing home for years, and Cal perched on a brocade couch, wishing he fit in just a tiny bit better.

"Where's Avery?" Nascha asked, as though Avery had been a fixture in their lives for longer than three weeks.

"I told him to go away," Cal said, feeling like a child.

Nascha rolled his eyes heavenward, and a muscle in Cal's jaw twitched. Damn it, this *wasn't* a bad grade, or a new alternator for the truck, or a shitty day at work. Nascha and Keir had very casually ended Cal's *identity*. They'd taken his troubles away, but they'd taken his family and his pride and his vision of who he was with them.

How was he supposed to be someone to Avery if *he* didn't know who that person was supposed to be?

Cal leaned forward, taking his weight on his elbows, and caught Nascha's eyes with the heat of his glare. He wanted *no* mistake about how angry he was.

"Do you have *any* idea what you did to me, old man?" he demanded, voice growing ugly, cracked, furious, and bleeding. "You and Keir were my *life*, and you just . . . just *stole* that from me?"

"We were killing you," Nascha said calmly.

"That was *my* problem!" Cal snapped. "You couldn't have fucking *told* me?"

"When, Calladh?" Nascha asked gently, and like a dose of radioactive coolant, Cal's whole name sucked some of the toxicity from his blood. "When you were busting your ass—*breaking* yourself—trying to keep us alive? When you were . . ." Nascha pursed his lips and shook his head. "When you were falling in love?" He smiled then, black eyes shiny. "Oh, that was wonderful. That was the reason the gods let old men live, Cal. So we can watch young men fall in love. You . . . you became this . . . this whole other person. Every dream your parents and I had for you—and that we betrayed—was suddenly there alive in your face." Nascha shook his head, a man lost in wonder, and Cal thought miserably that he hadn't even been strong enough to look at Avery's face as he'd pushed him away.

"But . . . but Keir—did he even know?"

Nascha nodded earnestly. "Oh yes. When you were laid up, Cal, you know I took my medicine every day. And it wasn't magic—I still had bad days—you were there. But I had a lot more good days. And you left to bus tables one day, still sick with fever, hands shaking, but we had no food. You needed your tips that day. We had nothing. And

Keir said, 'Uncle Nascha, if there were any gods, they'd make Cal's life easier.'"

Cal made a hurt sound. "But . . . you did all this—I mean, the bank accounts, the two different places—how did you *do* all that?"

Nascha smiled, suddenly about twelve years old. "Dottie had her tablet, Cal. Do you *know* what the internet can do for you?" Suddenly he laughed, the delighted sound of the dirty old man. "Porn. Man, I'm telling you. There is the *best* porn on that little magic box."

Cal narrowed his eyes. "Nascha, did you buy yourself a computer?"

Nascha nodded. "Oh yes. I had one waiting for me when I arrived." Then he sobered. "It's late afternoon, Cal. I'm not always at my best now—you know that. But if you want to know how, it was then. I called my friend, Raw, and . . ." Nascha's voice grew soft, grew affectionate, and he glanced over his shoulder.

Cal followed his gaze, and he saw a behemoth of a man, as tall as he was wide, body dwarfing an extra-large electric cart. The man smiled softly at Cal, like he'd known him once, and nodded, his long gray braids hardly moving with the motion.

"Raw?" Cal asked, wondering about Nascha's equal-opportunity porn.

"Raw," Nascha said. "It had been too long." He cleared his throat. "Anyway, Dottie helped me—she's not getting any younger, and as much as she's appreciated the money to supplement her social security, she was ready to not be our babysitter anymore. So she looked up things like escrow and interest rates and going property rates, and together, we assembled . . ." Nascha's smile this time was the wily old gambler " . . . a *lucrative* proposition for our family."

Cal nodded. So many sides of Nascha—so many parts of the old man he'd missed in his hell-bent effort to keep the man fed, to keep his parents' roof over his head.

"I don't know how to feel," he confessed nakedly, most of his anger spent. "I . . . I . . ." *I miss Avery so damned bad.* Nascha and Keir, yes—but God, the relief at not being their leader anymore. If he'd had room in that relief for shame, there would have been a lot of that, but just as there'd been no room in his worry for hope, there was no room for the shame in the relief.

"Feel however you want, Cal," Nascha said with a grin. "You have the world at your feet. You can go to school, or build your own home on a smaller plot of land, or—" he sobered "—or live in a tiny apartment with a happy young man who is probably very hurt right now."

Cal closed his eyes. "Yeah," he said, too lost to fight it anymore. "Yeah. That last one."

"Have you visited Keir yet?"

Cal shook his head. "No." A sort of weak wave of tears washed over him. Not enough for sobs, just a freeing stream, cleaning out the anger, freeing him from confusion.

"Well, let me know when you and Avery go. I can come with you." Nascha smiled. "We can have a picnic."

"I'll do that," Cal said with a weak smile. *Avery, would you still talk to me if I asked?*

He and Nascha talked for a few more minutes before Raw wheeled up to the two of them.

"Badger, it's time for dinner," he said, and from the tone of his voice, Cal could tell that Nascha had not always remembered dinner since he'd arrived.

"Cal, this is Rawlins. You used to know him a long time ago."

Cal looked at the elder and shook his head. "I . . . birds," he said, remembering the seeds of that long ago dream to help wild animals. "I remember birds. And . . ." A pretty Native American woman with a warm laugh. "A girl named Kitten."

Raw and Nascha shared a smile. "She's not gone," Rawlins said.

"No," Nascha agreed. "That's a wonderful thing."

Call stood, unsure of himself. Nascha patted Raw's cheek, though, and for that moment, they were in their own world.

"Bye, Nascha," he said, feeling lost.

Nascha looked over his shoulder. "Come visit," he urged again. "Bring Avery. It will be good."

The two of them wandered away, Raw in his scooter, Nascha by his side, and Cal left the facility feeling slightly less lost.

Avery, if I asked you, would you come?

Well, maybe it would depend on how he asked.

CHAPTER EIGHTEEN

THE RIGHT BED

A nd one day, about a week after Avery had watched his boyfriend's life implode and had been ordered rudely away from his living room, Avery walked out of the Stomping Grounds and Cal was just outside.

He was leaning against the wooden rail to the boardwalk, watching anxiously as people left the coffee shop, and when he saw Avery's face, those black, obsidian eyes got so big, and his lower lip trembled.

Avery gaped at him. He'd spent the past week nursing a grudge, crying into his pillow, whining to Gi-Gi online, and telling himself that Cal's rejection—and his fucking cruelty—had nothing to do with Avery personally and everything to do with the shit that had been building in his life since before Avery was in Kindergarten.

But none of it had helped him get over the sting of the meanness about money, or the shouted "Just go!" until he saw Cal's face when he walked into the sunlight.

He charged right into Cal's space and cupped his cheek. "You look like shit," he said, not caring if he was gentle or not.

Cal nodded. "It's been sort of a week." His mouth twisted, like he was trying to make light of things. He cupped Avery's cheek in turn, and his thumb brushed the healing cuts in Avery's lower lip. "You look fantastic."

Avery jerked away. "Don't be mean," he muttered, and Cal caught him by the back of the neck and held on.

"I'm sorry," he said. "Avery—look at me. Look at me, please."

Avery stopped resisting, and the awfulness of Cal's shouted words moved just a little so he could look Cal in the eyes.

"I *was* mean," Cal said softly. "I was. You said it yourself—when we're hurt, when something comes out of left field and crushes it, we can be . . . awful."

"I—"

"You weren't awful. You kept being afraid that what you did to Billy—that was who you were. But you . . . God, I was so awful to you. And you just kept trying to help. So I'm being fucking serious," he said, smiling bitterly. "I have *never* seen someone who looked so damned good in my entire life."

Avery stayed, because he wanted to believe, and because Cal's hand felt so good there. So warm. Keeping him grounded.

But that didn't mean he didn't have some pride.

"You've been gone a week," he said, feeling pitiful.

"I know," Cal acknowledged quietly. "If I was someone else, I'd be telling you to ditch my ass, because you didn't deserve that."

Avery swallowed a big fat lump of I-needed-to-hear-that, but it left his throat raw and his eyes watery. Cal pulled him even closer, until their foreheads were almost touching.

"You're right," he agreed. "I didn't deserve that." God. All he'd ever wanted was to have someone care how he felt. Here was Cal, caring what his words had done, caring about the damaged he'd inflicted. Avery had said he'd be there when the ugly in Cal's heart was gone. Here Cal was, proving that his heart was as it always was. The giant fish under the surface of Cal's life had hurt them—but it hadn't destroyed them.

"No," Cal whispered. "You deserve sweetness. You deserve to be cared for. All the things I told you I would give you if I could—I can now. Let me give them to you."

"Is that why you're here? To offer me riches?"

Cal bit his lip. "I *did* deserve that."

Avery shook his head. "No. No you didn't. That was my last . . . last barb. I promise. What *are* you here for?"

Cal let out a short, self-conscious laugh. "Well, to make up, among other things."

Avery pulled back and eyed him suspiciously. "Like what things?"

Cal turned and gestured vaguely to his truck. "I've got this bed," he said, in his terse way. Avery looked over his shoulder to where the bed frame—the hand-sanded, hand-oiled bed frame Avery and Cal had slept on together that one night under Cal's roof—stuck out of the back of Cal's pickup, with the mattress tied, cushioning the pieces against the bed of the truck. There were boxes too, and what looked to be like all of Cal McCorkle's life, packed solidly into the back of the pickup.

"Oh my God!" Avery said, the enormity of what Cal had needed to do in the last week sort of hitting him like, well, a big piece of wood. "Where are you going to put that?"

Cal turned to him, a sort of agonized look on his face.

"See—that bed frame, the dresser, all my clothes—everything I own but the dory—is in the back of that truck. 'Cause if Keir and Nascha weren't in that house, why would I want to live there?"

"Oh Jesus. *Cal*—what are you going to do?"

Cal's smile went crooked. "Now I asked myself that about sixty zillion times," he said, his voice getting bubbly underneath. "And what I answered myself was, uhm, 'I don't know.' But every time I asked myself that question, I kept hearing the question wrong."

Avery couldn't have run away then if Mt. Olympia had erupted in one big bang. "How did you hear the question?" he asked, eyes wide.

"I heard the question, 'What are you going to do *with Avery*?'" Cal said, that crooked smile making another appearance. "So, you know, I figured . . . I mean, you're just starting out, and now *I'm* just starting out, and maybe, you wouldn't mind *us* starting out together. I mean," and the half smile disappeared, leaving simple appeal written all over his face, "my parents were in school when they met. And they got their degrees, you know? But they decided that whatever they did, they had to do it together, and they had to do it here. So, uhm . . . I may go back to school, or buy some property I can live on forever, or . . . I don't know, take tourists fishing. But, uhm, I want to do it together. And I want to do it here."

Avery's own smile was more than a little bit broken in the middle. "Until we can't?"

Cal shook his head. "That's not good enough," he said seriously. "That . . . that lets one of us do what I just did, and"—his voice broke—"I don't ever want to go through another week like that again."

Avery wrapped his arms around Cal's back then, ignored all that self-inflicted advice about pride and space and not suffocating Cal with his need.

Cal *needed* him.

"Until forever," Avery whispered in his ear.

"Yeah," Cal muttered roughly. "Until forever."

They held each other, shaking, in the middle of the boardwalk, and the town of Bluewater Bay ebbed and flowed around them. Beyond Cal's shoulder, Avery could see the ocean, and the islands and the sky, but those weren't the things he'd come for.

What he'd come for was right there, in his arms, needing him with every breath, until forever.

The bed just *barely* fit into Avery's tiny one-room apartment, but since Avery hadn't had a dresser, and the cot he'd been sleeping on had wrenched his back, he wasn't going to complain.

They had a bed, and a hot plate, a cheap wooden table that came with the place, a small refrigerator, and, most blessed of blesseds, wi-fi.

They weren't going to live there forever—they established that as they carted Cal's stuff up the back stairs to the apartment. Hell, they might not even stay there through Cal's time in college, because who *knows* what better kind of apartment would come along then. But for right now, it was perfect, mostly because it only took them two hours to move Cal's bed in, and get the rest of his meager belongings into the room and mingling with Avery's same, sorry state of material affairs.

And *after that* they had the rest of the night to fuck like lemmings, make love, touch each other tenderly, and bang like a screen door in a hurricane—all of which they did in sort of a haphazard, mix-and-match manner that left Avery unsure as to whether he was going to get the tender lover one moment or the aggressive top the next.

It was the most exhilarating time in bed Avery had ever spent. Without the weight of the world on his shoulders, Cal made love like the Native American god of sex, whomever that may be.

At the end of round three, they fell back against the sweaty sheets, Avery's head pillowed on Cal's shoulder, and caught their breath.

"So, do *you* have extra sheets?" Avery asked, thinking they were going to need to go to the Laundromat soon. As they'd stood in the room with the bed made up, Cal had reached into his pocket and shyly produced negative test results. Avery had tackled him right then. The resultant mess was highly gratifying, but, well, sticky.

"I do, actually," Cal said, sounding proud. "They're in one of those boxes over there."

"We can change those later then."

"I'm thinking."

"God, Cal. How many people do you think heard us do that?"

Cal's evil chuckle told him that Cal was also thinking about the people trying to drink coffee underneath them at the Stomping Grounds.

"Probably the whole town," Cal said with satisfaction, playing with the curls in Avery's hair. "Especially that last time when you screamed when you came."

Avery couldn't even be embarrassed about that. "Well, the whole town knew we were broken up," he said practically. "Now they know we're not."

He turned and looked at Cal's profile, loving the dreamy smile on his face when Cal acknowledged that was probably true.

"Avery?" Cal said, that smile intact.

"Yeah?"

"Do you have to be drugged to say you love me?"

Avery rolled over a little and licked a sweaty brown nipple. "No," he said decisively.

"'Cause I love you. I mean, I didn't say it before because—"

"You're a man."

Cal snorted. "Yeah. So that. But I love you."

"I love you back."

Cal sobered and rolled to his side so they were face-to-face. "Do you love me enough to visit my brother in the loony bin once in a while?"

Avery nodded soberly. "A week ago, I would have lived with you in a tiny house with your brother. I won't mind visiting him now."

Cal's expression was not nearly as guarded as it had been nearly a month before when he'd picked Avery up from the side of the road. "Really?"

Avery nodded. "Yeah. This bed, man. I'm telling you." He grew serious, staring into Cal's eyes and realizing he meant every word about forever. "It's like this place. And you. It's magic."

Cal shook his head. "It's not magic. It's *you*, Rescue Puppy."

Avery felt an irrational stab of hurt. "I'm still 'Rescue Puppy'?"

"Oh yeah." Cal nuzzled his ear. "'Cause you rescued *me*."

Avery wiggled, pretty much all sexed out, but totally susceptible to that hot breath in his ear. "I'll rescue you until forever," he said, thinking that he'd make sure Cal never lost touch with the family that had sustained him for so long.

Cal pulled back. "That's a deal," he said, making it like a vow. "Until forever. Like the sea and the sky."

"And the earth and the mountain," Avery said, knowing those things were in his bones now too. "Until forever."

As vows went, they weren't bad.

"I don't like him anymore," Keir said belligerently, staring at Avery across the table. "He got in my way."

Avery could feel Cal's deep breath. "And you hit him, so you're even."

"The doctor said I can be mad."

Avery fought the urge to grimace. They hadn't been able to bring Nascha this first time to visit. Keir's doctors had asked that he only get a few visitors at a time, and Cal sort of thought Avery and Keir needed to make things right. But Avery had also wanted to be with Cal as they'd met with his principle psychiatric physician—who had, in fact, said that Keir could be mad. Unfortunately, the man's point had been that Keir had the right to be angry with what had happened to him as a child, but that he needed to use his words instead of his fists.

The shrink had told Cal and Avery point-blank that it could take years to get to the bottom of what happened—something as simple as a bad day of teasing could have twisted inside Keir, become magnified and distorted, until it became the thing that drove him, made him dangerous today.

In the meantime, he was kept in an all-male ward—even his attendants were male—and as Avery thought about the women he'd met recently, he had to be sort of sad for Keir. He'd had Dottie, but somehow, her age seemed to make her safe. Avery knew *his* life would be really colorless without August, Tori, or Gi-Gi to talk to. He thought Keir might need that sort of softening influence in his life.

But first he had to not be a danger to that influence, either.

"So," Avery said, "do they let you watch *Avatar*?" He was hoping Keir would warm to him again. After all, he and Cal had started because Avery and Keir had bonded.

Keir glanced up suspiciously. "No," he said, his voice wavering. "Nascha had me write up all the things I wanted in a place, and I forgot *Avatar*." He hit his forehead with the palm of his hand. "*Stupid*!"

"No!" Cal said, going to grab his hand. "Look, we'll talk to your doctor. Avery, do they have DVD sets?"

Avery nodded. "Yeah, Keir—we can get you some DVD sets maybe, okay? I know you get a television, even if they don't get cable, so we can—"

Keir looked at him, naked gratitude on his face. "You could make it so I could watch the show?"

And Avery felt it, that connection, the vulnerability that had kept Cal tethered to his brother's side through six long, painful years, despite all of the reasons he'd had to send Keir away and sleep easier at night.

"Yeah," he said, smiling uncertainly. "Me and Cal, we could make that happen."

Cal's nod over Keir's head was grateful. "I'm going to hug you now, Keir, is that okay?"

"Really strong around the chest," Keir said bluntly, and Cal did, tucking his chin next to Keir's neck. Keir didn't return the hug, or pat Cal's hands, but he did relax in his arms.

Avery could relate; Cal made him feel safe too.

They had to leave soon after that—Keir was allowed visitors every day, but only for short times. The doctors said he needed to adhere to the structure of activities they had outlined for him. Apparently he'd needed that sort of activity structure for years, but Cal had been too busy to provide it for him. Watching Cal's face as the doctor had told Cal what his brother had needed, in contrast with what he'd gotten during that time, had twisted Avery's stomach.

Avery had never in the world felt that much of a failure about something—especially not something he'd been trying so hard to do right by.

Watching Cal hug his brother now, Avery knew, with certainty, that wherever their life took them, it would always end back in this area, where Cal could hug his brother, and Keir could look outside his back door and see the place he'd always known.

Avery was good with that.

They left soon after, and Avery caught Cal looking around the grounds again.

"He said they take him for trail walks every day," Avery said.

"I know."

"He said he gets TV time—once we get him the DVD sets, he'll be happy."

"I know."

"The doc said they could start introducing things, books, other shows, movies—he'll get a variety of things to think about."

"I know."

Avery grunted. "Look—I'm not complaining. I just need to know—is it going to hurt you this bad every time we come here?"

Cal's eyes flickered toward him, and his mouth pulled back into that flat line Avery remembered from their first acquaintance. "Yes," he said without equivocation. "Is that . . ." his voice wavered, "is that going to be a problem?"

In answer, Avery clasped Cal's hand tighter and raised his face to the sky. "Can we take the dory out still?" he asked. Cal continued to work at the hotel restaurant a few days a week, because he liked to keep busy, but he hadn't been out to fish since the day he'd come home and found Keir beating Avery into the mud.

"Yeah," Cal said, pulling Avery from *that* unpleasant memory. "Why?"

"'Cause I think we should make that a tradition. That we come here, and our emotions get all twisted up, and then we go out on the boat. And then go out to dinner." Because now that Cal had money, they'd been able to do that. Not a lot, because they had so many things they *could* do with Cal's money—and Avery's as well—that they didn't want to squander it before they made the decision. But enough— enough that Cal remembered what steak tasted like, and why having a beer with dinner wasn't out of the realm of possibility. Enough to make Friday nights something to look forward to, and not another long night in a succession of them. Maybe they could change their going-out-to-dinner day to the days that they saw Keir.

Oh! "And we can tape the show and watch it after dinner!" Because now that Cal had time, Avery was introducing him to this whole concept called leisure moments and that included *television*— and the one show Cal seemed to have any interest in whatsoever was *Wolf's Landing*. Avery was working on expanding his repertoire—so far he was showing a promising attachment to *Arrow* and *Grimm*, but first and foremost was *Wolf's Landing*. The show that had brought them together—and the show that had made Avery believe, even in fiction, that there were people out in the world as good and as noble as Cal.

Cal tugged on his hand and pulled Avery into his arms.

"Of course the show," he said, smiling faintly. "I like traditions. They're like legends—they go on until forever."

"And us," Avery said, because that thought comforted him more every day.

"Yeah."

"Good. We'll make it a tradition, then."

"Until forever."

Avery closed his eyes and accepted the kiss, and yearned for the moment it would be him and Cal, and the sea and the sky and the wind.

Sometimes, they got to be the heroes in their own lives.

Explore more of *Bluewater Bay*:

riptidepublishing.com/titles/universe/bluewater-bay

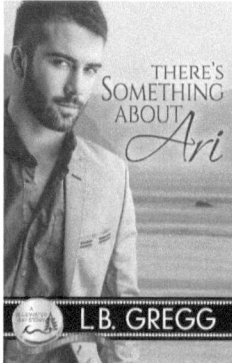

Dear Reader,

Thank you for reading Amy Lane's *The Deep of the Sound*!

We know your time is precious and you have many, many entertainment options, so it means a lot that you've chosen to spend your time reading. We really hope you enjoyed it.

We'd be honored if you'd consider posting a review—good or bad—on sites like **Amazon, Barnes & Noble, Kobo, Goodreads, Twitter, Facebook, Tumblr,** and your blog or website. We'd also be honored if you told your friends and family about this book. Word of mouth is a book's lifeblood!

For more information on upcoming releases, author interviews, blog tours, contests, giveaways, and more, please sign up for our weekly, spam-free newsletter and visit us around the web:

Newsletter: tinyurl.com/RiptideSignup
Twitter: twitter.com/RiptideBooks
Facebook: facebook.com/RiptidePublishing
Goodreads: tinyurl.com/RiptideOnGoodreads
Tumblr: riptidepublishing.tumblr.com

Thank you so much for Reading the Rainbow!

RiptidePublishing.com

Choose your Lane to love!

Amy Lane has two kids in college and two in soccer, and an indulgent spouse. Together they exist happily in a crumbling suburban crapmansion, and equally happily with the surprisingly demanding voices who live in her head.

She loves cats, movies, yarn, pretty colors, pretty men, shiny things, and Twu Wuv, and despises housecleaning, low-fat granola bars, and vainglorious prickweenies.

She can be found at her computer, dodging housework, or simultaneously reading, watching television, and knitting, because she likes to freak people out by proving it can be done.

Connect with Amy:

Website: greenshill.com

Blog: writerslane.blogspot.com

Facebook: AmyLaneAnonymous

Twitter: @amymaclane

Goodreads: goodreads.com/amymaclane

Enjoy more stories like
The Deep of the Sound
at RiptidePublishing.com!

Wallflower	*Poster Boy*
ISBN: 978-1-62649-037-6	ISBN: 978-1-62649-131-1

Earn Bonus Bucks!

Earn 1 Bonus Buck for each dollar you spend. Find out how at
RiptidePublishing.com/news/bonus-bucks.

Win Free Ebooks for a Year!

Pre-order coming soon titles directly through our site and you'll
receive one entry into a drawing for a chance to win free books for
a year! Get the details at RiptidePublishing.com/contests.